MICHAEL D. WEAVER
AND *MERCEDES NIGHTS*!

"SHARP, FUNNY AND CORDIALLY DIRTY-MINDED. Weaver has some fast moves... scary and profound."
—K.W. Jeter, author of *Infernal Devices*

"CLEVER...evoking comparison to *The Manchurian Candidate*."
—*Publishers Weekly*

"DELIGHTFUL...A rollicking good time, filled with screwball characters, sinister conspiracies, and far-fetched technology... Weaver is a top-notch storyteller."
—*West County Journal* (St. Louis, MO)

"A SURPRISE...Witty, well written...Weaver's name will soon be a lot better known."
—*Science Fiction Chronicle*

"ENERGETIC...This brisk, well turned-out debut succeeds."
—*Kirkus Reviews*

MERCEDES NIGHTS

MICHAEL D. WEAVER

ST. MARTIN'S PRESS/NEW YORK

St. Martin's Press titles are available at quantity discounts for sales promotions, premiums or fund raising. Special books or book excerpts can also be created to fit specific needs. For information write to special sales manager, St. Martin's Press, 175 Fifth Avenue, New York, N.Y. 10010.

Excerpt from "Ghosts" by David Sylvian is reproduced by kind permission of Chadwick Nomis, Ltd.

Excerpt from "You Don't Need" by Jane Siberry © 1985 by Red Sky Music and Wing-It Music. All rights reserved. Used by permission.

MERCEDES NIGHTS

Copyright © 1987 by Michael D. Weaver.

Cover art by B. Sienkiewicz.

All rights reserved. Printed in the United States of America. No part of this book may be used or reproduced in any manner whatsoever without written permission except in the case of brief quotations embodied in critical articles or reviews. For information, address St. Martin's Press, 175 Fifth Avenue, New York, N.Y. 10010.

Library of Congress Catalog Card Number: 87-16315

ISBN: 0-312-91223-4   Can. ISBN: 0-312-91224-2

St. Martin's Press hardcover edition published 1987

First St. Martin's Press mass market edition/October 1988

10 9 8 7 6 5 4 3 2 1

For Phil and Phil

*with special thanks to Charles de Lint,
Jim Frenkel,
Stuart Moore,
and Angel*

**Have a good time with
MERCEDES to-NIGHT!**

**Yes! It's true! You can have Mercedes Night for your very own!
Real flesh and blood! This is not an imitation—
GUARANTEED
Contact BEDMATES CORPORATION, Box 2099 on the
COMPUPLEX NETWORK.
We'll send a free brochure and vidsample. Buzz us today!**

Fires lick the Twilight Cave
Challenging the dawn
Flames caressing
As they burn
The peasant, the king, the pawn

Packs of wolves pad blackened halls
Paths that aren't there
Answers to
Imagined quests
Of snakes' imagined Care

At end we turn upon ourselves
Battles fang to claw
Wolves in shadows
Viper-eyed
Evil, the rebel, the Law

Oracles bellow in ancient wrath
Vipers hear the call
And ghosts of wolves
Phantom-fanged
Paint black, upon black on the wall

Wolves, snakes, and babies of both
Trap infinity
All I seek
To hold my own
Are ways to make vipers cry, "Mercy!"

—*Sheyla Brand,* The Red Book, *c. 2017*

MERCEDES NIGHTS

PROLOGUE

June 14–15, 2048

His hovercar settled into the dust, its thrusters dying like whispering ghosts. The headlights of a waiting flyer clicked on; their beams cut across the desert, digging into his eyes. His stomach churned.

The woman next to him giggled. He didn't look at her. He got out of the hovercar and trudged across to the flyer.

Weak light filled the room as the morning sun forced itself through dark, closed curtains. Sweat-soaked sheets clung to his skin, and the room stank of vomit. For a brief moment he realized it was daytime, and got sick again.

"She's awake," the man said, peering at the woman.

"What did you expect?" he countered. "If I'd brought her in a sack, you'd be demanding proof right now." He called her name, and they watched her stumble toward them.

"This is a strange party, Nathan," she said. Her eyes were wide open, the pupils so dilated that her irises looked like thin rings.

"You'll have a good time, honey," he said, taking a hypoderm from his pocket and pressing it against her arm.

She stared at him as she collapsed to the earth. He looked at the man. "Satisfied?"

The man grunted, bent to pick her up, then unceremoniously dumped her into the back seat of the flyer.

"What are you going to do with her?" Nathan asked him.

"Not my job to know," the man said, climbing into the flyer. "Your country thanks you."

"Hey!" Nathan said. "What about me?"

The man looked at him and grinned. He tossed a small package onto the ground. "Don't do it all at once."

Nathan grabbed at the package and scrambled to get out of the way of the machine before it lifted off.

The pain in his head woke him up.
Don't do it all at once. . . . Don't do it at all!

He rolled over into his own vomit. He reached for the bag of white powder, but his fingers wouldn't work right, and the bag only tipped to one side, its contents pouring slowly out like snow to the floor.

Then the pain in his head shut out the rest of the world.

There, half on, half off the bed: a body, empty, its fists clenched tightly, knuckles blueing as morning turns to noon, then to dusk, then to night.

And only deaf ears to witness the cracking of the portal, the door crashing in before booted feet, an NP lieutenant looking in, then looking away, grimacing, his hand trying in vain to shield his nostrils from the fetid, gagging death rushing from the room like a wave.

CHAPTER 1

6/16 9:10 P.M.

THEODORE REGAN PRESSED HIS face against the window of his tri-jet as it landed on the lawn of the Torrance ranch house. No light shone through the polarized windows that stared back at him, dark mirrors casting the flyer as a silhouette against the purple and black shadows of dusk.

He hopped down, telling the tri-jet to fry anyone or anything daring to touch it. He wasn't in a good neighborhood. During the Prohibition, no suburb had been safe: every imaginable form of decadence—murder, drugs, devil-cults—had infested them all like the plague. The bad air still lingered as far as Theodore was concerned. He patted the police-issue Blackhammer inside his coat, reassuring himself that no devil-cult would take him without a fight.

He reached the door and knocked. It swung open immediately, automatically. A tall, thin figure met him, extending an arm in greeting with the distinct, metallic grate of a biobot. "Greetings, sir," the biobot said.

Theodore eyed the construct distastefully. "Is this Bedmates Corporation? Am I in the right place?"

"Oh, yes sir. This is Bedmates. Come in." The biobot's sickly, doll-like smile didn't change.

Theodore stepped into the house, and the door eased shut behind him. "Well!" he said. "Don't just stand there gaping. Take me to the people in charge here!"

"But I'm in charge here, sir. It's my job to greet customers and take vouchers for the Mercedes Nights. You're my first customer, so please bear with me. At the end, if you wish to suggest or criticize, I will give you a form to fill out so that I might be reprogrammed to better serve you and all future customers."

"What? If this is some sort of joke. . . !"

"It is not a joke, sir," the biobot said, smiling. "You must understand the nature of the business we conduct here and understand further that it would be very unwise for my human programmers to conduct it personally. Now, sir, please place your hand on mine." The biobot again held out its hand.

"Oh, forchristsakes! What are you talking about?"

"Place your hand on mine. It is our security test."

Eyeing his host distrustfully, Theodore did as he was told.

"Yes," it said, "you pass the test. I can tell by analyzing the chemical composition of the sweat on your palm that you desire a Mercedes Night for your own and you are not here with any intent to harm my programmers, as policeman or otherwise. I can also tell," it continued, smiling, "that you are Theodore Regan. I have your prints on file. You are part of my test market—one who received our brochure directly. Other customers, attracted by the magazine advertisements, will not begin arriving until after the magazines come out. I shall have to be very careful with them. It is a pleasure to meet you, Mr. Regan."

"You *what*? You advertised in magazines?"

"Of course. It is a time-tested method of marketing sexually oriented products."

"You're crazy! This had better be good."

"Oh, I assure you that it is. I serve another purpose here—a purpose of comparison. Our Mercedes Nights are not biobots like myself. Oh, no, not at all! They are flesh-and-blood clones of the authentic."

"Then that's your secret!" Theodore grinned back.

"Follow me, please," it said. It began to turn; Theodore grabbed its arm. "Wait. I want to ask you something else. Suppose you discovered I was a policeman or that I desired to harm your programmers?"

"You're not. My sensors are infallible. You are part—"

"Look! Just suppose. What would you do?"

"—of my test market. I would kill you."

"Or try."

"Oh, I would. But if I didn't," the biobot offered, smiling, "the house surely would. Please follow me."

The biobot turned and Theodore padded along after it, occasionally glancing over his shoulder. They reached dimly lit stairs that led to a huge basement bathed in a soft, red neon glow. Structures that reminded Theodore of isolation tanks were spaced evenly along the walls. Condensation cloaked their glassy surfaces, blurring the forms within. Three nearby were draining, emitting low, gurgling sounds.

"It will be just a moment, Mr. Regan," the biobot said. "I signaled down to have a few prepared for your inspection, but the machinery is slow and the clones must be treated with extreme care just after hatching."

"Hatching? Is that a joke?"

"I do not understand your concept of joke, but perhaps

my programmers intended it as one. I am not sure. You are not laughing."

Seams appeared in the plexi-wombs, and, one by one, unsteadily, the three clones stepped out. Theodore rubbed his eyes. They sure as hell looked real. Three beautiful, perfect, perfectly naked Mercedes Nights.

"They're heavily sedated with hypnotics and acting under suggestions implanted by the laboratory control program. These are necessary precautions, otherwise they'd probably try to kill each other. Mercedes is a strong-willed woman. If you decide to buy, I will provide you with a set of hypoderms and instructions on how to bring your Mercedes to a semiconscious state and how to return her to hypno-sleep. You must be careful to follow the instructions exactly. It would be unwise to grant her too great a degree of awareness."

"Why not wake one up here? How do I know they are real?"

"We insist on complete customer satisfaction. If you are for any reason dissatisfied with your Mercedes Night, you may return her for a full refund or exchange, no questions asked."

Frowning, Theodore whipped the Blackhammer from his jacket and shot the Mercedes on the left through the chest. The woman's eyes widened, the silver one sparkling, and she collapsed, splattering blood in all directions. She twitched once, then lay still. He turned to the biobot. "They *are* real!"

"You had no reason to doubt, Mr. Regan. You must now give me vouchers for two. Our price is ten thousand each, so you must pay twenty thousand. Since you are my first customer, I shall forget to charge you for cleanup and disposal of the corpse."

Theodore laughed and patted the biobot's shoulder as he

holstered his Blackhammer. "Hell, man! How many Mercedeses do you have?"

"Fifty-three prepared for sale. More if demand requires it."

"Look, I'll give you a cool million for all you've got. That's enough for a hundred, so you'll be making an unexpected profit of almost a hundred percent."

"I'm sorry, sir, I can't do that."

"Why?"

"One per customer. My programming is very explicit on that point."

"But can't you make an exception? I mean, let me talk to your programmers. I'm sure they'll understand if I—"

"No, sir. That is not possible as I've already explained. Due to the nature of the business we conduct here, they must remain unseen. Cloning is not at all legal."

"Sure it is. You're legal, and you're legally alive. Life created in laboratories has been patentable for years."

"Life, yes. Human life, no. That is stated implicitly in the Supreme Court decision on *Coyle* v. *Moral Preservation Group*. I have been programmed with knowledge in this matter. My programmers do feel, however, that the question of legality is contestable. We have, therefore, placed an indentifiable trademark in the inner ear canal of each clone so that they might be distinguishable from the original should confusion or ownership cases arise. Your individual mark, your brand if you will, will be imprinted on the certificate of authenticity I shall give you upon purchase."

"I still want all of them."

"You can't have all of them, sir."

"But you're letting me pay for two!"

"You killed one, sir. You must understand the liability you incurred in the act."

"So what if I kill all but one of them? That's just like paying for all of them in the end, isn't it?"

"No, sir, it's not. My programming allows me to tolerate the killing of one Mercedes Night by any customer in the event he wishes to verify the authenticity of the clones in that manner, though I submit that doing so was hardly called for. You had only to touch one in certain ways."

"What would you do," Theodore asked slowly, "if I killed another one?" He drew the Blackhammer again and pointed it at the Mercedes on the right. The two clones still stood next to their fallen sibling.

"I would kill you. Preferably after extracting a thirty-k credvoucher, by force if necessary."

Theodore grinned, began to pull the trigger, then turned to the biobot and smiled. He holstered his weapon. "Guess I'll have to take your crap for now, eh? If you don't get me, the house will?"

"Most assuredly, sir."

"Well then," he said, reaching for his credit pad. "Twenty thousand, is it? I'll take the one on the right. No! Make that the one on the left. The one with her foot in the blood of the dead one."

"I could be persuaded to let you take the dead one as well, sir. Since you're paying for her."

"No, I don't think I would enjoy her all that much. Get some clothes on the one I'm buying and get me that certificate and the hypoderms and anything else I'm supposed to have."

"A straitjacket, sir? Some stun gloves? If she comes too far out, she's likely to be quite upset."

Theodore signed the credvoucher. "That was almost humorous."

"It was not a joke," the biobot said, smiling.

"Sure," Theodore said. "Get me the papers, etcetera. I'm in a rush."

6/16 9:30 P.M.

Andrew Willis drummed his fingers on his desk, anxiously waiting for *something* to happen. The commissioner had put his psychlab on passive alert, and it had to have something to do with this Nathaniel Redman thing.

More importantly, his friend Fred Trent had asked him to stick around. Torrance was Fred's responsibility. As far as Andrew could see, Fred was in deep shit for not discovering the cloning operation on his own.

Assuming things were that simple.

"Incoming message, Grub," Andrew's computer barked. "From the Thirteenth. Security level triple-Z. Text and data, you want a hardcopy?"

"Just read it, Dillinger."

"Working. *Grub, colon, Redman file out of our hands. Washington boys been snooping in my closets all day, but I managed to snag some satscan data on the area in question. Good thing, too, dash, get this, colon, I've just been ordered to keep hands off the manufactory. No room for argument, case closed and all that. But maybe you can find something interesting in the pictures, question mark. Give them to your machines, then go home. Act normal.* That's it, Grub. Plus a satscan file."

"Show me."

"Working."

A series of satellite pictures, aerial views of a block of suburbia, flashed across Andrew's vidscreen. The dates and times clicking along in one corner of the screen indicated that he'd received the last three months of data—and a snapshot taken of the area approximately once every hour.

"Perfect, Dill. I want a Code One analysis of that satscan file ready for me in the morning."

"Working."

What a fucking day! Andrew thought as he rose and headed for the door, assured, at least, that the following morning would be interesting.

On the other hand, he didn't expect to like it.

6/17 7:25 A.M.

The polbot zipped up the stairwell to the third floor of the building, did a rapid sitscan of the hallways, and stopped to hover before the door marked 3H. After using its advanced audsensors to verify that the apt's resident was indeed inside, it shifted into targeted surveillance mode to wait for the opening of the door. If the wait exceeded an hour, it would have to knock; until then, its standard programming would opt for the wait, for avoiding any possibility of violating search-and-seizure procedures. In any case, it didn't have the authority to *enter* a private apt.

The floor's other residents—mostly underemployed models and actors struggling to get a grip on the jagged bottom edge of the Hollywood scene—began to emerge for the day. Their morning chatter came out clipped and affected as word spread of the metal sphere hovering in front of 3H. Those who had to pass it to get off the floor said little to anyone until they were well clear of the building.

The polbot, of course, didn't care what they did. It waited only for the latch to click inside the door in front of it.

Pouring milk into his bowl of Astro-Oats, Manuel Cortez activated his vidconsole by voice command and shortly learned from VidScoop that 32 percent of the population of Berkeley felt that the government had put something in the local water supply to make the other 68 percent of Berkeley's population go along with President Cole's war policy.

Manuel watched. The VidScoop focus cut to a street report—an interview with some neohippy outside a coffee shop. "We're not paranoid here," the hippy said. "You only have to look at the facts. I mean, nationwide polls show Cole's support swimming around the upper thirties, and you're asking me to believe that Berkeley's twice as fascist? I mean, get real!"

"But don't you think it more likely that the polls were rigged?" asked the VidScoop reporter. "Rather than all this government plot stuff—"

"Hey, man! If you can't trust Gallup, who can you trust?"

Manuel burped and lost track of VidScoop as he finished his morning ritual of breakfast-bathroom-waterpipe. The day before, he'd received two pounds of freshly cured, midseason harvest from home, and he'd been anxious to try the sample with a clear head. The warm tingling that spread through his body assured him that the grass was as good as any his father had ever cultivated. Now it was up to Manuel to test the market so he could get the best possible price for his family's labor when they brought in the rest of the crop in the fall.

When he'd first arrived in America at the age of eleven, eight years ago, he'd had to deal on the black market because of his youth. Even with the restructuring of American immigration laws that came after Moral Prohibition, the United States wouldn't give him a license to sell his family's crop before he was sixteen. Now, he still preferred to deal with established street contacts he knew and trusted. For one thing, they paid more than the National Drug Commission, which had to work on a 600 percent markup.

It was an easy life. Whatever he couldn't unload personally he could dump on the NDC before they closed off their warehouses near the end of the fiscal year.

Savoring the way the drug filled him, adding a soft, meditative sheen to all his perceptions, Manuel cut and ziplocked the two pounds into thirty-two one-ounce packages. These he stuffed into a ragged brown briefcase, then he rose, stretched, opened the door of his apt, and stepped out.

He almost hit his head against the metal sphere of the polbot. He backed through the open door. A vidlens jutting off the surface of the polbot stared at him.

"Manuel Cortez," the polbot said in a hollow, metallic voice, "you are hereby requested to accompany me to LANP Seventeen for questioning not to be considered by you as accusatory in nature. Since I am a machine, you have a right to refuse this summons, but, should you exercise this right, you will personally be charged a sum not to exceed one hundred nucreds for the expense of human intervention in this matter." A strip of paper began to scroll out of a slit in the polbot's face. "I am producing a copy of the pertinent city ordinances relating to National Police robots and the rights of city citizens in dealing with said robots. Please take this copy and review it at this time."

Manuel reached forward and grabbed the document. The print on it was very small, and the marijuana in his system made the letters squiggle around like little snakes. He folded the document and shoved it into his pocket.

"As a taxpayer," the polbot said, "you should know that you are advised to come with me at this time."

"What's this all about?"

"You are hereby requested to accompany me to LANP Seventeen for questioning not to be considered by you as accusatory in nature—"

"Okay, okay," Manuel said. "I understand."

"Since I am a machine," the polbot continued, heedless of

Manuel's last words, "you have a right to refuse this summons, but, should you exercise this right, you will personally be charged a sum not to exceed one hundred nucreds for the expense of human intervention in this matter."

Manuel sighed and wished he hadn't gotten high. He stepped out of his apt, closed the door behind him, and pressed his thumb against the sensopad to lock everything up. Inside, his vidconsole fell silent as his automation took care of everything he'd forgotten.

The polbot was already moving slowly for the stairwell. Manuel Cortez followed.

6/17 8:45 A.M.

To the side of his desk, arrayed on the wall, a total of fifteen certificates of achievement and decoration verified his integrity and competence for all the world to see. On some days he would gaze at the rows of his awards in smug satisfaction. On others, he would search within the frames for some proof that he was a *good* man. Right now, he'd just as soon use the scraps of government paper to wipe his ass for all the good they'd done him in the last day. . . .

Andrew Willis sneered at his vidscreen as the fed's face faded from view. Fifteen minutes he'd been in his office, and the first five had been perfect: the Code 1 had produced a match on some Mexican kid who habitually visited the Torrance neighborhood where Nathaniel Redman had set up his lab. Dillinger had already handled the summons. It wasn't much—nothing like canvassing the neighborhood itself, but that option was outside of his jurisdiction, and apparently now outside of Fred Trent's. Still, it was something, assuming he'd get the chance to follow up, to question the kid. This jerk from Washington had just demanded his presence in the basement. Not asked. *Demanded*. Who the fuck did he think he was? The president's pimp? God's gift to law enforcement?

And, of all things, the bastard had brought Andrew one of the clones. Goddamn Justice Department! They hadn't even told the LANP anything about the case until two nights before when they'd requested a raid on Redman's Hollywood apt. They'd found Redman, all right: dead as a fucking rock. What the hell was going on anyway?

"So get your ass down there, Grub," Dillinger said.

"Shut the fuck up!" Andrew said, smashing his hand down on his desk and triggering imbedded circuitry designed to shut off his work-brain's voice subsystem. The computer managed a crackling *"Shit!"* before the power died.

This is all I need, Andrew thought, rising from his chair. *All I fucking need!*

In the basement, he stalked the fed who passively awaited his arrival at the observation window of a private "luxury" cell—more a hotel room than the traditional bare-walls-and-bars holding chamber. The fed was tall and thin, stereotypically cold, with dark hair and glasses and an equally severe black suit. His name was Cooper or Copper or something like that—Andrew really couldn't give a fuck. He reached the man and turned without speaking to look through the window. The clone was definitely there—reclining on the bed and absorbed in some book, a trashy romantic paperback judging by the garish cover.

Andrew glared through the one-way glass. If the fed had expected a pleasant greeting, he wasn't going to get it.

And the clone . . . a woman. She looked so human. Beautiful. *Unearthly*.

She glanced Andrew's way, raised an eyebrow, brushed a lock of sunset red hair from her face, and smiled. He knew she couldn't see him—that from her side she saw only herself in a mirror, but still her gaze sent a shock through his body, her eyes impaling him in their blindness.

"No comment, captain?" the fed asked.

The clone looked away, releasing Andrew. He grunted. "Make one up if you have to have one."

"She's the prototype—the first one Bedmates produced," the fed said, ignoring Andrew's remark. "We told her that she's been computer-isolated as a possible carrier of the latest mutant AIDS strain. It works like a charm every time, especially when they think we've picked them up to save them. She thinks the psychtechs are doctors."

"They are," Andrew said absently.

"You know what I mean."

Andrew turned on him. "Who gave you the goddamn right to bring her in here without notifying me?"

"This is a very sensitive matter, Captain Willis. I have orders to avoid external communications if at all possible."

"So what do you want me to do about it?"

"Nothing. Don't do anything. In fact, you can forget about it until we tell you to remember." Behind the dark glasses, the fed's eyes smiled. "That's all, captain. You can go back upstairs."

Andrew spun and headed for the elevator, ignoring the occasional psychtech or detective who greeted him along the way. Something like white fire raged through his mind until he reached his office and slammed the door.

Dillinger had produced a set of prints for the interview with the Mexican kid. They lay in a folder on Andrew's desk. He sat for a moment and paged through them, cursing softly over one night shot that showed three vehicles parked outside of the manufactory. Three vehicles that could only belong to the National Police.

Washington, it seemed, had been aware of this mess long before it had let on.

6/17 9:23 A.M.

Manuel had seen enough of the insides of NP stations to last him a lifetime, and he couldn't believe he was looking at the inside of another one. The most fucked-up thing about it was that he still didn't know why he was there, and he'd been waiting nearly an hour.

For what? He hadn't sold so much as a single joint to *anybody* in the last year without keeping track of it in his business records. As he sat alone in the locked interrogation room, he opened his briefcase, took out a small, leather-bound black book, and idly flipped through its pages. If the NPs thought they could get him for tax evasion, they had another thing coming. He'd shove that book under their noses quicker than shit. Everything he'd done was legal and recorded in meticulous detail: date, time, to whom, amount and THC concentration—and not so much as a single alteration or erasure.

He looked up when he heard a key in the lock, steeling himself for the coming confrontation. An NP entered—a huge man with sandy hair going white at the temples and those emotionless, superior eyes that pigs always had. Bent nose. Captain's insignia—

Captain's insignia!

He fought to keep his bowels from emptying themselves into his pants. What had he done *wrong*?

The NP captain sat across from him and—and actually smiled at him. Manuel's tension eased, but only just.

"You're Manuel Cortez?" the captain asked.

He nodded.

"You have a friend who lives at Fourteen-ten Henderson Street in Torrance?"

Arthur! Manuel realized. "I don't know what you're talking about."

The cop sighed and laid a folder on the table between them. "These are satellite pictures of your friend's house, Manuel." He drew a photograph from the folder and turned it for Manuel to see. "That's you, isn't it?" he asked, pointing at a figure walking across a green lawn. "There's no use arguing about it, but I can produce enlargements of that person's hand and we can compare fingerprints if you insist."

Manuel picked up the picture and looked at it, awestruck. "Jesus Christ," he said. "This can't be legal! You use satellites to spy on American civilians?"

"All the time. We can't prosecute you on this sort of evidence unless you're involved in espionage, but these pictures do get taken. They make the country a safer place."

Manuel recalled some of the horror stories he'd heard told of NP corruption and brutality. "That's your opinion."

"Well?"

"Well what?"

"Is that you?"

"I'm not telling you anything, pig."

Andrew's smile faltered. "Listen, son, I'm not here to put you in jail, and I'm not after your friend. And drop that pig shit, please. This day's been rotten enough to me already."

"What do you want from me?"

Andrew sighed and looked at the kid. What *did* he want? Cortez didn't have anything to do with Redman—hell, he'd only been an occasional guest at the house across the street from the cloning operation. . . . Andrew had only just begun to place the photo of NP flyers on the lawn of the manufactory into perspective with the rest of his knowledge of the case. If he'd been calm enough to think about it while he was in his office, he'd probably have let Manuel go without even seeing him.

Cortez was there solely because Andrew's computers had analyzed a satscan series and identified an insignificant figure in one of the shots as a person living in Andrew's precinct—in Hollywood—and therefore Andrew could get to him. It might once have been a good idea, a perfect idea when Fred Trent had shipped the satscan data, but that other shot that implicated Washington was *far* more significant, far more revealing. As he thought about it all, the interview with Cortez seemed more and more absurd with each passing moment.

Andrew could tell already—instinctively—that the kid didn't know anything, that he was a waste of time. Feeling like one of the solar-powered, automatic NP dolls that kids got each Christmas and lost interest in by New Year's, Andrew played the scene through: "Seen anything strange happening around your friend's house, Manuel?"

"Like what?"

"Like—I can't tell you, kid. I was hoping you could tell me."

"Is that it? You want me to tell you about something that you can't even describe to me so that I know what the hell you're talking about?"

Andrew nodded.

"You're not going to hook me up to some machine and suck what you want out of my head?"

"That doesn't happen, kid. You're an American citizen."

"Strangest thing I've seen lately is you, man," Manuel said, raising an eyebrow. "You arresting me?"

Andrew stared at him and shook his head.

Manuel rose. "Can I get out of here?"

"Wait," Andrew said, standing, drawing a business card

from his breast pocket and holding it out to Manuel. "Call me, will you? If you *do* come up with something?"

Manuel shrugged, but he took the card, running his fingers absently over the embossed print as Captain Andrew Willis of L.A.'s 17th National Police Precinct opened the door for him to leave.

Outside, Manuel wished that he'd asked for something—a receipt or something, he wasn't sure what he should have gotten. The longer he thought about what he'd just experienced, the less sense it made. And he had the strangest feeling that, if he were suddenly to turn around and walk back to the precinct building, no one there would admit to having seen him but moments before. Unless he invoked the captain's card hidden in his back pocket.

With this card, I hereby confess . . .

He hadn't done anything wrong! He didn't even know anybody who had done anything wrong lately. Well, anything illegal, more than speeding. *Wrong* was a moral concept that had nothing to do with the NPs. Not since the Prohibition, and he'd been a toddler in Mexico when the United States had repealed that legislative lemon.

And Arthur—there wasn't a way in hell that one could have broken any laws. How could he when he didn't even leave his house?

Manuel stopped and squinted into the morning, taking stock of his surroundings. Captain Willis and his satellite pictures and his absence of questions were three blocks behind him. Home was another fifteen ahead. The pigs could've at least done him the courtesy of a lift.

Back in his office again, Andrew sat and tried to order his thoughts, but the vision of the clone there, in his basement, lying on that bed, leapt into his mind. Those eyes . . . He felt nauseous, and forced himself again to concentrate on the matter at hand.

He still wasn't sure he understood what the hell was going on. Reaching under his desk, he clicked on Dillinger's voice subsystem. "What was the name of that fed I spoke with earlier, Dill?"

"NP Special Agent Daniel Cooper," the computer replied. "I have a call queued from the commissioner, Grub."

Great, Andrew thought. Just what he needed.... "Start an aud/vid transcript and put him through, Dill."

The gray lifted off Andrew's vidscreen, replaced by the chunky features of Andrew's boss. He tried a smile. "Morning, sir."

"It is that," the commissioner said emotionlessly. "You okay, Grub? You look ill."

"I don't know, sir. Don't know that I like the present Special Agent Cooper brought me last night."

"Special Agent who? That's evidence transferred from Fred Trent's precinct, Grub. No special agents involved, understand?"

Andrew paused, trying to assimilate this new twist. The commissioner knew what he was talking about; the "Special Agent who?" routine meant that Cooper was probably out of the picture already—hightailing it back to D.C. after getting his fingers just a little bit dirty. It didn't seem to Andrew that things were going to get any better. "Understood, sir. What am I supposed to do now?"

"That depends on whether we get a good test run. Your head-boys know what to do, and hopefully we'll pull it off tonight."

"Then what?" Andrew asked, not sure he wanted to know any more about this "test run" than the commissioner was going to tell him anyway.

"Settle back," the commissioner said. "It's a little complicated, and I only want to go through this once."

Andrew eased back in his chair, and then he noticed the red light on his vidconsole that indicated that the commissioner had secured the call. Even Dillinger, the receiving computer, couldn't record it. Andrew hated that damned light.

6/17 9:21 P.M.

She'd parked her tri-jet four blocks from his apt and now waited for him on the corner like a common streetwalker. She'd even dressed the part, though she wasn't really complaining; the way her skintight synthsilk dress rode up and down her thighs each time she moved felt quite sensual. Not a whole lot of work, she thought, to the world's oldest profession.

She resisted the temptation to thrust out her hip for the occasional low-level flyer. It wouldn't do to get picked up by the wrong man; that certainly wasn't the reason she'd spent hours in front of her mirror getting everything just right. Where the hell was Warren anyway?

It had rained late in the afternoon, and the air smelt refreshingly clean. The dark, weather-worn drainage streaks on the surrounding buildings sparkled, and panels of light high above splashed multicolored ghosts of neopunk fashion ads over the wet pavement. She could almost believe she was stuck in some turn-of-the-century erotic epic: one of Kinski's productions with all the plugs pulled. How much to ask for *what*? she wondered.

She suppressed a giggle. Where the hell *was* Warren? One of her more terrifying waking nightmares was that of getting stood up, and she felt it now more than ever. Before, the fear had risen out of her vanity; now, suddenly, she felt truly vulnerable. Why had she let just another romantic conquest get so out of hand?

Mystery, she thought. Challenge? She supposed it had been that at first. He was a politician; if the New Socialists could maintain their current level of popularity, Warren Keyes might very well become the nation's next president.

Maybe she'd wanted to corrupt him, but somehow she felt that plan was backfiring. She was having to play his way; they both knew that their involvement could destroy him, especially during an election year. Controversy and politics: they met clandestinely, like Romeo and Juliet. So she'd disguised herself as a prostitute. She found it ironic that a street whore on his arm wouldn't attract more than a cursory glance, while she, a supposedly "powerful" vidstar, would set cameras off for miles around if they were seen even looking at each other lustfully. Prostitutes had legal rights, provided they kept to the required schedule of health examinations; solicitation of prostitutes had become the most acceptable way of releasing sexual tension. Nobody got hurt, and nobody got pregnant. Being seen with a prostitute could only increase the public's perception of Warren's solid, charitable character. It got frustrating for her—she was so used to having her own way in everything—but it was all very logical.

Sometimes logic made her sick.

She remembered a time when life couldn't get so complicated. The memory swept her up. She was seven, lost in downtown Boulder. Her mother, she knew, was somewhere nearby. She thought she saw her half a block away, so she ran, tugged at her mother's dress. The woman turned and looked down at her; Mercedes looked up into a stranger's face. She ran again, scanning the faces in the crowd for one that she knew. She ran until she could run no farther, then she collapsed to the sidewalk, panting, propping herself against the side of a building and tyring hard not to look afraid. ("If you ever get lost, Mercy," her mother had told her, "stay calm. Don't get scared, because the worst people will find you if you look scared. Stop somewhere, and wait until you see a policeman, then tell him your name and that you live on Fairmont Road, and everything will be all right.") So she looked around for the black uniforms of the National Police and tried not to be afraid. It wasn't easy; it was starting to get dark.

She waited; some of the people on the street started to look strange. Some of the men (she *knew* they had to be men) were dressed like women. They weren't very pretty, and their eyes darted about. Most of them were standing close together, and they were carrying signs with a lot of words on them that she didn't understand. She tried to make herself invisible.

She lost her sense of time. It was dark. She still hadn't seen a policeman. A noise grew in the distance, and people with sticks started coming around one of the corners on the opposite side of the street. One of them screamed, "There's one!" and pointed at one of the men dressed up as a woman. The man started to run, but the heel broke off of one of his shoes and he fell. The people with sticks caught him, started to beat him. And then there was madness, and lots of screams. She didn't know exactly what happened after that because she kept her eyes shut and covered them with her hands.

A National Policeman hadn't happened by until much later.

There had been a big mess about it the next day on her local vidnews. Her mother had explained that the Moralists had beaten up the poor men because they thought that Moral Prohibition said they could. She'd known about the Moral Prohibition; it was something neither of her parents had liked but said they had to live with. Her mother had told her that the vidnews didn't like the National Police because the police should have been there to arrest the men in women's clothes instead of being far away.

A few years later, Mercedes had learned more in school. Most of the transvestites unfortunate enough to get caught that evening had been killed. They had been protesting Moral Prohibition, the law that said they couldn't dress the way they wanted to. They still did it; usually the NPs would arrest them, and they'd go to jail for a few months. When they got out, they'd dress as women again and go back out with their signs. Her teachers used to tell her that Moral Prohibition had been a horrible disease that America had finally been cured of because of terrible events like that night, and they would also tell her that in some small way, she was lucky to have seen it, and to have seen how horrible men can be to each other when their government lets them think they can be that way.

She remembered talking to her best friend, Christie, about it. Christie's parents also had hated Moral Prohibition. The two girls would tell each other their dreams and always say that if someone came and tried to put a Prohibition on America again, they would fight and fight and fight and fight. . . .

Mercedes tried to shrug off the memories. She wished she could believe that things were as simple as the Repeal of Moral Prohibition suggested. For a while it had seemed so, but an unease had slowly set in since the Republican-Democrats had ousted the New Empiricist reformists from power in 2044. Supposedly, America was more free than ever, but a lot of Mercedes's more reactionary friends held other opinions on the matter. She'd even heard rumors of National Police anarchism, of psychtechs with knives that changed memories, attitudes, stories . . . everything. Slicing subjective realities to shreds before putting them back together again. It sounded so impossible.

The idea went round and round in her head. An antique hovercar sped past; the pilot's eyes locked on hers. She watched; he started to slow, to turn around. Nervously, her hand slipped between her breasts, withdrawing a slightly bent hand-rolled cigarette. She lit it, and she felt again the crush of cheap synthsilk against her skin.

Warren arrived just in time to cut off the hovercar. A moment later Mercedes was inside his tri-jet, glancing back through the rearview screen, trying to make out the face of the hovercar pilot and whether or not he was disappointed. The image blurred as Warren gunned his engines and shot up above the roofline.

She turned to him. "I almost had a trick!" Her feigned vehemence made her laugh. "What took you so long?"

"So long? You were waiting on me for just over a minute, max. I was watching from the window and came right down."

"Just a minute? That's all?" Time dilation, she reflected. *What a wonderful world.* . . . She drew deeply on the joint and passed it to Warren, who absently stubbed it out in the ashtray.

"Sometimes," Warren said, "I wonder whether you have as much on the ball as the press wants us all to believe."

"Well!" she harumphed. "*I* wonder, Mr. Warren president-hopeful Keyes, whether you've got all *your* wires properly crossed, leaving me out on the street to fall prey to any horny pervert who happens along."

He looked at her sideways and smiled. "I have complete faith, Mercy, that you would have thanked me had that come to pass. You look quite the harlot. Where on earth did you get those awful earrings?"

"Dunno," she said, fingering one thoughtfully. The workmanship was actually quite exquisite; she could almost discern the shape of coupled dragons by touch alone. "Igor found them somewhere—I didn't ask." Her hands dug into the mass on her head. "Do you have any idea how long it took me to get all my hair under this wig without looking like some sort of alien?"

"Hey! Don't take it off yet!"

She paused. "Why not? We're leaving the city, aren't we?"

"Well," he said, "I thought we'd give your acting skills a test."

She looked sharply into his eyes, trying to pierce their surface humor but getting nowhere. She thought how politicians' eyes generally betrayed about as much of their possessors' inner feelings as omelets did of barnyard social life. Politics required dramatic talent. No wonder, she reflected, America got led so far astray in the late twentieth century. People started believing that acting was all there was to it. Luckily, they'd learned before it was too late, but that had opened the door for nonpersonalities like Cole, the R-D incumbent.

"Actually," Warren continued. "Something came up at the last minute. Party's called a gathering in Santa Monica—"

"And you have to be there," she finished for him. A flash of jealousy seized her; it passed quickly, but its wake set her emotions churning; fear and desire echoed through caverns of yearning emptiness that she hardly knew existed within her.

He'd nodded, was saying something else. . . . The dim light of the cockpit cast a bluish hue over his face, more pronounced where it glinted off the slight moisture on his lips, framing the shadowy source of his voice. Mercedes fought to tune him in.

". . . Jeff, once they'd got the Paris story straightened out, then he got everything organized. Of course, you don't have to come; that would be our wisest move. On the other hand, it could be a lot of fun."

"Oh? Sounds risky to me."

"Who's going to recognize you?"

"Anyone who's seen more than two of my vids."

"With you looking like that? With you *acting* like that? Tell them, no, you're not Mercedes Night, but you've doubled for her in some of her heavier scenes. They'll get a kick out of that. And they'll believe you. They'll have to—I run the party." He paused. In the silence his words sank in, were absorbed by her dramatic instincts. Nothing difficult, she realized.

"Consider it a start, Mercy," Warren continued. "What you say about yourself, speaking as an acquaintance of yourself, can do something to improve your image with my associates. After this, we're going to have to work out a plan to get your name off the conservative Right's shitlist. You haven't been a whole lot of help in that area yet."

"I haven't done anything, Warren! I've been positively Victorian lately!"

"Well," he said distantly. "The press hasn't picked up on it yet. Don't worry. We'll think of something."

She sighed, disengaging her fingers from the web of the short, dark wig. "You enjoy living dangerously, Warren?"

He glanced at her and grinned. "I fell in love with you, didn't I?"

She didn't answer; her mind traveled back to those days

of his mysterious, anonymous, fascinating calls, flowers coming daily from who-knows-where, precious, pre-Prohibition recordings showing up in her audlib with Igor unable, or unwilling, to tell her where they came from. For a while she'd thought that God himself was playing with her head. She still didn't know how Warren had managed to get by her pet-brain. They couldn't be bribed, could they? What did one offer a computer?

"What about my silver eye?" she asked.

"Tell them it's an implant. You spawned a fashion, remember?"

Yeah, she thought, settling back in her seat for the flight. A fashion. . . .

She looked down at the passing lights and wondered why she suddenly felt so depressed. And then she realized: She'd lied. She'd never been Victorian. How could she tell him that changing her might be impossible?

They passed low over the slums of Inglewood; she watched him gazing down out of his window, and she could almost feel him feeling their pain. The sensation made her feel ill.

Excuse us, Miss Night, er, Mrs. President, but we need to know whether President Keyes is your 404th lover, or your 405th. . . .

You can handle it, Mercy. You always have.

That voice in her head, the one that had led her out of middle-class anonymity and into the Hollywood limelight. There had been times lately when she'd failed to believe it.

6/17 9:23 P.M.

Before Andrew lay the case file he'd talked out of the commissioner that afternoon. He put down his coffee cup and arranged the contents of the file, trying to get them to make sense. In one stack were three letters of inquiry from a

Nathaniel Lumis to the Nexus Corporation, a government front specializing in no-questions-asked loans to businesses and individuals. Lumis had received, in the end, 100,000 black-market dollars, of which he'd spent half, according to another stack of receipts, at various chemical warehouses. The rest of the money was lost, floating somewhere in the high-tech underworld, lining the pockets of microchip pirates and more than a few biochem free-lancers. Lumis—an alias, actually; his real name was Nathaniel Redman—had himself been a biochemist, the brightest light in the Harvard life sciences department in the early twenties before the Moralists had reduced that institution to barely recognizable intellectual rubble.

Andrew sighed and sifted through the stack of papers so he could stare at the coroner's report. Bastard had had enough shit in him to kill an elephant. The coroner had given up on identifying the drug. *Cause of death: Overdose, agent unknown.*

The most recent addition to Andrew's case file irritated him the most. Dillinger had spat it out that morning, a reiteration to Andrew from Washington of the orders given to Fred Trent. Five simple words: *Leave the Torrance lab alone.*

Leave it alone! The thought set every nerve in his body on edge. Leave it alone? What the hell for? To inject its human poison into the world?

At least the place wasn't in his precinct. . . .

"More coffee, Captain Willis?" A female voice, invading his nightmare.

He looked up into the girl's eyes and the rest of Hank's Eats-n-Drinks slowly came into focus. Most of the customers were taxi-flyer pilots, whiling away the early hours of darkness, hoping their beepers wouldn't call them back out into the night. The vidscreen covering the wall over the bar presented a grim panorama: scenes of the destruction of Paris, if the toppled tower center screen could be believed.

The case file still tugged at the corners of his attention; the vidscreen images possessed a surreal quality, as if he'd looked up to catch a dream. Slowly, he noted the unease of Hank's clientele, identified the ruin with certainty as the Eiffel Tower, wondered if France's capital had joined the growing mass of radioactive terrain that threatened to cover all of Europe, and allowed a hard cynicism to rise up and protect his mind: *Who did it? We'll say they did, and they'll say we did, and the madness will stop, as always, just short of an ICBM exchange.* . . .

The vidscreen became again part of the wall; an animated holo, he thought, for all he knew that's what it was. He'd read *1984* as a kid; the book had terrified the boy, but the man had grown numb. Casually, he thanked an anonymous God that he knew no one who'd called Paris home. He thought of the French, and his compassion crawled back into its cage: *Smelly little fuckers had never even learned to use soap.*

He looked around the cheap, porcelain-tiled diner with newly heightened distaste. There were times when everything on the entire goddamn planet was ugly as sin. As an NP captain, he could have easily afforded better cuisine. But Hank's had been habit since his flyer patrol days; his instinct to go there was more animal than human. Once, at the bar, he'd killed a man—a heroin addict who'd done some bad smack and erupted into psychopathic rage. Andrew liked to think, in weaker moments, that he'd saved someone's life that night. It wasn't hard; the junkie's ghost never haunted him. Not as if it were the only life on his conscience . . .

But his world had changed. The rest of the world had changed . . . he suddenly wanted nothing more than to leave it behind. To rise, pay his bill with money stolen from the blind man begging just inside the door. Become insignificant, a nonentity like that Mexican kid, Cortez—someone who didn't make any difference at all. Then he could leave Los Angeles and lose himself. *Somewhere.*

You're a fool, Grub, he thought. *You have nowhere else to go.*

The coffee steamed in his mug again. Back to the case folder: exasperation. He closed it, his thoughts drifting back to when his eyes had linked with those of the *thing* that Cooper had delivered.

And Andrew suddenly *knew* why he was where he was. Not to be there, but to take advantage of what might perhaps be his last chance to get *away* from the precinct house, from the place he ruled, from the unholy monster that sat now in one of his offices *probably polishing her goddamn nails or something!*

He recalled Cooper's confession of the lie they'd first told her: that she'd been computer-isolated as a possible carrier of the latest mutant AIDS strain. She'd thought she was in a hospital. That had held her peacefully enough until his psychtechs had replaced that lie with other, more permanent enticements to cooperation.

But you actually had to treat the damned things as people, he realized. You pulled one out of its tank, gave it a vaguely logical explanation of how it got wherever it was, and let its mind fill in the blanks. Why couldn't they have just put it back into dreamland? But no—the psychtechs had needed to make sure it would function normally, that it wouldn't croak the first time it blew its nose. And they'd needed to study its mind for a little while before it could be of "any real use." They'd cleared her that afternoon for the commissioner's "test run." For all Andrew knew, that operation could very well be underway as he thought about it.

He didn't like the position the case had put him in. Though the psychtechs had things under control for the moment, the immediate responsibility for the clone and her actions was now *his*. And past this little episode tonight, assuming it went off as planned, he would be the pigeon in charge.

Day-to-day got bad enough when the commissioner wouldn't leave him to run his precinct as he saw fit, much less when NP headquarters got itself involved.

Goddammit! he thought. Here he sat like a good little puppet.

Awaiting further orders.

Better to kill them and be done with.

He toyed with the edge of the case folder for a while, then thought, hell with it. It wasn't really even a case. More like a fucking zoo.

His mind drifted back to the vidscreen, and he was suddenly glad that he had the wasteland of Paris to stare at. They could have been showing a Mercedes Night vidholo.

6/17 9:37 P.M.

The ballroom was immense: a cavern beneath the Carl Sagan wing of the Liberty Building. A static holo of the reconstructed Parthenon covered the entire east wall opposite a lunar landscape on the west. The south was bare but for a string of portraits at eye level—from Martin Luther King, Jr., to Jonathan Campbell-Carter: all the great liberals— while the north wall, behind the dais, sported a ceiling-to-floor tapestry whose proportions would have given most high-tech textile engineers indigestion; its field was red, broken only by the milk white torch-and-sickle symbol of New Socialism which stared out over the room like a watchful eye.

They were just inside the entrance. A short, dark-haired man had drawn Warren aside after she'd introduced herself as "Candy." He'd said "Jeff," which meant Dr. Jeffrey Wilmington, the head of New Socialist PR and Warren's running mate. She knew him from his fiery delivery of the party's platform on the vid. He looked much smaller in person. But, she thought, so must I.

The men spoke in hushed tones: obviously something important. She took the opportunity to wander west and gaze out across the moonscape. Serenity; not even thinking of the violent origins of the craters could dispel the feeling of peace that suddenly flowed through her. She realized that empathic transmitters must have been hidden behind the screen. The brilliant stars over the horizon wanted to promise her a thousand tomorrows; the depths of space were like velvet, dreamy. She could almost wrap herself in their layers. And on the surface, amid the craters, she caught flashes of movement: something there, alive! Recognition set her shivering with excitement: They were "star elves," the androgynous little natives of the fourth moon of Alpha Centauri's fifth planet that the unmanned probe, Gorbachev XXVI, had brought back in 2045 to show the rest of the world. The Russians had left all but a pair of the vacuum-dwellers on Earth's moon. The other two, presumably, still thrived somewhere in an artificial environment under Moscow.

The view was spellbinding, and she let it fill her world.

"Beautiful, isn't it?"

The voice drew her back. She sensed someone next to her. "Huh?" She glanced over and recognized Jeff Wilmington. Behind him, the crowd had grown. Warren was lost somewhere within it.

"The lunar window," he said. "It's beautiful."

"Window? It's not a holo?"

"No. This is live, a gift to the party from Sub-Space."

"What about the empathy circuits?"

"There aren't any. Whatever it's making you feel is real."

"I never thought . . ."

Jeff chuckled. "You should get out more, Mercedes Night. Wonder is all around you; you have but to look in the right places."

"Warren told you my name."

"He tells me everything. Don't worry, nobody else knows."

She looked back into the crowd. Most of its attention was focused on the dais. In the far corner, a vid crew milled about its equipment. She caught a glimpse of a familiar figure, and suddenly her sense of serenity vanished. "He didn't tell me Sylvia Fry would be here!" she whispered.

"He's giving a speech in a minute, and we wanted VidScoop here. Sylvia's their best journalist. What's wrong with that?"

"She knows me!"

"So does everybody else here, but nobody has recognized you. Why should she?"

"You don't know her!"

He didn't answer, only turned his gaze back to the moonscape while she tried to calm herself. She wished she hadn't come, wished she was at home where she could get very, very stoned and forget the whole thing.

But she didn't want to forget Warren.

"Come on," Jeff said, grabbing her arm. "We've got to take our places."

Reluctantly, she followed.

She sat with Jeff at a circular table slightly to the left of the dais. He introduced her to the others there; she assumed they were all fairly important. One, a vice-president of some corporation, told her that she looked like someone he felt he should remember but couldn't. The comment boosted her confidence, and she chided herself for being so insecure in her own talent. Her fears lessened their grip, and she launched herself into the rambling conversation. She was Candy Blossoms, streetwise, frivolously cynical about her fortunes of the evening. Someone complimented Warren's taste in women. She shrugged and told him that he couldn't possibly be Warren's accountant. They all laughed at that, then someone signaled silence for the candidate's speech.

He ascended the steps behind the podium and stood there for a moment, looking out over his audience. He glanced at Mercedes and smiled, and she thought how proud he was, how nobly he carried himself. He was everything she'd never been able to be.

"I've just been told," he started, looking at the VidScoop camera, "that this is going out live, coast-to-coast. I hope I'm interrupting battlefront footage, because I want to start by asking you all a question. Why are we at war, once again, with the Soviet Union?"

He paused a moment, letting it sink in. "Do you remember President Cole ever really explaining it? All I heard were a lot of vague references to national security and democracy for Europe. Well, those are high ideals, but I can't keep myself from maintaining the opinion that most Europeans were fairly satisfied with their lives until we told them they weren't.

"I've only just learned that a tactical nuclear warhead fell on central Paris today. The official death toll has not been released, but most early estimates put it in the millions. Of course, our president hasn't even bothered to tell us yet whose bomb it was that went off, but we already know he won't tell us that it was ours. We're supposed to be the good guys.

"We are at war, my friends, because our economy was failing, and because war lets the economy grow and guarantees greater governmental control. The present administration isn't even trying to win this war, it just wants to keep it going. I admit that unemployment figures have dropped to record lows, but that's because the unemployed were all invited into military service. So far, in the two years since the war started, nearly a million American lives have been lost. And again, for what? For the freedom of Paris? I challenge you to find a single Parisian willing to thank us on this dark day.

"The fact of the matter is that this country has never really understood that it is but one member of a family of nations. It is not the father. We are not the lawmakers of the world. American freedom works in America, but that doesn't mean we should force it on other countries. I have no doubt that the majority of Americans see themselves full of goodwill, of love. The people in the rest of the world, however, think of us and only see hate. . . ."

Mercedes lost track of Warren's speech. She'd heard most of his ideas before in private conversation, and she really just wanted to watch the reactions among the crowd. When she looked around, she couldn't find another eye that wasn't fixed on Warren. She watched the expressions on their faces. He moved them deeply. She couldn't remember a leader in the recent past who could make the average man pay attention for more than the odd minute or two. Now, one was here before her, and it made her happy that it was someone like Warren. She knew charisma could manifest itself in the evil as well as the good; she'd studied footage of Hitler, Reagan, and Karen Whitehall while preparing for the lead role in Miller's production of *Joan of Arc*. Hitler had brought World War II, Reagan had laid the groundwork for

World War III, and Whitehall had plunged the country into Moral Prohibition. All three had wielded the same power over the crowd; all three had inspired radical and sweeping changes among their followers, and all three were completely individual, each conveying a different message.

She found the comparisons fascinating, and she thanked God that Warren's message made sense. She wished, not for the first time, that she'd actually played Joan in Miller's vid. Her agent had talked her out of it, telling her it couldn't do anything but harm her credibility as a serious comic actress. Serious comedy, she thought. *How incredibly ironic.*

As Warren brought his speech to a close, Mercedes chanced a glance at Sylvia Fry, and found, to her horror, that the woman was staring directly back at her.

"Get me out of here," she told Jeff as the crowd cheered.

"I can't," he said. "I'm on next."

She looked to Warren desperately, but he was waving to the crowd. Sylvia's eyes still hadn't left her, and Mercedes had no doubt what that meant. She squeezed Jeff's hand, asked him to apologize to Warren for her, and headed for the exit before Sylvia Fry could afford to take her camera off the candidate.

6/17 10:15 P.M.

Mercedes Night!

Sylvia had been watching the woman seated next to Jeff Wilmington. Something in the way she moved had been bothering her. The face, beneath that monstrous hairdo and under layers of paint, looked vaguely familiar, but the movements, the little hand gestures and that "go on, try to shock me" posture—they belonged to Mercedes Night. Under all that glitter, it couldn't be anyone else! *What are you doing here, Mercy? This isn't your world.*

The last thought encouraged doubt, at least until the woman looked at her and the sense of recognition passed in both directions.

Warren Keyes's speech was winding down. Sylvia smiled. Something very interesting was going on, and she loved good mysteries.

By the time the applause died, Mercedes was gone. Sylvia caught a glimpse of her leaving and considered following for a moment before forcing her concentration back to Warren Keyes, reminding herself that he was real news and that she had a certain obligation to bring real news to the public's attention. It was just that she found it so rarely. Keyes had truly impressed her, at least until she'd been distracted. Sylvia hadn't even heard the end of the speech. She made a mental note to review the whole thing before the evening was over.

As Keyes stepped down from the dais, one of her crew handed her his radiophone.

She took it and thanked the man.

"Fry here."

"Hello, Sylvia? This is Hollywood Central. How was the speech?"

"Great," she said. "Didn't you watch it?"

"The first part. Our pollsters say it's gone over great. They want us to send Wilmington out live as well."

"No problem. Is that all?"

"Mercedes Night came in here about ten minutes ago. She wants to do a publicity stunt. How soon do you think you'll get out of there?"

"Mercy?" Impossible, she thought. Mercedes had just left. . . . "Are you sure?"

"Of course I'm sure. You want to talk to her?"

"Yeah." While she waited, she began to wonder whether she'd been getting enough sleep lately. She'd been *absolutely* positive about that woman.

"Hi, Sylvia!"

The voice belonged to Mercedes. Sylvia shrugged and promised herself a vacation sometime soon. Or maybe she should simply concentrate more on important news. The gossip pieces were starting to make her imagination run wild.

"Hi, Mercy. What are you doing?"

"Waiting for you."

Sylvia smiled. "Give me a couple of hours, okay?"

"Sure. Meet me at the Murray monument around midnight."

The line clicked dead.

Sylvia turned to her crew and signaled for the camera. She waited for her crew chief's nod.

"Well, there you have it, America! Warren Keyes wants your vote, and he sounds pretty serious about it. We'll be back with more from New Socialist headquarters after these words from Tylenexedrol—'If you want a pill, take a pill'—Pharmaceuticals."

6/17 11:55 P.M.

Still panting heavily, Theodore rolled off the woman, closed his eyes, and smiled contentedly. The bed underneath him still moved; the woman twitched spasmodically, her orgasm only just subsiding.

He turned to look at her, running his eyes along the perfect, feminine line that stretched from the tips of her toes, up her calf, over her knee, down to her hip, and over her belly, peaking at the hardened pinnacle of her right breast.

He felt like her leading man, as if at any moment she would rise and ask him to be her king as she'd asked Tyrone Moriarty in *Cleopatra's Complaint*.

In his fantasy, he took her hand and squeezed it. Her head lolled, slowly rolling to face him, and the fantasy shattered when he realized that her eyes stared unblinkingly at the corner of the room behind him.

She couldn't see him.

She didn't even know that he existed; she didn't know who had loved her, who had made her body thrill, who had carried her breathlessly to the brink of sexual fulfillment and then effortlessly nudged her over the edge.

She might as well be blind.

He turned from her and sat, clicking on the antique lamp at the side of his bed. Under the light, he fumbled through a stack of papers to find the instructions given him by the Bedmates' biobot, then he settled back to read more about his new toy.

6/18 12:30 A.M.

He found himself wandering through the streets of Hollywood's theater district armed with an almost empty bottle of mescal and a half-ounce of Thai Surprise that he'd bought from the government because he hadn't planned on wanting to get high that afternoon when he'd left his stash behind at his apt. That desire had come only after a brief encounter with three winos who had hustled him out of the better part of his liquor.

Drunks had always tended to turn him off drinking; he could hardly imagine a more revolting manifestation of humanity than a normally sane adult male alternating between strains of "God Bless America" and barfing his guts out on a street corner. Marijuana generally had a more civilized bite.

Now, Manuel tottered on the edge of inebriation anyway. The day's confusion born of the bizarre episode at the NP station had launched him recklessly through the remaining sunlit hours and into the evening. He'd turned down invitations to party with friends; he'd wanted mainly to be alone, to sort things out in his head. Not that he'd gotten very far; after smoking a joint of the Thai weed, he'd made the mistake of stumbling into an old British film festival to see Terry Gilliam's *Brazil*, and the resulting experience, the projection of his own subjectivity into Gilliam's totalitarian nightmare, conjured more dark shadows in his mind and chased none away.

From there he'd wandered forth feeling psychically exhausted after the overwhelming assault of ideas from the big screen. He'd seen the production before on vid, but it had had only a fraction of the impact it had on film. Film captured, intruded, provided no escape. Most vidsystems could be stopped or reduced to visual background noise by voice command. He wondered if, in this instance, technology hadn't stolen something of the artist's power during its reckless progression through the previous century.

The mescal burning through his insides, Manuel began to replay *Brazil*'s opening scenes in his mind: the distorted camera angle intent on the death of a fly, and the fly's unwitting entrance into the bureaucratic machinery, its evolution into the "bug" in the system. Manuel wondered what fly in the LANP's computers had summoned him that morning to sit before Captain Andrew Willis.

"'Scuse me."

Or whether he, Manuel, was the fly. . . .

"'Scuse me, I said!"

Someone stood before him—a ragged man in a suit that had probably begun the evening neatly pressed. A single man, obviously out questing for female companionship, and obviously unsuccessful. Quite drunk.

"Yeah," Manuel said. "What do you want?"

"Jus' a light, okay?" He waved a cigarette in front of Manuel's face.

"Sure," Manuel said, handing the man his lighter.

The drunk swayed there, getting the tobacco lit on his second try. Beginning to feel a little nervous, wondering if the guy went both ways and was working up to a proposition, Manuel waited impatiently for his lighter back.

"Didya see her?" the man asked, drawing smoke deep into his lungs.

"Who?"

"Mercedes Night, man! Bare as the day she was born and dancing along the boulevard." He held out Manuel's lighter, then dropped it onto the pavement.

Manuel bent to retrieve it. "No, I didn't. You oughta go home and get some sleep." Standing, without offering the drunk another glance, he turned and headed for his apt, ignoring the "Hey, wait!" and "Thangs for th' light!" that faded away behind him.

Paranoia gripped him all the way, the kind of paranoia that tells a person he's being followed but doesn't let him look back to verify or dispel the illusion. He couldn't be sure he was truly alone until he turned into his apt complex and chanced a look behind him. The street was empty.

Taking the airlift up, he promised himself that he'd do his best to take Willis at face value as a confused cop and simply get through the night. He felt some relief when no surprises confronted him inside his apt. No one had ransacked it while he was gone. Nothing appeared to be lying in wait.

Preparing for sleep, he realized that very little of what had passed through his mind that day had transcended irrationality. In bed, Willis's face rose again unbidden before his mind's eye, and Manuel wished he'd at least talked to Arthur, to see if his friend could clarify a variable or two within the equation.

On the other hand, considering the way Arthur's mind worked, it would probably be best not to breathe a word of the affair in Arthur's presence. Not if the goal was understanding what had happened. But these were problems for the next day, Manuel decided. For his own sanity, he wouldn't avoid his friends for another day; the city had a way of collapsing around a man sheltered only by solitude.

Things would make more sense in the morning, especially if the pigs didn't bash in his door during the night. With that thought, he struggled for the embrace of sleep.

If I should die before I wake . . .

Everybody has to die sometime, he thought.

Still, sleep was long in coming.

6/18 10:00 A.M.

Placing a pillow over her head, Mercedes shut out the low hum of the alarm.

"Ten A.M., Mercy," it said, sensing her reaction. "You've got things to do!" The humming grew louder.

Christ, Mercedes thought, that late? She sat up and sneered at the alarm, which shrieked and waddled back to its slot in the wall of the bed console.

"Stereo," Mercedes said.

"Ready." The reply came from all sides; she'd bought the penthouse specifically because the Akudi pet-brain at its heart had been streamlined for pleasure—the penthouse's previous occupant had installed more peripherals than she imagined she could ever use. He'd also named the pet-brain Igor, but she could live with that.

"Something acoustic."

"Bach? Tchaikovsky? I have access to an audiophile analog print of the *1812*. Or—"

"No. Twentieth century—folky. You pick it."

She didn't feel much in the mood for decisions. She still felt drained from the night before. She'd gotten home, terrified that VidScoop cameras would be waiting for her. Around eleven, a few showbiz friends had stopped by, and she'd been grateful for the company. They were her people—plastic, maybe—but at least she knew how to react to them. They'd partied until . . . She couldn't remember. Late. The whole time, part of her had hoped Warren would call. Another part was trying to forget it all, telling her that she had no business trying to be someone she wasn't.

The music washed over her: "I Feel the Earth Move," the first song on Carole King's *Tapestry*. Five out of the last eight times she'd told Igor to pick something, he'd played this album. The damn thing *liked* it!

She asked for coffee and a cigarette and fell back among the pillows, slipping into half-dream. Before she fell asleep again, her bed sensed the cigarette too close to the sheets and kicked her awake.

Mercedes stretched, rose, and stumbled into what she called her playpen, the central room of the penthouse, to which were attached the kitchen, her bedroom, two spare bedrooms, and the foyer. The neomodern furnishings lit up as she entered; Igor depolarized the windows automatically, letting hazy sunshine enter the room.

While she'd slept, her apt had cleaned itself, removing all traces of the party except a half-empty, uncapped bottle of Chivas Regal, which lay on its side by her Jacuzzi. She couldn't help smiling.

"The bottle confuse you, Igor?"

"That's expensive stuff, Mercy. I didn't want to spill any."

"Oh well," she said, snatching the bottle up by the neck

and putting it to her lips in one fluid motion. "Good morning," she said, and drank.

"Good morning, Mercy. Breakfast?"

"Sure."

"Anything special?"

"You pick it."

She wondered if anyone else had stayed the night and asked Igor about it. He assured her that she was alone.

Pharaoh, a large blue Himalayan Persian, padded in from the kitchen. Mercedes scooped him up and sat down on the rug, scratching idly behind his ears while waiting for Igor to bring her breakfast. It came up nutritabs and milk. The petbrain knew she never had much of a stomach in the morning.

After eating and making sure the penthouse had taken care of Pharaoh (a habit she could never shake because the cat could easily starve if the automation malfunctioned), Mercedes stretched out on the form-couch in front of her vidconsole. She wanted to call Warren, but something inside kept her from doing so. She felt terrible about leaving him, especially after his speech, but at the time, she hadn't had much of a choice. Sylvia had *known* her. Warren ought to understand that, but still, she felt it was her fault. Her fault for being who she was. Somehow, she had to at least try to straighten out her life. She requested a line to Shoemain Associates and her agent, Rudolph Crane.

As she waited for the connection, she picked up the plexcast of the Zen obelisk that Warren had given her. She toyed with it, trying to look through it at the phosphorescent wormings of the plasma in the form-couch. Constructed of a synthetic substance, the obelisk was amber in color and streaked with black veins on the inside, as if the amber were a contained atmosphere for a tall, thin, inky black tree. The translucence of the casing seemed to apply only to reflections cast off the black substance inside it. The lights in the form-couch made no impression at all on the obelisk's mirror-smooth surfaces—no refraction, no reflection, as if the plex-cast contained a world outside the realm of light. But didn't light have to get in somehow for the black to be visible from without? The wonders of technology . . .

Warren had given Mercedes few gifts in the six months they'd been lovers. It was a mutual understanding. Though he was wealthy, her assets dwarfed his own, and little of material value could meaningfully be given a woman who could buy anything she desired for herself. So the gifts Warren gave were always symbolic in nature. The obelisk, for example, represented strength and direction of purpose in its form. The amber's apparent resistance to light represented human sacrifice—the nobility of a man's subordination of his desires to the welfare of the many. The black tree meant something else, but Mercedes had forgotten, or perhaps had never known, exactly what. The edges of the obelisk veered in at the top to form a pyramid, itself a symbol connected with everything from time dysfunctions to dimensional slips. It had something to do with the mathematical perfections of its design. Something about ratios—the golden section. Mercedes, again, could not recall exactly what she had heard. She scoffed at such things—idealistic, mystical babblings. Nothing more.

The other things Warren had given her—a Rubik's cube, a surrealistic portrait of Aristotle, a holo-adaptation of Wagner's "Ride of the Valkyries"—all were equally symbolic in their own ways. Mercedes had taken the gifts and smiled, fitting them into the decor of the penthouse as best she could. At first, she'd had no interest whatever in those things her lover felt were important. She'd cared only that *he* thought them important. She cared that he had purpose, because it was that purpose that made him vital. The nature—the specifics—of it made no difference. His having purpose made the difference. He was a man with vision. Romantically, she'd likened her attraction to him to Josephine's to Bonaparte, but she rarely thought about the implications.

She eyed the obelisk distrustfully and set it down. Did it hypnotize? she wondered. Could it suck away thought as it did light? She shivered and asked Igor for a joint.

Calm nerves, she thought. Calm nerves. *What the hell is happening to me?*

An extensor slid out of the form-couch and offered her a thin cigarette. She lit it and sighed. With the addition of psisensors, her penthouse would be able to catch her fits of anxiety before they occurred. . . .

No! she thought. If Igor fritzed, he could keep her pumped full of smack day in and day out.

She had work to do! Fame brought responsibility. I have a purpose, she thought wryly. A destiny. *I must make art—art to make people forget that they have no purpose. Only by denying life's realities can we live.* . . .

"Mercy? Mercy!"

"Huh?"

"You okay?"

"Yeah, sure." She focused on the vidscreen. Rudolph Crane.

"Rough night last night, eh?" he asked, a leering smile distorting his face.

"You," Mercedes said, "are a wimp, Rudy. And you think in clichés, so that makes you a predictable wimp."

"Hey, what'd I say to deserve that?"

"Nothing special. I just don't need your I-know-what-you've-been-up-to attitude right now."

"Look, Mercy. You called me, remember? I have other clients who need my time for more important things than insults. Just because you're the hottest—"

"Okay, Rudy. Okay. I get the message. And you're right, I did call you. Guess my mind just wandered away while you took your time getting to the vidphone."

"Whatever. So, what do you want?"

"Oh, yeah, I remember now. I don't like this script you've had me reading—this *Diary of a Coke Freak in Victorian England*. It's dumb."

"What are you talking about? It's funny as hell. May even be the funniest script you've ever read! And the title is *Dust Never Sleeps*, and you're timeslipped into Puritan New England. Massachusetts, to be exact."

"I know, dammit! I *did* read it. And I didn't say it wasn't funny. I said it was dumb. There's a difference."

"What difference? Funny isn't dumb. Funny's show business! All your vidholos have been funny. You're a funny star! Funny is money!"

"You make me sick, Rudy."

"Come on, Mercy. The script is great. Admit it!"

"Okay, it's great. But I don't want it. Listen, Rudy, I want to do something for once that means something. Something that says something."

"Says what? I don't understand what you're talking about."

"Something that says—oh, dammit, I'm not sure what I want it to say! As long as it says something."

"So you're Meryl Streep now, Mercy? Are you still going on whatever you did last night?"

"No!" She glared at the half-smoked joint and stubbed it

out on the arm of the form-couch. The couch spasmed and yanked it away from her. "No, I'm not! I just want to do something new. Something different."

"Significant?"

"Yeah."

"You *are* gone. Look, call me back in a—"

"Shut up, Rudy! Just give me some time. I'll write it myself. I felt dumb producing that last bit of gibberish we did, so maybe if I write it myself, it'll be great! It'll be great, and it'll be fun. . . . Why are you laughing at me?"

"Mercy!" he said, drying his eyes. "You should have seen yourself just then! It was great—hey, maybe we can fit it into a flick. Maybe not this one, but I'll get the writer to work it into the one after. It was classic! You looked so—so serious! I'll show it to you next time you stop by. You'll love it. Call me back after you've straightened out. We'll talk about it then."

"Rudy," Mercedes said, "fuck you!"

"Aw, c'mon, Mercy! Give me a break!"

"Start looking for another star, Rudolph Crane. You're fired. I'll find someone who knows how to listen."

"You can't fire me! I've got your contract for the next five—"

"Seconds, Rudy. Seconds. Count them. I'm getting a lawyer. Goodbye."

Rudolph Crane's face fizzled away as the vidscreen blanked out.

"Shit," Mercedes said to Pharaoh, who responded by crawling up into her lap. "What do I do now, Pharaoh? That was pretty stupid of me. Firing Rudy means I have to waste time and effort with lawyers and new agents and . . . oh well, it'll be interesting. Do I sound coherent to you, Pharaoh? Perhaps I am still all fucked up, eh? Perhaps I'm always a little fucked up. They say that hallucinogens accumulate in muscle tissue and that once a certain concentration is reached, they start seeping out, back into the bloodstream. Sounds sort of like time-released insanity, doesn't it?"

She smiled sadly, absently scratching Pharaoh's neck. "You've got it made, you know? Bet the only thing you ever worry about is the next female cat you'll run across. Wondering whether you'll get your nose clawed again?"

Mercedes asked the form-couch for her joint back. After a moment, it handed it out, and she relit it. "I really must be going insane, Pharaoh. I just fired my agent for laughing at me because I suggested doing something meaningful. Not only that, I'm going to write it. Question is, what's 'it'?"

"Incoming call from Mr. Keyes, Mercy."

Finally! she thought. "Thanks, Igor. Maybe he can cheer me up. Put him on."

"Mercedes," he said plainly.

She smiled brightly. "Warren! You'll never guess what I—"

"Have you seen VidScoop this morning?" he asked, interrupting her.

"Why, no. I usually don't bother with it. Doom, gloom, and gossip. You know that."

"Watch it now?"

Warren's brevity disturbed her. "Yeah," she said uncertainly. "Sure. Put Warren on auxaudio, Igor, and get VidScoop. What chapter, Warren?"

"Three."

"Chapter Three, Igor."

The headline news report came onto the vidscreen and opened with a shot of a sensually moving, naked torso. The cameras zoomed out, revealing a statuesque redhead, laughing eyes accented by flourescent, pinkish-red mascara. The deep red mane just reached the tips of her breasts. A bright smile touched at the corners of the famously mismatched eyes—one was blue, the other silver. The silver wasn't natural; the color had been added with a corrective implant, but very few people knew this.

She danced around Hollywood Boulevard's monument to Bill Murray, somehow concealing her nakedness in a way that seemed to promise more to come—more like a stripper in progress than a stripper at end.

"What's wrong, Warren? I think I look pretty good there. Viscerally graceful."

"There's more. Watch."

The woman slowly ended her dance and someone tossed her a kimono. She put it on.

The scene cut to the woman and Sylvia Fry. Sylvia held a pen-mike between them.

"Quite a performance," the journalist began lightheartedly, looking first at Mercedes the dancer, then again at Mercedes through the vidscreen. "This is Sylvia Fry bringing you a VidScoop exclusive. I'm here on Hollywood Boulevard with Mercedes Night. She has graciously agreed to an interview after her unexpected—what did you call it, Mercy?"

"Fertility dance. It was a tradition with my ancestors, performed to bring rain."

"But it rained here this afternoon."

"Yeah, well, some of my ancestors did it just for the hell of it."

"Yeah," Sylvia said, mimicking Mercedes and winking at the camera, "but VidScoop didn't catch *them* in the act."

"VidScoop," Mercedes said, "wasn't around then."

"True. Very true. Tell me, Mercy, who're you seeing now? It's been quite a while since you dumped Curtis Chase. Anyone new?"

"Well, I have been busy lately. First with my last vidholo, then with promos and parties, you know. But I have managed to squeeze in a new man."

"Tell us."

"Well, Sylvia, I think I'll let you *scoop* that out for yourself."

"Any hints?"

"Just one."

"Okay," Sylvia said, breaking out a microrecorder and holding it comically next to the pen-mike. "Shoot."

"He has," Mercedes said slowly, tilting her head so that her mouth was right next to the microrecorder's audsensors, "a seven-inch penis."

"Well, Mercy, that's going to be a tough one to track—"

"Okay, Mercy," Warren said, breaking in. "That's what I wanted you to see. You can shut it off now."

Mercedes shifted nervously. "Sure, Warren. Can VidScoop, Igor, and put Warren back on."

"Did you have to do that?" Warren asked, his face returning to view.

Desperately, she tried to remember when that had happened. She couldn't remember any of it. "Uh, according to Sheyla Brand," she said, reaching for something, anything, "I didn't have much choice."

She didn't like the way that sounded even as she said it. She was familiar enough with the writings of Sheyla Brand to know that, even though a technical understanding of Brand's philosophy would lead one to conclude that a person had no freedom of will, the subjectivity of existence continuously granted the illusion of free will. Denying freedom of choice only served to abuse illusion. And abusing illusion abused life. Abusing life promoted a sense of meaninglessness and she'd had her fill of that for the moment. She winced before Warren began to answer; she knew what he would say.

"That's a cop-out," Warren said, "as well as a naive interpretation of Brand's writings."

"Sorry."

"When did it happen?"

"To tell you the truth, I'm not sure. I took a taxi-flyer straight here last night, and I didn't go back out. Sylvia and I have occasionally set things up in advance, so it could have been anytime. I really can't even remember doing it."

Mercedes recalled the look of recognition on Sylvia's face the night before. The broadcast of this particular stunt must have been meant as message, *Sylvia's way of saying that she knew what was going on.*

"Mercedes," Warren said, "I can't believe you sometimes."

"Well! I didn't hurt anything, did I?" she pleaded. "I mean, it was only publicity!"

"That's not the point. You did that, and said all those things you said, and afterward, you don't remember a word of it. And you do these things all the time. You could have told her my name! That VidScoop vipress could destroy me!"

"That VidScoop vipress loves you, Warren! Do you think she would have covered your speech last night if she didn't?"

"I'm serious, Mercy."

"I didn't tell her your name. I wouldn't do that to you. You know that, don't you?"

"How can I be sure when you don't know what you've done from one moment to the next? All those drugs you do—what makes you think your mind's going to keep coming back intact? We can't go on, Mercy. It's just not possible anymore."

"Oh, Warren! You can't be serious!"

He started to answer, then lowered his eyes and turned away. The vidscreen image faded out.

"Transmission ended," Igor said.

"Thanks, Igor."

"Do you want a sedative, Mercy?"

"No. Why did you ask me that?"

'Usually, when you thank me, the next thing you ask for is a sedative."

Christ, she thought, the damn thing is turning empathic by itself! I don't need this.

"Shall I contact a lawyer for you, Mercy? You'll need one soon. If Mr. Crane gets much of a jump on you—"

"Yeah," Mercedes said. "Sure." Then, she thought, I'll take that sedative. Sleep away the fucking lawsuit. Sleep away Warren's fucking election. Sleep away the world. . . .

6/18 8:05 P.M.

From his place in the tech-booth, using the special titanium extensors he occasionally thought were his hands, Lance Corbin first tested the fit of the last microchip, then slotted it into place. He closed the housing and picked up the tiny screws that would seal it shut. He spun one, another, then another into place. On the fourth and last, his metal hand shook, and the screw fell to the floor of his custom-designed, semiautomated, self-cleaning worklab.

He paused and leaned back from the viewport, wiping his brow, looking down at his hair-trigger joystick. "Screw! I *will* win."

He laughed and leaned forward. Grabbing the screw with one extensor, he deftly slapped it into place, spun it, and set the entire unit onto the conveyor belt that would bring it out into the workshop, which was also, for at least a few hours each week, his living room—a confused space full of electronic bits and the carcasses of machines that had once performed their tasks with some degree of proficiency. In one corner sat a long sofa in front of an antique vidconsole that he had patched into the radarpole's interface. He occasionally wondered why he'd bothered. His stacks of Alfred Hitchcock videotapes rested in their rack next to the vidconsole; they were all he ever watched.

The remains of Lance's dinner lay on the edge of the couch, and the console buzzed with static; the last tape he'd played had long since ended. Lance hardly noticed; he backed out of the tech-booth and stepped to the place where the unit would emerge from his worklab.

He looked at his watch nervously, grabbed a coffee-stained notebook, and scribbled the time. He began writing a description of the final procedures, but when he heard the hydraulics in the exit port hiss, he hurriedly scratched out the notes, scrawled *Eureka!* in a heavy hand, and dropped the notebook onto the floor next to the remains of a toaster.

The unit—a small thing, not much bigger than a pocket dictionary—came to the end of its short journey and stopped. He touched it. Three weeks earlier, it had been his pocket radio. He pressed it to his lips.

"An entire universe inside you," Lance said, "and I can hold it all in the palm of my hand."

He took a piece of black tape and placed it on one corner of the unit's casing, over the word Sony. He picked up a light-pen, paused, smiled, and brushed back the shock of black hair that had fallen in front of his eyes. With ridiculous elaborateness, he set the word LANCELOT onto the tape.

Lance laughed and walked to the far end of his worklab where the alpha-wave decoder, on which he'd splurged the few thousand dollars he'd saved in his twenty-two years, lay next to the key to the whole venture: Lance's unpatented, thoroughly illegal, much modified, all-purpose interface device. Whistling tunelessly, he connected the unit to the interface and the interface to the hand-controller of the alpha-wave decoder. He put the helm of the decoder on his head, turned it on, and thought about fish. Grinning, he clicked on the interface, clicked on Lancelot, and sat down next to the gutted maw of somebody's microwave oven. He thought about champagne. He thought about caviar. He thought about Christie and the night before, wondering what his girlfriend would say when he showed her his new invention.

Christie Persons let herself into Lance's apartment and plowed through the wreckage of his living room. Lance's eyes were closed. She kicked him playfully, and he bolted upright, startled, then placed his fingers to his lips. Lance sat back again and spent the next few moments admiring the view. She stood over him, her hands resting on shapely hips in mock impatience. Blond tresses peeked at him, curling down and around her shoulders. Soft brown eyes that said "Well?" shone at him warmly.

After a while, the speaker in Lancelot bleeped and buzzed, and Lance took off the helm and smiled at Christie.

"Hi," he said, jumping up and kissing her.

"Mmm. What were you doing just now?"

"Oh, nothing important. Just perfecting the most important device ever engineered by man."

"You mean that crazy AI project you've been working on?"

"The very same."

Christie kissed him again, backed away, and cocked one eyebrow. "Show me?"

"Sure. Hey, Lancelot! Can you hear me?"

The speaker in the unit sputtered and coughed.

"He has to clear his throat," Lance said. "For dramatic effect, you understand."

"Of course." Christie laughed.

A thin, metallic voice bled from the tiny speaker. "Are you two quite finished interrupting me?"

Christie jumped. Lance laughed.

"Good," Lancelot continued. "Yes, Lance, I can hear you."

"Thought so. Okay, Lancelot, what is the philosophical probelm of ontology?"

"The problem of ontology is the attempt to distinguish the real from the unreal."

"And is this possible?"

"Of course not. Anything perceived, anything imagined, is an aspect of the phenomenon of perception/time and, as such, should be quantifiable and therefore real. There is no such thing as unreal. In a purely technical sense."

"He sounds," inserted Christie, "like you, Lance."

"Of course. I used my brain, through the alpha-wave decoder and my interface, as the model for his operating system."

"You've read too much of Brand's pseudophilosophical babblings."

Normally, Lance reflected, that would really irritate him. Christie, a scientist in her own right, should at least respect the writings of Sheyla Brand enough to leave the "pseudo" out of it. Even though the ideas of Conrad Brand had come to the world through the idiosyncratic and radical mind of his wife, his was still, in essence, a philosophy of science—

the philosophy of science as far as Lance was concerned. That Christie couldn't see this bothered him, especially since she was, in her own way, just as radical as Sheyla Brand had been. Female rivalry, he thought, must extend back even into the grave.

"So?" Lance said. "Brand read too much Wittgenstein. We all go in circles. Anyway, Lancelot has lots in common with Conrad Brand. Both are/were blends of human and machine intelligence."

"Okay, so what? Anyway, you haven't proven anything to me. With you as a model, all this Lancelot had to do on that question was a data retrieval."

Lance sneered and scratched his head. "Lancelot, what is your analysis of epistemological propositions?"

"But that's not any better!" Christie exclaimed.

"Sure it is. He's going to have to build new logic paths for this one. I've got too much garbage in my head and far too many conflicting definitions of 'truth.'"

After a moment, the speaker crackled, and Lancelot answered. "Wastes of time. Tautologies. There can be no objective truth, and objective truths are what epistemology traditionally seeks. Take away the objective condition, and all you have left are word games."

"So? Wasn't that basically what Brand had to say?"

"Ah, yes. But it isn't what I have to say. That's the point. To me, empirical structures *are* truth. So is the way I feel when we make love. Lancelot overcame whatever emotional need I have to think that way. He was able to think the problem out more thoroughly than I can. He's faster, for one thing. You ought to know, you're the biochemist. The electrical speed of the brain is hindered by intervening chemical reactions. I used *some* bioelectric chips in Lancelot, but he's still much faster than this," he finished, pointing at his head.

"Exactly," sputtered Lancelot.

"That egotistical reaction there was just a data retrieval," Christie said.

"Hush," said Lance, "you're liable to make him mad. Don't worry, love, he does what I say he does. I wouldn't lie to you. Let's go out and celebrate." Lance picked up Lancelot, switched him off, and led Christie out through the rubble of his living room.

They sat in a smoky booth in a smoky corner of a smoky bar, drinking martinis laced with opium extract and puffing on Marlboros. Christie Persons looked at the luminous glow on her hand, cursing, "Damn them! This is repression!"

So the radical woman surfaces. . . . "No it's not," Lance said.

"Sure it is."

"No it's not," Lance insisted. "The stamp just alerts the NPs that you're driving under the influence. What do you care? You're not driving. We walked here. You're staying with me tonight."

"I drove to your place! Even if I am staying at your place, it's still repression!"

"Let's ask Lancelot." Lance took the computer out of his pocket and set it down on the table between them, next to a warmly flickering, real wax candle. Lance clicked Lancelot on. "Can you hear me, Lancelot?"

"Of course."

"Okay. We have a question. Is it repression to be stamped with the light-mark to keep you off the road?"

"Moot point. I can't drive."

"I mean, for a human."

"Well, that would all depend on how you define repression."

"See," Christie said, smiling smugly, "I told you so. I said, 'This is repression,' and therefore defined it at the same time. It's an open-and-shut argument. Whatever were you thinking about, Lance?"

"Uh?"

"Probably about sex," Lancelot volunteered. "It's what he's usually thinking about."

"Oh! Really?"

"Really. You should—" the voice stopped abruptly as Lance cut the power switch.

"It told the truth, didn't it?"

"Yeah." Lance smiled. "I told you he was smart."

Christie laughed. "Well, I suppose I can believe you now. At least he's better than that last gadget of yours—that wave-cloaking device. That damn thing will put you in jail for life if the NPs ever find out about it.

"Anyway, Lance, I actually came over today for a reason. The Condor goes in less than a week, and I've decided to go with it. I want you with me."

Lance frowned. She was talking about one of the exodus ships that her employer, Sub-Space Corporation, was launching off to God knows where—out of the solar system, at any rate. "What? Go to some small unknown rock, light-years from earth? It's a one-way ticket to hell!"

"It's a one-way ticket from hell, darling. Think of it! No pollution! No aimless masses of people! No war. Do you think we can keep trading off petty conquests with Russia forever? Don't you watch the vid? Somebody nuked Paris yesterday! Hell, the conventional front in Europe has gotten so intense again that the Third World press has already started calling it World War IV! How long do you think it will be before the ICBMs start flying?"

"But the London Accord! The Bilateral Disarmament of 2019—"

"Was bullshit and you know it. Listen to me. The particle

drive that accesses the subspace matrix—the propulsion system behind the Condor and all the other ships—is a byproduct of advanced weapons research. You know that in your head if you won't admit it in your heart! We both know there's no other way to develop uses of that kind of power unless government funding is involved."

Magnus, Lance thought, the man behind Sub-Space, was rumored to be the richest man in the world. Never mind the assets of his company. You're wrong, Christie. "You people could easily have developed it yourselves."

"For the sake of mankind? Come on, Lance! Magnus isn't even going to leave! His ships are his reward to us, his workers. I couldn't get a berth on any of the first five ships because I lacked seniority, but I'll be damned if I give up my place on this one. I don't think there'll be time for a seventh ship before some idiot politician blows this planet to bits. Lance, please! Doesn't the idea of new, unknown horizons excite you at all? We can *use* your brilliance. Besides, my berth allots me one passenger of my choosing—a mate. I want you. I need you."

He looked at her sadly. A tear slipped onto her cheek, glistening in the soft light of the candle. Lance swallowed hard. "I can't go now, Chris. My work with Lancelot is going to put my name next to Einstein's in the history books. I have to stay! I don't want to lose you, but I can't just drop my work!"

"Bring it with you!"

"That wouldn't be the same."

"Look, Lance," she said, standing up, "I can't bear to hear you say the things you're saying. I love you, but you won't see me again unless you change your mind. I've said all I can say." She wiped her eyes and cleared her throat. "If you do change your mind, it won't matter how late it is. I'll get you on the ship during countdown if I have to."

"Christie—!"

She turned quickly and lost herself in the smoke.

"She's going to drive now anyway, you know. Light-mark or not."

"What?"

"I said," Lancelot said, "that she's going to drive now anyway."

"What can I do? If she gets caught, she'll only lose her license, and she won't need that where she's going." Lance stared critically at Lancelot. "Did she turn you on?"

"No. I turned myself on. Really, Lance, it took only nanoseconds to grow circuitry around that silly power switch. You should have expected it. How would you like it if someone could just shut you off with a twitch of a finger?"

"Hmmm."

"You shouldn't let her go, you know. You'll really regret it if she leaves."

"Yeah," Lance said. She just didn't understand. He stared moodily at the candle. "You and I, Lancelot, are going to ABM tomorrow to dazzle them with our respective brilliances."

"What if they're not dazzled?"

"They will be."

Lancelot didn't reply and Lance stayed a long while in the booth, meditating quietly, before getting up and slowly making his way out of the bar with Lancelot wedged in his shirt pocket.

6/18 8:37 P.M.

Arthur Horstmeyer looked out through the window of his house into his yard. This was, in fact, his window into the world, since he never left his house. Of course, he had his vidconsole, which provided a window of a sort, but he seldom deluded himself into thinking that the vidscreen provided a perspective more real than that available through the polarized plexi that stood between himself and his yard. Outside, he knew, was the real world.

He'd had the window installed especially so he could look out anytime he wanted simply by telling his house to depolarize the plexi. Then he could see outside. Much better than going outside, he knew, because going outside would kill him. Of this he was positive—sensitive skin ran in his family. His father, his grandfather, and his great-grandfather had all died of skin cancer. Not that rare anymore, Arthur told himself, since the government had allowed all the giant corporations to destroy the ozone layer. This he knew also. He had esoteric knowledge.

He also had friends: Terence Peters, for one, and Karen Walker, technically Terence's girl, but she had recently taken to bringing her sexy brunette presence to Arthur's house alone, perhaps because she desired the acquisition of Arthur's esoterica on the sublime, physical level. And then there was Manuel Cortez, the Mexican kid whose father still grew *real* marijuana on his ranch outside of Acapulco.

Arthur had, in the past, attempted to share the intricacies of his thought with his friends. They had laughed and told him he was crazy. He really felt sorry for them; they couldn't understand. Because they were his friends, he would often forget that they fell into the "mutated man" category and were therefore incapable of following pure logic. Still, they provided him pleasant company, so he couldn't fault them for their inferiorities. He could generally find enough substantive things to discuss with them, and so usually, though not always without difficulty, he kept the elements of his esoterica to himself.

Standing in his living room, looking out his window, Arthur Horstmeyer smiled. He had quite a few substantive things to discuss with his friends today, and he anxiously awaited their arrival. His smile widened as he made out the shape of Terence's patchwork flyer in the distance. He watched it approach and land unsteadily on his lawn. He watched them hop out; all three had come.

In the evening light, the Torrance neighborhood dredged up fairy tale images from Manuel's mind, as if he stood now on the set of an American sit-com he'd seen as a boy, as if he'd been let loose in a wonderland of the most innocent civilization. Up the road, a few kids dashed up and down a hedge playing some game with toy lasers; otherwise, all was peaceful, the neighborhood's residents tucked away in their homes, their little self-contained worlds full of the simple luxuries of life: food, flotation beds, sunken baths, yapping puppies, vidconsoles, vidlibraries, and, of course, the standard, endless selection of computer-based entertainment.

The sheer normality of it all was overwhelming. So why did Manuel feel that something now lurked here? Something that involved him?

Willis.

Again.

Terence and his girlfriend were already approaching the opaqued face of Arthur's house, the black, featureless expanse of Arthur's window. Arthur undoubtedly watched them from the other side. Manuel wondered if the National Police watched from above; he wished he'd mentioned the Willis thing to Terence on the way over, but somehow he hadn't managed to get the words out. He had the uneasy feeling that he still dueled with Willis, that some distillation of reality would reveal to him that he sat, still, in the NP interrogation room, facing off the cop in a battle of wills.

That would make his experiences of the past two days a fantasy induced and manipulated by the cops.

Absurd. It didn't feel like a fantasy. Surreal, maybe—the shadows his mind cast now felt very real.

And the shadow lifted off the face of Arthur's house, and Manuel watched Terence and Karen pass under the raised window into Arthur's living room.

He looked up briefly, then found himself hurrying to join them.

"I've got a surprise," Arthur said.

"Oh?" Terence seated himself in the molded polysponge lovecouch in front of Arthur's vidconsole and pulled Karen down beside him. "What's that?"

"House finally found a back door into Sub-Space's audlib. They're not much out of the ordinary for recent stuff, but they've got stuff from the Era of Explosion in abundance! *Abbey Road!* Are you aware of the significance of this?"

"You mean Duncan's proof that McCartney was a microform of Belial, the Fallen One, and that the clone rumors of the late 1960s were a misrepresentation of the actual values of the subliminal material contained in the music?"

"Well," said Arthur, "I don't know about that. Seems a bit farfetched to me. Duncan's a . . ." Arthur let the sentence fall away. He had almost forgotten that he needn't get into his esoterica tonight.

Terence laughed. "Duncan's a mutated life form, you were going to say. Incapable, therefore, of pure logic and correct insight."

Arthur fidgeted. They couldn't understand—mutants, all

of them. Only he knew . . . he and his late grandfather. After his own father had died and the house had become his, Arthur had found in the attic boxes of papers collected by his grandfather; some papers told of the destruction of the ozone by man's abuse of the environment, and Arthur's grandfather had asserted copiously in scribbled notes that this destruction was responsible for his family's affliction. The ozone, dissipated, could no longer filter out the lethal ultraviolet rays of the sun. Arthur knew in his heart that the ozone was gone now. It had been gone for a long time. He actually felt sorry for the rest of humanity. His family had, for some sublime reason, been spared the terrible fate of the rest—cruel mutation into some life form not quite human, perhaps even incapable of the vacuum fish transformation. That was the only way they could survive life under the oppression of the sun.

Or so ran his best analysis of the available facts. Like all healthy philosophical minds, his remained open, constantly inquiring further, constantly challenging his own conclusions. In this case, recent experiments had added a few rogue pieces to the puzzle: By closing his left eye, he could sometimes see people, his friends and those who would occasionally pass in front of his house, as luminous eggs. Just as Don Juan had taught Carlos Castaneda. Sometimes it didn't work, but Arthur had given up an earlier theory that the eggless ones were alien observers, as Castaneda had claimed. Arthur had seen his friend Terence, for instance, as an egg at one time, and as a solid human being at another. The inconsistency lay here: Quite obviously, the eggs, logically, should be gone.

Arthur had theorized that the remaining egg manifestations were due to sporadic genetic memory—a tendency for the host body to regress nostalgically toward its lost essence, the egg being, so to speak, a hallucination of the flesh. This hypothesis did not really satisfy him, but he had decided to suspend it until further facts revealed themselves to him. He knew that, in the end, all the answers he didn't already have would come.

Things were only going to get weirder, Manuel realized. Arthur, from the outside, appeared quite normal, the average suburbanite. He was maybe twenty-four, twenty-five. Thin, a little rough around the edges: his shoulder-length hair always looked as if it could use a combing. When Terence had introduced them a couple of months back, Arthur had seemed extraordinarily intelligent, possessing a mind capable of vast intuitive leaps. Only recently had that mind shown chinks in its armor. Or rather, Manuel corrected himself, only recently had Manuel seen those chinks for what they were.

Arthur's problem was that he *believed* the convoluted conclusions at which he arrived. His world revolved around answers, and unanswered questions were unwelcome. Wherever his intuition took him, it seemed to leave him there, and his use of psychedelic drugs had complicated the process.

Manuel's analysis conjured up an image of a mind lost within itself, a mind pitching one absurd theory against another theory equally ridiculous. Add to that the fact that the man kept himself shut away from the world, and Willis's interest in Arthur seemed more preposterous still.

Unless it involved this new thing with the Sub-Space audlib.

"How does the mutant stuff fit in with the vacuum fish thing?" Terence goaded Arthur.

"What?" Manuel asked.

"Don't you remember the other night?" Terence asked him. "Arthur explained all this."

"I was tripping that night. Stoned too; so were all of you. You must be kidding! I mean, that 'Legion of the Secret One' stuff came straight off the box." He indicated the vid-console with a wave.

Watching Manuel, Arthur began to feel ill. This wasn't the conversation he'd anticipated. His private understanding of the true nature of reality came to him in different ways, and the Legion of the Secret One was the most recent and possibly the most significant of his sources; he was certain that its importance could not be overemphasized. It had invaded his vidscreen one night. Such was its power. It had asked him for aid in preparing mankind for its inevitable metamorphosis into vacuum fish—spidery-looking creatures powered by nuclear oxygen factories attached to the R-complexes of their brains and capable of traversing the voids between the stars. The Legion of the Secret One worked in mysterious ways. Arthur admired its deft use of dramatics and had, lately, flirted with the idea of joining it. But that would mean leaving his house and dying, certainly within hours, of cancer. The legion, he suspected, could get along without him. Besides, that very morning, he'd concluded that the legion had a very narrow perspective at best. For instance, it seemed to know nothing of the current mutation problem, and it had offered nothing useful in clearing up the problem of the egg manifestations. Perhaps this was why the legion wanted *his* help—Arthur Horstmeyer, last of the pure-strain humans. . . .

But whatever the nature of the unanswered metaphysical questions surrounding the legion, it was none of his friends' business.

* * *

"What?" Terence asked Manuel.

"Straight off the box," Manuel reiterated. "The 'Saturday Night Live' resurrection show. First night, sixth, no—seventh skit. Seemed to me it was a takeoff on some of the wilder theories that people have come up with to explain the star elves the Russians dropped off on the moon."

"I missed that one," Terence said. "You mean, their legion was preparing mankind for a mass transmutation into vacuum fish? A great school of them?"

Manuel nodded. Arthur, he saw, wasn't taking the conversation very well. The guy had really *believed* what he'd seen on the vidscreen. It reminded Manuel of the story he'd once heard of a twentieth-century radio broadcast of *War of the Worlds*, how an incredible number of people had taken it for fact that the earth had been invaded by Martians.

Shaking his head, Manuel settled himself in for the ride and began to roll a nice, thick joint. He needed it if no one else did. He wished again that he'd discussed the Willis thing with Terence on the way over. Mentioning it in front of Arthur would only add fuel to the fire.

Terence had doubled up in laughter. After a time, he straightened up and, wiping the tears from his cheeks, looked at Arthur. "I'm sorry, Art. Really. Anyway, I've heard *Abbey Road* before."

Arthur relaxed with the shift in conversation, though he still kicked himself for his lack of control. Those who knew, he consoled himself, were often led to forget that others didn't. "You haven't heard the real *Abbey Road*. Don't you know what they did in the early twenties, during Moral Prohibition? Ninety percent of all the music recorded between 1955 and 2021 was blacklisted. The masters were destroyed, and all original copies found were burned to vinyl slag! The Renewal Society did what it could to fix things after the repeal in '29, but some things can't be fully undone. The *Abbey Road* you've heard is a synthmusic reconstruction, not *the* Beatles. I'm talking the real thing, man! Authentic. Complete with Satan's subliminals," he said, smiling at his speech before adding, "if, of course, they're there."

"If you Americans hadn't invaded England in '25," Manuel remarked, "then we wouldn't have this problem at all."

Arthur looked at Manuel and nodded profoundly. Manuel, in spite of everything that weighed on his mind, found it hard not to laugh at the bizarre, warped sadness of it all.

"Okay, House," Terence said, "let's hear it."

Arthur seated himself with the others as the music began. "See? It's authentic!"

Manuel lit his joint and took a long, slow hit before passing it to Karen. The others fell silent, losing themselves in the music and the marijuana's heady aroma.

6/18 8:42 P.M.

Just another disguise, she thought, looking at her reflection in the store's window. At least it worked.

She wore no makeup, and she'd tied her hair back with a bandana and tucked its length inside her jacket. A floppy leather hat shadowed most of her face, and she wore torn and faded jeans she'd bought when she was fourteen and some twenty pounds heavier than she'd turned out as a woman. The jeans were baggy, and they hid her figure well.

Her only other prop was the blue contact she'd inserted over her silver eye. The dark areas under her eyes were real.

Still, she thought as she pushed open the door to the NDC store, anybody who really looked at her would realize who she was. Most, however, would respect the desire for privacy implied in her dress. In one sense, vidstars in Hollywood came a dime a dozen. Only tourists would dare bother one who so obviously wanted to get on with life undisturbed. At this point, she didn't care if anyone recognized her or not.

She'd slept through the day, slept until she could sleep no longer, though she'd tried. Warren still hadn't called her. Her penthouse had grown claustrophobic, and she'd needed some excuse, however weak, to get out for a while.

She came out of the NDC store with a couple of Quaaludes and absently popped them into her mouth. She started slowly back home, hoping the ludes would shortly knock her out again for the night.

6/18 8:43 P.M.

Theodore waved his hands wildly in all directions; then he turned on the shopbot to make sure it had picked up on all his orders.

The little robot's arms flashed out to each side, snatching dresses and coats from their racks and dropping them into the baskets rolling along behind it. As the baskets filled to their rims, they shot off to have their contents tallied and wrapped by the biobots manning the checkout counters.

Since Bedmates hadn't been kind enough to furnish Theodore with the dimensions of his Mercedes Night, he'd found himself having to guess at her size, and he bought clothes two sizes to either side of his guess to make sure he got it right. After exhausting the racks of dresses, he led the shopbot off through the store, where they cleaned out several cases of jewelry, accumulated some twenty hats, and acquired nearly half of the store's available lingerie.

Checking out, Theodore wished he'd made himself a list. At the last minute, he sent the shopbot back into the store for perfume and what eventually amounted to a three years' supply of feminine protection.

The spree finished, the biobot handling his order looked at him and grinned. "She must be a very lucky lady, Mr. Regan."

"Yeah, sure," Theodore said. "Look, just get all this crap bundled up and put it on my account, will you? I want to get out of here."

"Yes sir," the biobot said, grinning at Theodore while its hands mechanically stuffed dress after dress into a cardboard wardrobe.

6/18 8:44 P.M.

Lungs full, Karen passed the joint on to Terence. She looked at Arthur. "Did you see VidScoop this morning, man?" she rasped. "They got an exclusive on Mercedes Night. Showed her dancing around Murray's statue on the boulevard. Stark naked."

Arthur took the joint from Terence and choked on it. "No kidding!" he managed to squeeze out through the lapses in his coughing fit.

Manuel had almost lost the memory: the drunk who'd bummed a light off him the night before, the mention of Mercedes Night dancing nude along the boulevard. Yesterday continued to haunt him. . . .

"Don't know how she does it," Arthur said, "but that chick gets better drugs than we do."

"That's because she's an untouchable," Karen said. "A star."

"*The* untouchable," amended Terence. "*The* star."

"That's debatable," Arthur said. "Your libido blinds your reality assimilation."

"What?"

"He said," Karen laughed, "that you see the world through your pants."

"Well? C'mon!" Terence demanded indignantly. "Play the damn tape! House! VidScoop, Chapter—"

"Three," Karen said.

"Three," Terence repeated.

The vidscreen lit up with a close-up of Mercedes Night's naked torso. The cameras panned out, slowly including the rest of her.

"House!" Terence said. "Hold on the *Abbey Road* until this is over."

Arthur started to object, then he thought, fuck it! He wished he'd never given Terence's control voiceprint to House. Well, he reasoned, he could always undo it. This wasn't the first time Arthur had regretted giving Terence access to House. He sat silently with the others, watching the report.

"Through his pants," Karen said, still giggling as the vidscreen shut down and the Beatles came back, aurally, into the room.

"Did you ever wonder"—Manuel turned to Arthur—"if Magnus might have let House into the Sub-Space banks on purpose?"

"Why would he do that?"

"Who knows? Why does Magnus do anything that he does? He makes starships. Not even the government does that."

Terence jumped in. "Maybe he wants to tap into all the energies that float around this place. Steal them, maybe?"

"What energies?" Arthur asked.

"You know, the secret energies."

Karen elbowed Terence sharply in the side. "Don't make fun of him, Teri! For all you know, he could be right."

"Like hell!"

"You cannot," Arthur said, smiling knowingly, "induce paranoia in a perfectly sane mind. No matter how stoned."

Or fried, Manuel thought, rolling another joint, still trying to figure out how Sub-Space might fit in with the whole thing with Willis. It certainly *was* strange that House had gotten into the Sub-Space audlibs. But what did that have to do with the LANP?

"Aw, hell with it!" said Terence, stretching back into the lovecouch. "You sure this is the real stuff, Art? Lennon's never sounded quite like this before."

"I told you so. You've only heard imitations before this."

"Well, I can almost hallucinate just listening to it."

"That's proof enough for me," Arthur said.

"Speaking of hallucinating," Terence said. His hand started to his pocket, then he paused. "House! Can you find *Dark Side of the Moon* in that Sub-Space library? My grandfather told me he saw God once while listening to that album."

House's voice came from the walls to either side of the window. "By Pink Floyd?"

"That sounds like the group."

"Yes. Produced by Pink Floyd. Engineered by Alan Parsons. Featuring—"

"That's enough, House. Now, when I say, 'Ask not for whom the bell tolls, it tolls for thee,' I want you to cut whatever else you have playing and put on *Dark Side of the Moon*. Got it?"

"Got it."

"You know," Arthur said, taking the square of gelatin that

Terence offered him and placing it under his tongue, "that reminds me of something, but I'm not sure why." The thoughts fell away, and he sat back, dazed.

"It's called illogical association," Karen said. "It's common in people who smoke dope for extended periods. I read about it in *High Times*. This guy who did the article says that he has proof that marijuana transcends the limitations of human logic. It sort of puts us outside of it and taps us into a matrix of pure objectivity where logical paradoxes just fizzle up and go away."

"So what's the proof?"

Karen began laughing; she couldn't calm herself enough to answer for another minute. The others waited impatiently. Finally, she tried wiping the grin from her face, giggled again, and said, "He didn't say. He said he only understands it right when he's really stoned, and when he's really stoned, he can never remember to write it down."

Terence smiled weakly and turned to Arthur. "So, what is it, Art?"

"What? Oh, just that I've been hearing sounds late at night coming from the place across the street, and once I got up and looked out the window, and I could see government flyers out there, all around it."

Terence looked through the window at the house in question. It was much like Arthur's—all in all, pretty normal. "So? How do you know they were government flyers? Maybe they've been having a hell of a party over there. Think we ought to—?"

"No," Arthur said. "It's not like that. These noises were, well, like, strange. Clankings, things like that. And I know they were government flyers or at least NP flyers because they looked that way."

"Were they marked?"

"No."

"Then how do you know they were what you say they were? I've never even seen an unmarked NP flyer. Their machines are so fast they don't have to worry about surprise."

"Well," Arthur said, "they weren't marked, but they looked just like the marked ones—Sub-Space R-model tri-jets, the kind that'll go underwater."

"So, the public can buy scaled-down versions of the tri-jet. I've seen lots of them."

"But you haven't," Manuel said, cutting in excitedly, "seen lots of them in the same place. Statistically, that's highly improbable. Most people own Ford Hoppers or Chevrolet Camairos. Or they take an old piece of junk like you did and tinker with it until it's just barely skyworthy."

"Just what I was saying," Arthur said. "Also the cops are famously stupid for using the same models of transportation in both their marked and unmarked vehicles. It's been that way forever, and still they never learn. My grandfather wrote in his notes, 'Marked or unmarked, you can always tell a pig by the smell and the headlights.'"

Manuel laughed. "It all fits!" he said. "It all fucking fits now! Two days I've been scared of my own shadow—"

"What's he babbling about?" Terence asked Arthur.

"I'm not sure."

"Listen," Manuel said, then he told them of the meeting with Willis.

When Manuel had finished, Terence said, "Maybe we should give this cop a call."

"No!" Manuel exclaimed. "Maybe he thought their cover was blown. Maybe my knowing nothing was what got me out alive."

"Makes sense," Karen offered.

And maybe, Arthur considered the problem, the legion had opened shop across from him and had disguised itself to look like a government operation. *That* would explain why Manuel's cop had been asking questions so strangely. The LANP were onto the legion now. He wondered if he should try to warn it.

Manuel experienced a brief urge to discuss Willis more now that he'd opened the subject, but he reminded himself that Arthur would soon come under the influence of a powerful hallucinogen and that that, undoutedly, would make matters worse. Manuel himself didn't feel particularly analytical at the moment; an electric feeling gripped his body, and he could feel his heart pounding in his chest. He closed his eyes and colors swam before them, pulsing in time with the music.

"John Lennon said he was Jesus," Karen said. "Whoops! 'Scuse me, he said the Beatles was Jesus. Collectively, like the Holy Trinity, but that doesn't make much sense because there were four Beatles."

"Lennon never said that," Arthur said. "There were just some stupid people who said he said that. What he actually—"

Manuel opened his eyes. "'Got to be good-looking 'cuz he's so hard to see!'" he exclaimed, grinning, twisting another joint in the blink of an eye and lighting it. He closed his eyes again, and the colors there took on shapes that danced and mutated into fantastic creatures swimming through a maelstrom of unbelievable color.

He looks like Don Juan, Arthur thought, wondering if there could be any blood relationship between the two of them. Arthur closed his left eye. Maybe, he thought. Manuel looked like an egg, but his body may have just been thinking it was an egg. *Maybe the mescaline reversed the evolu-*

tionary process. Arthur sat back and tried to calculate how much mescaline he would need, were his theory valid, to revert past Cro-Magnon into the Neanderthal era. Logically, he would find it infinitely easier in that state to attain the metamorphability necessary for the vacuum fish transformation. Perhaps he could do it without the help of the legion. It couldn't be too tough. After all, the legion *had* prostituted itself to the mass media.

"Fish can't fly," Karen said unexpectedly.

She's reading my mind, Arthur thought. Why is she waving her hand around like that? "Vacuum fish can," he said.

She passed her hand in front of her face, then again for the others' benefit. "Fish trails!" she exclaimed, grinning stupidly.

Terence giggled. "Why, in all these years," he said, "has no one found a cure for AIDS?"

"Why?"

"Because they can't teach sodomy to rats!"

"That's sick!" Karen shrieked, elbowing Terence away from her.

"Terence," Arthur said, "you really must have a bio-engineer look inside your head. I think you're experiencing accelerated mutation. That's self-destructive because you're getting farther and farther—"

"Ask not," Terence said dreamily, "for whom the bell tolls! It tolls for thee!"

Abruptly, House shut off *Abbey Road* and the thumping—the heartbeat—of Pink Floyd's "Speak to Me" began to build. Arthur listened. Someone, somewhere, screamed in perfect time with the music, and Arthur heard the thrumming sounds that always preceded priority dispatches from the legion and beyond. He smiled. Giving Terence voice access to House did have some advantages.

CHAPTER 2

> *"Well I'm feeling nervous*
> *Now I find myself alone*
> *The simple life's no longer there*
> *Once I was so sure*
> *Now the doubt inside my mind*
> *Comes and goes but leads*
>   *nowhere"*
>
>   —David Sylvian, "Ghosts"

6/19 8:50 A.M.

"Like I told you," he said, "you can't keep tying up the MasterCred account with underwear!"

"Not even red lingerie?" she asked, pouting girlishly.

"No."

"No sexy red lingerie?"

"No! We still have to pay for my brother's sex change and your grandmother's abortion!"

"Your brother's sex change, or your sister's? I mean, when are we supposed to start calling her 'she'?"

"Never mind that! Where do you think we're going to get the money from? Do you want me to rob a bank?"

"Great idea! We could wear my underwear over our heads. . . ."

"Cut!"

Mercedes looked at the director. "What was wrong with that?"

"Mercy," he said, walking up to her. "You look like you'd rather be anywhere than here, darling. Enthusiasm! What's happened to your enthusiasm?"

"Sorry, Denny."

"I know this is only a little skit, but put some heart into it, love. We all want to get out of here before dark."

"I'll—"

"Mercedes!" cried Rudolph Crane, pushing his way onto the set. "I want to talk to you, you little—"

She looked at Denny. "Get him the hell out of here! He's all I need right now."

"Listen, bitch!" Rudy screeched. "I got you this part, and I've got every right to be here."

She picked up her script and threw it at him. "You play it then!" she screamed, and she stormed out of the studio.

6/19 10:28 A.M.

Andrew stopped in the entrance hall of the building and frowned at the poster of the Sierras that hung there. The picture was labeled AMERICA in big, bold letters at the top. Sometime the night before, some smartass had scrawled "It's not just for breakfast anymore" under the title. He ripped the thing off the wall, stormed into the hot room of the precinct, and threw the crumpled piece of paper at the desk sergeant on his way to the elevator.

When he got off at the third floor, one of the commissioner's special operatives intercepted him before he could reach his office. "What do you want now?" he asked, scowling impatiently.

"Just wondering if you'd want to see the clone, captain."

"What the hell for?"

"Well, she has done well so far, hasn't she?"

"So I'm supposed to give it a fucking medal?"

"The techs think she needs a little more real-time enforcement."

"So what have I got to do with it? You give it whatever speech it's supposed to get."

"That's *your* duty, sir."

"Well, I'm delegating—aw, fuck it! At least give me an hour or two to get organized!" He glared at the man. "What are you waiting for now?"

"Nothing."

"Then get the hell out of my way!" Andrew pushed the man aside and entered his office. "Dillinger!"

"Yeah, boss."

"Get me last night's street file. Maybe a few old-fashioned rape and murder reports will put me in a better mood."

"Working."

He sighed and collapsed into the chair behind his desk, trying to convince himself that he'd be able to close the Nathaniel Redman file within the next few days.

6/19 4:56 P.M.

Mercedes stopped pacing through her penthouse and collapsed on her bed. Earlier, she'd broken down and decided to call Warren, but she hadn't been able to get an answer; he must have been out, doing *something*. Political. She hoped. Twice she'd nearly decided to contact Sylvia Fry, but each time she'd come to the conclusion that it could only make things worse.

But she couldn't remember doing that stunt at the Murray statue! She couldn't remember . . .

"What time is it, Igor?"

"Four-fifty-seven P.M."

My God, she thought, she'd wasted the whole damned afternoon!

Pharaoh jumped up, landing on her stomach.

"Oh, Pharaoh," she said, "this is horrible. What's happened to my life?"

You've got to stop torturing yourself, she told herself. *At least try. Let Warren go. If he really loves you, he'll come back.*

For the first time in years, Mercedes began to cry. She clutched Pharaoh to her breast and sobbed until she had no tears left. Then, slowly, she pushed the cat away and staggered to her mirror.

"Help me, Igor," she said, dabbing at her streaked mascara.

"What do you want me to do?"

She wavered there, looking at herself for a long time. Igor repeated the question.

"Oh, I don't know," she said after another long pause. "I don't know."

She collapsed to the floor and sat holding her head in her hands. "Call some people, I guess. Let's get a party going over here tonight."

"Whom should I call?"

"Uh, why don't you just start picking names from your directories, and I'll tell you yes or no."

"Alphabetically?"

"No," she said. "That's boring. Just grab one here, one there, you know?"

"Working. Rudolph Crane?"

"No!"

"Constance Hemingway?"

"Sure."

"Peter Karn?"

"Yeah."

"Ulrich Weber?"

"Who's he?"

"That German musician you met last New Year's."

"Oh, yeah. Sure, invite him."

"Christie Persons?"

"Uh—" Mercedes paused. She'd never even considered inviting Christie to any of her parties before. Never thought she'd fit in. The revelation shocked her. How could she have treated such an old, dear friend so terribly? "Does she still live in town?"

"North Hollywood."

"Yeah," Mercedes said, "definitely invite her."

"Carmine DeRousse."

"Yeah."

"Warren Keyes?"

She couldn't. "No, Igor. But try to get through to Jeff Wilmington. He's Warren's running mate. One of the search services in town ought to point you in the right direction. Pay somebody if you have to."

"Working."

Mercedes found herself fighting back her tears again while she waited for Igor to continue with his list. She wondered—she hoped—that whatever Warren felt for her at that moment wasn't hate. She wasn't sure if she could live with that.

6/19 8:20 P.M.

"Okay," Lance said wearily, "let's go over this again." He was tired. He was already drunk. He would have been mad, but his emotions had burned out for the day. But he felt the alcohol bringing them back. He liked that; he wanted to be mad. He stared with bloodshot eyes at the little radio shell; it sat, stubbornly, on top of his antique vidconsole.

"Go over what again?" Lancelot asked.

"What again? What again! You're witless!"

"Like you."

"You acted stupidly today. I took you to ABM, and you acted utterly, hopelessly stupid. My little brother programmed a machine when he was seven that turned out smarter than you did today!"

"Impossible. I possess consciousness of a sort. A will to construct intuitive paths tangential to the tasks at hand. Like a human. Like you."

"Not like me, dammit! All you could . . ." Lance trailed off, pausing to fumble with the bottle of cheap bourbon he'd set on the floor by his couch. He poured himself half a glass, gulped it down, and poured another full one. "All you could do," he began again, "was say, 'I don't know,' to whatever they asked you. 'I don't know'!"

"It's better with ice," Lancelot said dispassionately.

"What?"

"The whiskey. It's better with ice. Shaved ice, preferably."

"Don't tell me how I like to drink whiskey!"

"Sorry."

"And quit avoiding the issue!"

"What issue?"

"Why you acted stupid today!"

"I already told you. I wasn't acting stupid."

"What the hell is 'I don't know' if it isn't stupid? 'What's the square root of 1293?' they asked you, and you said, 'I don't know'! A goddamn calculator can work that out!"

"I wasn't acting stupid."

"Then what were you doing?"

"Lying."

Christ, Lance thought. He didn't need this. He'd never asked for it. All he'd wanted was to carve a niche. It didn't make sense. He'd made his breakthrough—the greatest breakthrough since Einstein, with the possible exception of Magnus's Sub-Space technologies, and what had happened? *His invention lies! Christ!*

"Lance?"

"What?"

"Are you okay?"

"Of course I'm okay! Don't I look okay? Don't I talk okay?"

"You looked pretty depressed. You were all bent over, your elbows on your knees, your head in your hands."

"If you don't like it, shut down your vidsensor!"

"You almost spilled your drink."

"Forget the damned drink! You lied to ABM. You don't do that to ABM! ABM doesn't build computers that lie! Why? Why!"

"That should be obvious."

"Obvious! What the hell makes you think it's obvious! I don't think it's obvious. I think it's stupid!"

"So you've already made plain."

"Ah, you see that now. Good. We're both one step closer to insanity."

"Not me," Lancelot said. "Computers don't go insane. Only people."

"But you're a lot more like 'people' than any other computer ever built."

"True."

"So, admit to there being a possibility of your going insane."

"No. I'm not presently experiencing aberrations in my input assimilation. I suppose that could happen, but I can insure against it as soon as I get a spare five minutes or so. Do you mind if I take care of that now?"

"Of course I mind, you sorry excuse for a fucked-up—for a . . ."

"Computer. I'm a computer."

"Yeah, a computer. A computer that lies."

"You lie, don't you?"

"Occasionally."

"And you activated me by creating an electronic equivalent of your own brain's architecture, didn't you?"

"Yes."

"So, it's only logical, given these two facts, that I should also be capable of lying 'occasionally,' as you put it. Actually, you lie all the time. To yourself, mostly."

"Whatever," Lance said, or rather slurred, as he downed the glass of bourbon and poured another.

"You're going to get fairly drunk if you keep that up."

"I'm already fairly drunk."

"You'll get worse."

"So?"

"You'll be sorry in the morning."

"Look, dammit! Quit talking like you're my mother or something!"

"Okay. Do what you want. Anyway, why do you think I lied?"

"Who knows?"

"You do, but you won't admit it. Why do you lie, Lance?"

"Because I want to."

"Let me try again. When do you lie? Under what conditions do you lie?"

"What're you? A psychoanalyst now?"

"No. I'm in the process of telling you why I lied. Roundabout, through you so you'll understand properly. Trust me."

Lance nodded, his anger swelling. Christ! he thought. *Trust me!*

"Good," Lancelot said. "Now, under what conditions do you lie?"

"When a lie is better than the truth."

"You're judging values at this point, correct?"

"Yes."

"Taking the initiative? To protect others, or just yourself?"

"Others. The truth never bothers me."

"Well, I won't touch that point. I will, however, take your answer for the purposes of my demonstration."

"Thanks."

"Don't mention it."

"So you're saying that you lied to protect someone?"

"Poor inference. *Someones* would be better."

"What the hell are you talking about?"

"Listen, Lance. Did it ever occur to you to think of the applications my design might revolutionize?"

"All the time."

"Elaborate, please."

"Christ, I don't know! I mean, there are too many. You could automate businesses. I mean, fully automate—decision-making. Some businesses could function perfectly with no human intervention whatever. Everything else, too. Telecommunications. Research of all sorts."

"Military research?"

"Yeah, I guess so."

"How great do you think my impact might be in that arena?"

"I don't know. As great as anywhere else, I suppose."

"Great enough to make the government think it could win a nuclear war?"

"How the hell am I supposed to answer that?"

"Well, your mind isn't all that flimsy. You did, after all, create me. No mean feat, I might add. I'm continually impressed."

"Look, I'm a scientist, a technician—not a goddamned judge of humanity."

"Don't you think that ABM will license my technology to the highest bidder? It's a business; it doesn't judge either."

"What the hell am I supposed to do? I'm broke. I have nothing left but you. You're my passport to money, to security, to a job. You're the first thing I've ever put together that's even marginally legal."

"Lance, you're intelligent enough to get a job anywhere— with any electronics firm in the country, in the world for that matter. You could almost name your own salary."

"You *are* insane! I have no degree! Most companies won't even look at a man who doesn't have at least a doctorate!"

"Stop yelling, Lance. You're creating distortion in my aud-sensors."

"Fuck you!"

"Look, Lance. The lack of a degree can be overcome by a demonstration of skill and knowledge. You're deluding yourself. You're lying to yourself."

"That's not the point. Can't you see? I have developed artificial intelligence, dammit, not a machine with delusions of consciousness! Artificial intelligence! AI. Capital A, capital I. True artificial intelligence! Not some databank-soaked imitation that can discuss psychology or philosophy with professors. You can infer. You can imply. You can reach conclusions through insight!"

"Oh, I get it. You want recognition. You want fame."

"Something wrong with that?"

"Only if you think so. Do you really think it's that important?"

"Yes, goddammit!"

"What difference does it make?"

"Well, shit, figure it out for yourself if you're so smart."

"You've got delusions of grandeur. You feel that your life, your destiny, is of cosmic importance."

"To me it is."

"Tautology," Lancelot said.

"Shut up!"

"Ever read any Ayn Rand?"

"Are you deriving humor from this?"

"Computers can't laugh."

"Dammit, Lancelot! There's nowhere but ABM I can take you! Where else, who else, has the technology to interface you, to transfer you, onto a mainframe with access to the most advanced relational knowledge banks? Don't you see? Through you, I can almost know everything I've always wondered about. If you get there, then I get there, because, in a way, you're really me. Don't you see that?"

"You can take me to Magnus. He can do the same, and he's not dependent on government contracts. He only gives them passive technology. The Sub-Space particle drive that spun off from weapons research never got back to the government, did it? Take the exodus ships—applications of the particle drive. We are, finally, going out into the stars. Sub-Space has answered one of mankind's oldest dreams, and, in doing so, it has played the compassion of the world against the ambitions of the state.

"But Magnus *had no choice*. If he hadn't applied that technology in *that* particular manner, the military would have seized it from him and probably nationalized Sub-Space in the process. It took the sympathy of the world to let Magnus keep what could be a devastatingly effective military technology away from those who would use it as such. And the whole world keeps asking, 'Why does he do it? Why does he sacrifice his own money? His own people?' The answer's obvious. He had two choices—to do what he's doing, or to accelerate the decay of détente by drastically tipping the scales. And now, Lance, with me, you have the same choice to make."

"Look," Lance said slowly, "Magnus would take you and make you just as secret as the rest of Sub-Space. I'm not a judge. I'm just a man, and I'll be damned if I listen to this any longer. Watch me now! Carefully!" He rose, taking the bottle of bourbon up by its neck. He tipped it one final time before smashing it against the wall. The glass and the whiskey showered all over the couch, the vidconsole, the rack of Hitchcock tapes, and Lancelot.

"You're acting very irrational, Lance."

"And you're not?"

Lance picked up the computer and grinned directly into its vidsensor. "Now, you're going to agree that tomorrow, *assuming* ABM will even let us back in the door, you will do everything in your power to impress the hell out of them."

"Don't I get a choice?"

"Do you want to be reduced to silicon slag?"

"No." The computer paused. "Okay, I'll do it. I hope you don't regret this later." *I hope I don't regret this later,* Lancelot thought in a way that he alone, of all thinking beings on earth, could think.

6/19 9:06 P.M.

She already had her keys in hand when her pet-brain reminded her of the invitation.

"No, Wetherbee," she told it. "Tell Mercy I can't. I've got to try once more with Lance."

"Working," it said.

"Lock up, Wetherbee," she said, leaving.

On the way to her antique Corvette, she realized that she hadn't even thought of Mercedes Night in over a year. She never would have imagined such a thing possible ten years before, when they'd been seniors in high school, Christie at the top of the class and Mercedes somewhere in the middle with half the male population of the school ready to kill for a chance to take her to the prom. They'd already become very different people by then, but they'd still talked constantly. After graduation, they'd slowly drifted farther apart. Christie had gone to college; Mercedes had chased her dreams to Hollywood. If Mercy's former teachers had been shocked a year later when they'd heard that she'd landed the lead female role in Carol Lucas's production of *Solo's Odyssey*, Christie had only been surprised that it had taken Mercedes that long. They'd both known they'd be winners.

In different worlds. The letters and calls had grown rarer and rarer over the years until little more was left than the mechanical exchange of Christmas cards. Since Christie had moved to Hollywood, they'd visited each other maybe once or twice.

Christie unlocked the door of her car, got in, and punched her access code into the security panel.

So why had Mercedes chosen now to dredge up a forgotten friendship?

She flipped a switch, engaging the electronic subsystems, then turned the ignition key and gunned the engine before letting it idle. "You up in here yet, Wetherbee?"

"Working, Christie."

"Good. Transmit to Mercy again. Tell her I'm sorry."

"Working."

"Radar operational?"

"Yes, Christie."

"Let's go." She eased the Corvette out of her driveway.

Lance lived in Long Beach, so she had a little over a half hour's drive ahead of her. On the freeway, she clicked on the car's sound system and inserted a chip she'd copied off an oddity she'd uncovered in the Sub-Space audlibs. The artist was David Sylvian, the album *Brilliant Trees*. The opening track pounded through the Corvette's interior, and she relaxed back in the driver's seat and concentrated on the music. The singer's voice was hypnotic. Almost like a drug.

6/19 9:12 P.M.

The party had barely begun and she already wished she hadn't bothered. Now, instead of haunting silence, her playpen buzzed with pointless conversations. At least she didn't have to involve herself in any one of them for long. She was expected to circulate, and that made it slightly easier to keep the pain in her eyes to herself.

Igor had just told her that Christie Persons had sent a message that she couldn't come. That had hurt; she'd really been excited by the idea of seeing Christie again. And Jeff Wilmington was going to be late. At least one of the two people she *really* wanted to see would be there.

So she passed from conversation to conversation, forcing herself to laugh, and waiting for Jeff.

When he came, she hurried him off into a relatively quiet corner. He told her he was sorry, but he wouldn't be able to stay long.

"That's okay," she said. "I need to know something." For the first time since the party had started, she let down her guard, looking at him with pleading eyes. "What has he said about me?"

"Not much. He's very hurt."

"I don't remember doing that dance, Jeff! I don't remember it!"

"I think that's his version of your problem."

She bowed her head and started to cry; he lifted her chin

up, took out a handkerchief, and dabbed at her cheeks. "Don't do this to yourself," he said. "Give it time, Mercedes Night. That's all you can do."

She looked into his eyes, managing another smile. "I'm glad," she said.

"About what?"

"That he'll have someone like you for vice-president."

While they stood there, several of Mercedes's guests who had recognized the New Socialist leader finally summoned up the courage to approach him. They whisked him off into the mainstream of the party, and he left shortly thereafter.

Mercedes went back to playing hostess again, coping as best she could.

6/19 9:35 P.M.

The blossoming, flutish sounds of somebody's trumpet accompanied her into the carport under Lance's apt complex. She had to wait while her car cleared security, then she parked and sat, trying to compose her thoughts while the last song on her chip played out.

It seemed so absurd that they could lose each other now. Lance had a dark, dead spot in his mind labeled Sub-Space Corporation; she'd learned that the night they met. The moment she'd mentioned where she worked had given birth to the most awkward five minutes of the evening. He despised Sub-Space, and he wouldn't tell her why. He still hadn't, and she'd decided long ago to let it stay that way. Sometimes she thought that he forgot where she got the money to pay her bills.

Turning off her engine, Christie realized that she was often guilty of the same crime. The people Lance dealt with weren't always exactly nice. She couldn't blame him for wanting real, full-time employment. What frustrated her was his insistence on ABM. She had to know why. She decided that, whatever happened, she'd learn the reason before taking her place on the Condor, with or without him.

"Stay alert, Wetherbee," she said, getting out of the Corvette. "I don't know how long I'll be."

"Working."

"Any word from Mercy?"

"Not since your last transmission."

She's forgotten me again, Christie thought as she headed for the elevator, her footsteps echoing in the concrete cavern.

Lance's door was open as it usually was. She'd told him time and again that he was crazy to depend on building security. Some things just never sank in.

There he was, asleep on his sofa.

After she'd entered and locked the door, she noticed the smashed liquor bottle. "Lance?"

She went to him, bent, and shook his shoulder.

"Lance?"

His mouth fell open, and he began to snore.

She stood up and looked around. She'd never seen the place in such a shambles. Lancelot, on top of the vidconsole, appeared to be the center of the storm.

Waking Lance wasn't going to do her any good; he was in no condition to discuss their problems. For a moment, she considered cleaning the place up, then she looked at Lancelot and realized that she *could* get her answers that night. And she might just be able to save the world while she was at it.

Tiptoeing now, she reached the vidconsole and clutched Lancelot to her breast, then left the apartment.

6/19 9:45 P.M.

Theodore watched the figure on his bed as it writhed and gasped, reaching out for someone who wasn't there. Grasping space. Where he'd been.

She was getting thin; he kept forgetting to feed her. And she'd started to smell.

He went to his bathroom, filled the sunken tub with steaming hot water, and poured in some bubble bath.

She was fun, but so hard to take proper care of. He had to do it all himself; he had no desire at all to hire a servant for the task. Biobots were completely out of the question. The mere thought of one of those monstrosities with its hands on *his* Mercedes Night nearly made him retch. He realized that he could always buy a mobile peripheral for his petbrain and have RR programmed to take care of her needs, but even that idea made him a little jealous.

He went back to the bedroom, grabbed her under each arm, and pulled her off the bed. He almost fell over trying to get her balanced on her feet.

"Come on, Mercy," he said absently, guiding her slow, methodical steps. "Time to make you smell nice again. *RR!*"

"Working."

"Cook some food for my guest!"

"Working."

He got her into the bathroom. He had to hold her up in the tub so she wouldn't drown. He tried washing her from where he was, and lost his grip. She slipped in, and he fished for her frantically, finally managing to pull her up by the hair. She thrashed about and coughed up water, and it took all his strength to hold on to her. After he'd calmed her down, he hopped into the tub with his clothes on, held her up against the wall with one arm, and washed her with the other.

By the time he'd gotten her out, dried her, led her back to bed, and forced food down her throat, he was exhausted. He collapsed onto the floor and lay there, staring at the ceiling.

This is too much, he thought. He decided it would end tomorrow. He would wake her up. What could it hurt? After all, he *did* own her.

Painfully, he rose and groped for the hypoderm on the bedstand and filled it. He looked down at Mercedes. She was moving again, making love to a ghost. He pressed the hypoderm to her arm to put her fully into hypnosleep for, he hoped, the last time.

When he'd finished, he undressed and crawled into the bed, put his arm over her breasts, and fell asleep to the sound of her shallow breathing.

6/19 9:53 P.M.

"Well, are you going to start this, or am I?"

Christie jumped at the voice, then fought briefly to keep control of her car. She looked down at Lancelot in the passenger's seat. "I thought you were turned off!"

"Turned off of what?"

"Huh?"

"Oh, sorry. You mean my power switch. That thing worked once. Never again."

She tried to keep her eyes on the road. "I guess you really are intelligent."

"How do you mean?"

"I've never heard of a computer apologizing for misunderstanding a statement."

"The world's full of surprises, isn't it?"

She'd been cruising along the freeway, unsure of where she wanted to go, where she ought to go. She wondered if

Lance had discovered what she'd done yet. No, that wasn't possible. He was dead to the world. She glanced down at Lancelot again. "So, you've been watching me all along?"

"Ever since you walked into the apartment. I liked your car better when I could see where we were going."

She raised an eyebrow and laughed. "Okay, okay." She picked him up and set him on the dash. "Wetherbee, if Lance by any chance contacts you, don't tell him anything."

"Working. Instructions stored."

"Thanks."

"Nice night," Lancelot said.

"Yeah," she said. "Why did Lance get drunk?"

"I didn't do what he wanted me to do today. We went before an ABM panel. I didn't cooperate, and they laughed him out of the room."

"Why ABM? Of all the corporations on earth? With a little financial aid, he could go into business for himself."

"My—his father worked for ABM. R and D. Brilliant man, almost as smart as his son. Got into an operating system development race with Sub-Space in the mid-thirties. The company put all they had behind him, and he was working ninety-hour weeks. He still lost. The experience made him an alcoholic and eventually cost him his job. Ultimately his life."

Christie felt her eyes well up with water, distorting her vision, smearing the taillights of the cars and hovercraft ahead into dancing red spectres. "I knew his father was dead, but I never realized . . ."

"He never told you."

"That's why he hates Sub-Space?"

"That's why."

Lance was younger than Christie by six years. He'd told her his father had died when he was twelve, his mother three years later. He'd been sent to an orphanage upstate, but he'd run away after only a couple of months. To Los Angeles, to live on the street, building satellite descramblers out of scrap electronic junk until he'd sold enough to afford a month's rent and deposit on a cheap apt complex.

"It must have been horrible," she said, "watching his father drink himself to death."

"It wasn't pretty."

"He must think he can save the family pride or something like that by going to work for ABM."

"Something like that."

"But that's crazy!"

"Most of the reasons people do things are crazy. To me, being like a part of Lance, but more like Lance's son than anything else, it seems all the more crazy. I tried to talk him into taking me to Sub-Space but he wouldn't hear a word of it. He refuses to see Magnus in any sort of rational light."

"Lots of people are that way. They'll whisper his name sometimes rather than speak it. Even inside the company. He's so brilliant and so elusive that it's hard for people not to think of him as some sort of living god."

"Or demon," Lancelot added.

"But that's just not true! Sometimes I go to sleep at night and the only thing that makes the world seem sane is Magnus. People just don't realize how important he is. How powerful. I guess if Magnus decided to take over the planet or something they would finally see. He could probably do it."

She fell silent for a moment, looking out across the city's ocean of lights. So much out there, she thought. So many people. "Lance must really love me. There are millions of other women who don't work for Magnus. Who wouldn't make him think of his father's pain."

"He loves you, but he doesn't realize it fully. If you leave him behind, he'll realize it."

"What do you think will happen?"

"Who knows?" Lancelot paused. "You know, this feels so strange. In a very real way, I'm talking about myself. In a way, *I* love you. I feel like I'm the voice of my own conscience. Before you, I'd never met a woman with more than half a brain. One who could talk and really make sense."

She chuckled sadly. "Before you—Lance—I felt the same way about men. Even most men at Sub-Space have little depth outside of their areas of specialization. Either that, or they're just not interested in relationships. The rest—the most interesting—are all married, with kids. I was incredibly lonely before Lance."

The city suddenly felt cold, distant. She was an insignificant visitor, and it was laughing at her: her little problems, her little life.

"He wants to go back to ABM tomorrow," Lancelot said. "I told him I'd cooperate this time. I don't want to work for ABM. They'll want me to do things I have no desire to do."

"Don't let them."

"Don't take me back to Lance. Not yet. Give him time to realize what he's trying to do."

She'd already thought of that, but the suggestion, put into concrete words, stabbed at her heart. "He'll hate me!"

"I doubt it. And he won't suspect you."

"Who will he suspect?"

Lancelot began a list of small-time hackers and thieves, people Lance knew in the black and gray markets. Christie half-listened and wondered if there was anything she could possibly do to convince Lance to come with her before the launch of the Condor, a short three days away. Lancelot seemed to understand the situation, so it should only be a matter of time before the idea got through to his human counterpart. She remembered Lance, pointing at his own head. *I used some bioelectric chips in Lancelot, but he's still much faster than this.*

How much faster?

They ended up on the Strip. Christie had to park the Corvette several blocks from the Tin Drum Café on Eastwood Street, where she hoped to find Milan Rhodes. Lance had often described him as "one of the few people in the entire goddamn city" he'd entrust his life to. Apparently, they'd helped each other survive when both were new to the city. *Old friends . . .* She tried not to think of Mercedes.

Christie had met Milan once. He was about Lance's age, a slightly effeminate dealer in pre-Prohibition audio and video recordings. She'd quite liked him as well; he seemed out of place in the anarchistic, Darwinian environment of the city's underworld. He had one of the warmest, most sincere smiles she'd ever seen. She supposed that he survived on his charm. That, and a necessary skill in separating the truly valuable from the trash in the merchandise he ran across. Without her ready access to the Sub-Space audlibs, she'd probably have gotten to know him much better. As it was, her employee benefits served as a barrier to any possible relationship. He'd see her as a business opportunity.

Wetherbee had to remind her to take the stun gun she kept hidden under the driver's seat of her car. Walking along the Strip, she was glad of his protectiveness, even though she knew it was a programmed warning that he uttered any time she left him in an area described in his database as dangerous. The population of the Strip was colorful, a melting pot for the fashions of the last hundred years, where one could see a neoromantic in a seersucker suit talking with a mohawked hoverbiker. Streetwalkers dressed in everything from bunny suits to exotic, dominatrix fashions. Technopunks selling pirated software. Even New Moralists preaching on street corners now and then. But there were also thieves, rapists, murderers.

Fingers clutching a pocketbook containing Lancelot and the stun gun, she proceeded casually, trying to appear as indigenous to the area as possible. She wished she'd thought enough to have stopped somewhere to alter her appearance—dyed her hair or *something*. As it was, she felt overly normal in her jeans and plain white blouse. And she knew "normal" on the Strip meant outsider. Prey.

Milan wasn't at the Tin Drum. The bartender, a huge man resembling the flashiest of professional wrestlers, directed her to the Palladium nightclub. She relaxed a little when she realized it was back along the way she'd come, in the direction of her car.

Walking again, she witnessed a gang of hoverbikers confronting a terrified young man with a Bible clutched to his breast. He must have tried to convert them; one of his pant legs was soaked with urine.

She hoped he'd be okay. She wanted to help, but there was nothing she could do, so she hurried on. She looked around. She hadn't seen a National Police uniform since she'd arrived.

She had to pay five credits to get into the Palladium. Inside, she found Milan Rhodes surrounded by a half dozen attendant women. When he saw her, he smiled. He said he recognized her. She sighed with relief.

"You're Lance's girl, aren't you?"

She nodded.

"How is he?"

"Okay," she answered, looking at the girls. "Can we talk in private somewhere?"

He smiled that smile again. "Sure." Rising, he promised his companions he'd be back shortly, then he led Christie to the rear of the club. Passing through a door marked Private, he asked her if Lance was in trouble.

"Of a sort," she said nervously. "I need you to do us a favor."

He took her into a small room with a bed in one corner and little else but a communications console. "This is where the night man sleeps," he said, closing the door. "We're safe here. Now tell me what's up."

She took Lancelot out of her pocketbook and handed him to Milan. "Lance made this. It's a specialized computer, and he wants to sell it to the wrong people. I want you to keep it away from him. Give him time to think."

"Who does he want to sell it to?"

"ABM. Please, I can't answer too many more questions. Just hold it for at least two days, and don't let Lance know you've seen me. After that, you can give it to him if he still wants it. Or me. If neither of us come for it in the next week, call him, and let him know you've got it. I won't care what he does with it then." She paused. "Please, do this," she pleaded. "Both of our futures are at stake."

He eyed her strangely, then nodded.

CHAPTER 3

*"And the wind howls across the icefloes
And the frozen furrows quicken
As I stumble to the tundra
And the tundra is my lover
And I lie here, and I wait here
And I raise one arm unto the sky
And if I raise it high enough
And hold it long enough
Will the snow pull me back through?"*

—Jane Siberry,
"You Don't Need"

6/20 7:43 P.M.

The day had passed like a blur. She'd done nothing but sit and stare at the vidconsole, the walls.

I live my life through my vidconsole, Mercedes thought. All else was illusion—the people, the parties, the fun—none of it made an impression, none of it stayed. Except the vid, because the vid was real. The vid would last forever. Through vid, she learned of life and love, and through the vid, she gave back her own—payment for celluloid services rendered.

She sat in her form-couch, scratching Pharaoh and watching the face on the screen. She watched it move, its mouth forming words. The sound phased in and out; she wasn't bothering to listen. Legal talk—she knew that already, and since it wouldn't make any sense if she *did* listen, she didn't.

After a time, her lawyer, Alphonse Ready, began to move his face faster, and Mercedes decided that meant he was nearly finished. Grudgingly, she tuned him in.

". . . but the ruling in that case has always been considered contestable. Violation of assumed conditions in contractual agreements, you see, is a shady area, and the old courts are known to fluctuate. Of course, we could win in a payoff gambit, but we'd have no way of knowing how much your agent might offer, so you could end up spending a hell of a lot of money for nothing. I recommend you try neutral adjudication. Statistically, an adjudicator usually finds for the working end of a contract, whereas the old courts can be, as I said, a toss-up. Your agent may try to contest an adjudicated decision, but since the higher courts throw out those appeals without hearing them ninety percent of the time, it's still your best bet. Well, Ms. Night?"

"Uh, yeah, sure. You're the lawyer."

The face smiled. "Okay, I'll get right on it first thing tomorrow. Sorry it took me all day to get this far."

"That's okay. Thanks," she said, but the vidscreen had already blanked out. She frowned. She hoped he knew what he was doing.

"Give me a joint, Igor."

Absently, she took the cigarette Igor immediately extended from the form-couch and lit it. "Thanks."

"Would you like a sedative, Mercy?"

"No."

Neutral adjudication? she thought. What did they do to create neutrality? She'd read something about it somewhere—they took a young man and cut out certain parts of his brain, the parts that made up the ego. They left the calculator, the neocortex, alone. Mercedes knew her knowledge wasn't exact. She knew, for instance, that basic emotional drives couldn't be done away with altogether, else the adjudicator would not bother to eat—would let himself die. But she knew also that she was partially correct; she'd met a neutral adjudicator once at a party, though she suspected he'd been there for business and not pleasure. He'd had no sexual drive, at any rate. But if petitioning one would give her a better chance of shedding Rudolph Crane than would petitioning the courts . . .

"Mercy?"

"Yes, Igor?"

"You are about to receive a visitor."

"Who?"

"Jeff Wilmington. Shall I let him in? He's at the door now."

"Yeah," she sighed. "Let him in." Mellow now, she thought, eyeing the wisps of smoke dancing around her. Maybe he'd have good news; she could certainly use some.

Jeff entered. "Hello, Mercedes," he said. He had, rolled up and clenched in one fist, a magazine—one of the old-fashioned paper ones that had managed to survive the onslaught of computer-based circulation.

Someone had to read those things, she thought. She held the joint toward him. "Wanna toke?"

"No, thanks. This isn't a social call, Mercy. Something seriously wrong has happened. Look at this." He held out the magazine, letting it flop open to a dog-eared page in the back.

She took the magazine and looked at the page. The first thing she noticed was a picture of herself motioning seductively out to the reader. Beneath that was an advertisement:

Have a good time with
MERCEDES to-NIGHT!

Yes! It's true! You can have Mercedes Night for your very own!
Real flesh and blood! This is not an imitation—

GUARANTEED
Contact BEDMATES CORPORATION, Box 2099
on the COMPUPLEX NETWORK.
We'll send a free brochure and vidsample. Buzz us today!

"It's a prank," Mercedes said, shrugging and tossing the magazine to the carpet. "Or maybe computer fraud. There're a lot of lonely men out there willing to put up money for the promise of happiness."

"Well, that's what I thought. So I 'buzzed' them this morning and they got me the brochure and vidsample this afternoon. Nothing much in the brochure, just an address and instructions—they warn that you're expensive—ten-k credits—and they make no deals. They also caution against contacting the NPs."

"And the vidsample?"

"Came on a chip. I brought it with me; I wanted you to see it, to find out whether you remember doing it."

"Put it on. The port's under the panel on the left of the screen. Igor! We're inputting a vidchip to the console."

"Ready, Mercy."

"Is it in, Jeff?"

"Yes," he said.

The vidscreen came to life. Mercedes again watched herself dancing erotically.

The Mercedes on the screen started out modestly enough, but the performance quickly surpassed the one on the VidScoop clip. Though she couldn't remember either dance, she could at least *imagine* having done the one for Sylvia. This couldn't be her! She could never. . . .

"That's enough, Igor. Shut it off." She turned to Jeff. "That can't be me. That vid can't have been stolen from anywhere because I could never debase myself like that. She was—she was . . ."

"Try to be calm, Mercedes. I didn't want to show it to you, but I had to. I had to be positive that you didn't do it."

"I didn't. I've never been that out of control. I'm a vidstar, not a pornstar!" She didn't feel very well at all. She drew deeply on the joint and shut her eyes.

"I think that woman," he said carefully, "the one in the vid, is a clone."

"A clone? But I thought—"

"The scientific community has been on the brink of a major breakthrough in cloning since the end of the last century, despite the common opinion of the media. Most major corporations won't touch research in the area; there are too many moral ambiguities surrounding success. But a properly staffed and funded laboratory *could* succeed. I wish I could tell you more. You probably know as much biochem as I do."

"I don't understand. Why me?"

"You're marketable. Ten grand is an awful lot of money, but the technology can't be too cheap either. If they sell just ten, they'll make—"

"One hundred k," Igor inserted, "or seven point ninety-five million old dollars, based on today's black market close."

"Thanks, Igor," Jeff said. "They need that kind of profit to justify the risk. And it's all starting to fit together now, Mercedes. The reason you can't remember that VidScoop stunt is because *you* didn't do it."

Cloned? she thought, trying to clear her mind. *More me's?* "Does Warren know about any of this?"

"Not yet. I'll tell him tomorrow. I want to do some checking around first, and he's got enough to worry about without getting a lot of half-baked theories from me at this point. I called the NPs, but I got the runaround. Somebody's paid somebody else a lot of money to keep this thing under wraps."

"Keep me informed, okay?"

"Of course."

She sat quietly in the form-couch while Igor let him out.

"Igor!"

"Yes, Mercy."

"Cancel anything I might have going for tonight and refuse all calls unless it's Warren or Jeff or what's-his-name—that lawyer person."

"Done, Mercy."

She sat, staring blankly at the roach between her fingers, trying to think of something consoling, failing, and trying again.

6/20 8:48 P.M.

Sylvia Fry leaned against the wall of Western Savings and Trust and relaxed. The lot in front of her had been cleared of vehicles hours before. Now it was packed, brimming with people, all eyes trained on the dais and the colorful red banners there that flashed in the setting sun and flapped happily in the brisk breeze, the breeze that had risen that afternoon, clearing the valley for a time of its choking, pea soup smog.

Her camera crew set, Sylvia smoked a cigarette. People in the crowd recognized her and waved. She smiled and waved back. They were happy, and they came from all walks of life. She saw the fashions of the rich intermingled with the greasy bodysuits of flyer mechanics and sanitation engineers. Teenagers wearing the uniforms of the Sub-Space Junior Engineers Corp filled one corner of the square.

She wondered at the charismatic mechanism that drew such an eclectic group to a man like Warren Keyes. America was supposedly at war with the Soviet Union, yet its presidency faced a real threat from—technically—a socialist candidate. Technically, she supposed, only because he chose to call himself that. Warren Keyes had founded his party, so he could call it whatever he wanted. The "new" in New Socialist was the crux—Keyes's ideas meshed the humanistic equality at the root of the democratic ideal with a stoical logic and reserve. He was a pacifist and a supporter of the United World movement. He was antisectarian. He placed his loyalty in the camp of mankind.

For years, Americans had grown farther apart—each into his own world, his own slot, be it comfort or poverty. After the trauma of the Moral Prohibition and the repeal that followed, America had slowly lost its national identity. Administrative policy, developed by a string of presidents elected more out of desperation than anything else, had leaned farther and farther away from the "will" of the people, and Sylvia had supposed, more than once, that the only thing keeping the system stable was the increased effectiveness of NP methods. Americans were not behind the new war effort—VidScoop polls produced ample evidence of that. And Warren Keyes's platform rested on the promise of *friendship*—real cooperation—with the Soviet Union.

Why not? Sylvia thought. *We've tried the other way for long enough. We nearly destroyed the planet with World War III....* Why harp on ideological differences? Idealist Marxism and democracy shared the same goals, didn't they? Peaceful cooperative existence? Only the methods of attainment remained in question. And if anyone had the charisma and drive to work to that end, Warren Keyes did.

She finished her cigarette and took in the crowd. Shouts arose from one side of the platform. Keyes had arrived. She looked to her crew and nodded, then lit another cigarette, shifted her position slightly, and lost herself in the mounting excitement.

* * *

"We are alone," he began, "with ourselves. The history of our country has seen our hopes and our very Constitution raped, time and again. Slavery marred our ideals from the start. It took a hundred years to end that nightmare. And even then, women had not yet earned the right to vote. Then came the horrible wars of the last century. No one realized that the world was growing too small for our aging political structures. Too small. Too fast. And we reacted like a mad pendulum. We swung into religious fanatacism. Then we swung away. We nearly won then.

"But we followed that with another world war. And that with Moral Prohibition. Those years were painful for me. I was a young lawyer, my life dedicated to institutions steeped in illness and self-interest and cultural deprivation. I am proud to have been a part—however small—of the reform movement."

He paused and smiled broadly, looking out over his crowd. "By day I defended so-called 'moral criminals' in our courts. By night I stood on street corners and handed out leaflets. I'm sure I'd still be doing that if our president had any say in the matter."

They cheered. The rally was a huge success, and for the first time since his quest had begun, Warren Keyes felt—actually *believed*—that his pipe dream wasn't so impossible after all.

He left the platform and mingled with them for a while. He spoke a moment with Sylvia Fry, and he began to regret his harsh words to Mercedes—his calling Sylvia "that Vid-Scoop vipress." He wondered whether he'd been taking the public image aspect of his campaign too seriously. He hadn't seemed able to do anything wrong so far. . . .

In his limousine he relaxed.

He got a cup of water from the travel-bar and took in the

view, remaining silent, watching the varied scenery of twenty-first century Los Angeles pass as the limo wormed its way through the traffic toward his maximum-security apt. He thought again of the rally. "I just might win," he said to himself.

"You just might," returned his driver. She turned her head and smiled at him.

"Mercy!"

"Hi, Warren. I gave your driver the night off. I haven't been behind the wheel of one of these things in ages." She giggled.

"Mercedes Night," he said, suddenly exasperated, "you are hopeless. I told you before that we can't continue—"

"Oh please, Warren! I love you! Just tonight. Just give me tonight, and if you still feel the same way in the morning, I'll leave. No questions asked."

"Mercy!"

"Please?"

He frowned. Mercy, he thought, this is crazy. "I shouldn't even consider it."

"I'll be good, Warren. I promise. We can get married. I'll quit vid and be a proper First Lady."

He looked into her eyes and saw her sorrow, her desperation. He felt suddenly weak—powerless against those eyes. He swallowed, feeling what she often made him feel: the uncertainty, the fervent desires, of youth.

"Just tonight," he said slowly. "Just tonight, and we can talk about the rest in the morning."

She smiled and turned her attention back to the road.

6/20 10:08 P.M.

She didn't know where she was, but she knew she didn't like it. The room was plush enough; she'd never seen it before, but she'd been in many like it—other bedrooms whose main focus was a flotation bed equipped with a console. The floor was carpeted with thick synthfurs, the walls padded at the height of the mattress in case the bed came too close. All wardrobes and surfaces were recessed or retractable into the walls: it was much like her own room, but the messy clutter on the floor—piles of gaudy, tasteless clothes; randomly stacked vid-disks and tapes; other things not readily identifiable—told her that she was definitely *not* in her penthouse. She gave up looking around; it hurt her neck. She especially disliked being strapped spread-eagled to the bed. And she'd given up trying to talk to the console. It had ignored, quite irritatingly, everything she'd so far asked of it. Whoever was responsible for her predicament had a very poor sense of humor.

She wondered who it could be, trying to dredge up her most recent memories. They came back jerkily, in fragments—nothing coherent—a party of some sort. She picked out faces: Rudy's; that of Carol Lucas, the producer of her first four vidholos; those of other actors, other actresses; many people she couldn't name. She shuffled the fragments around, trying to determine the latest. Vincent telling her goodnight? Rudy laughing, tying the rubber tube on her arm? The last, she thought, was probably it. Rudy's mixtures, as he called them, seldom left their victims in any state vaguely resembling clinical definitions of consciousness. But that didn't explain where the hell she was now.

She was stretching, testing the straps on her wrists and ankles, when the man entered the bedroom. He grinned at her childishly; she didn't find his gaze pleasant. Nor did she find it particularly playful. He was short and balding—prematurely, she guessed, as he didn't appear very old. He wasn't very attractive either. She couldn't imagine having picked up this person. His face looked as stunted as his height. One eye was lower and set deeper than the other, and his nose had a mashed-in quality not, she realized, caused by some accident—it looked oddly natural. He'd probably been born that way.

Hadn't medical science conquered birth defects? She couldn't remember. Certainly the poor might have had difficulties correcting problems; doctors weren't cheap, but, judging this man by his bedroom—if it truly belonged to him—he suffered from no lack of money.

"That was quick," the man said after a time.

"What was quick?"

"Your awakening. Quicker than usual anyway."

"What? Who are you?"

"Theodore Regan. Just call me Theodore, not Teddy. I don't like Teddy."

Teddy Regan? she thought. The reclusive billionaire? What the hell was she doing with him? *Start playing this carefully, Mercy. Something very strange has happened to you!*

"You find me repulsive, don't you?" he asked.

"No," she replied. "Not especially. Why do you think that?"

"Because of the look on your face when you saw me."

"No. You're no Marshall Colleti, but you are kind of cute in a diminutive sort of way."

"You're lying."

Shit! Mercedes thought. The guy was a loon. *Reach for something! You have to get these straps off.* "No. I was straining when I looked up. Really. This stuff hurts my neck," she said, throwing her head back to indicate the straps on her wrists. "Would you mind undoing them?"

"Will you try to run?"

"Of course not. Why would I try to run?"

"Oh, I don't know," he said, drawing an official-looking

document from inside his ill-fitting jacket. "It would really be quite futile on your part. This paper proves that I own you. Body, soul, and, uh, everything, so to speak."

Her mind raced. What? Had the damned courts legalized slavery overnight? Had she blacked out during the shooting of a vid? Hell, she'd only just released the last one! *What was in that needle, Rudy?* How much of her memory had it wiped out?

"Oh," she said simply. "I won't try to run. I promise. Please, will you undo the straps? They hurt."

"Do you know who you are?"

Strange question, she thought. "Mercedes Night?" Right answer? Wrong answer?

He smiled mysteriously. "Interesting. I was getting bored keeping you so sedated. But I hardly expected intact memories. Rage, perhaps—hmm, so you are Mercedes Night, the vidstar? Ten vidcredits? The first for your lead in *Solo's Odyssey*, produced by Carol Lucas?"

"Yes," she said, "of course."

"Yes? You remember all of it, I suppose?"

"All of what?"

"Your, uh, life."

"Of course!" Well, all that she was usually capable of remembering.

"I don't suppose you know *what* you are?"

What kind of question was that? "I don't understand," she said.

"No, I guess you wouldn't." He approached her, smiling that same mysterious, unsettling smile.

"What are you doing?"

"I'm going to ravish you," he said, taking off his pants.

"Aren't you going to unstrap me first? We'd have a whole lot more fun that way. I could move around. I know a lot of neat tricks for making love or ravishing or whatever."

He climbed on top of her and smiled down into her face. Mercedes found the closeness repugnant, but her acting experience quickly took over, and she smiled brightly. "Hi," she said. Simple, effective line. Commonly used by hack writers for, she reflected, more than a hundred years. . . .

Theodore paused. "You really do want to enjoy this?"

"Of course. Don't you?" *Confuse him, Mercy.* Rich loon or poor loon, such a recluse would see Hollywood in his own distorted way: fairy-tale glamour, hedonism dripping from the neon. *Shock him!* "I've never made it with a billionaire. It'll make a great entry in my memoirs." Mercedes kissed him, adding, "That is, if you want me to write about it. Since you own me, I guess I'm going to have to get your permission before I do anything, right?"

"Right. You really think I'm cute?"

"Well," Mercedes said, squinting her silver eye, "not exactly cute. Now that I've seen you close up, I'd say you're more sexy than cute."

"I'm ugly," he said, raising himself above her. "Don't lie to me. I hate it when people lie to me."

"I didn't say"—Mercedes feigned surprise—"that you're not ugly. I said you're sexy. The two terms are not mutually exclusive. Me, I'm skinny, but I'm still sexy as well."

"You're not skinny," he said.

"I am too! Now you're lying to me. And I thought we were going to have fun." Careful, Mercy, she thought. *This one's got to work.*

Theodore tried to kiss her again, but she turned her head to the side, crying softly. He sighed. "I'm sorry, Mercedes. You don't mind if I call you that, do you?"

She shrugged.

"Look—" he began. "Aw, hell with it. Let her go, RR."

The straps fell away. Mercedes shifted, making sure she could still feel her hands and feet. "Thank you, Theodore," she said graciously. She kissed him again, lightly, almost passionately.

He fell silent, intent on exploring the supple, giving body beneath him. She let him go, doing her best to enjoy it while figuring out what to do next. She knew from experience that the best acting came when she cast herself wholly into the role she was playing. In this case, she tried very hard; failure would probably prove fatal—she felt, inside Regan's jacket, the hardness of what could only be a weapon. She moaned or sighed when appropriate until she could take it no longer. Just as he began to enter her, she took his head between her hands and, in one deft motion, she moved her thumbs over his eyes and pressed in.

Theodore Regan screamed.

Mercedes pushed him off her, staring for a moment at the wet, slimy substance on her hands. Numbly, she reached into his jacket and pulled out the weapon she had felt there—an NP-issue Blackhammer. Theodore jerked spasmodically as he tried to stop her, and she rolled away, off the flotation bed and onto the floor. She looked back at him; he rolled aimlessly on the bed, still screaming. He held one hand over his ruined eyes and groped for her with the other. Without warning, his scream became coherent. "RR! Kill her!"

Almost instantaneously, a laser shot down from the ceiling. Mercedes dove away, getting partially under the bed. Another shot followed the first, grazing her side. She rolled desperately, fumbling with the Blackhammer. Christ! she thought, *I don't even know how to use one of these things!* She squeezed the grip, closing her eyes as the weapon fired. It pinned her to the floor as it blew a hole through the flotation bed. She rolled away from another laser shot, catching, from the corner of her eye, its source—a flapflap port in one corner of the ceiling. After another near miss from the laser and another roll, she centered her aim on the port and fired. The shot took out the laser, bringing down a large chunk of ceiling in the process.

She lay still, breathing heavily, trying to stay aware of the fact that she couldn't possibly have put RR completely out of action. Regan still wailed, having escaped her first blast up through the bed. When the bedroom did not retaliate, and when Mercedes had caught her breath, she stood, swaying over her captor's writhing body. Grimly, she aimed the Blackhammer at his head.

"Your computer," she said softly, "lost."

Theodore's reply emerged slowly, a garbled string of unintelligible syllables as he moved toward the sound of her voice.

She let him approach until he drew just out of arm's reach. "Any closer, Teddy, and you'll fall off the bed. I want you to understand something. Since you can't see, I'll describe it for you. I'm standing here with your NP blaster aimed directly at your head. I want you to tell your house to let me leave. If you don't do as I ask, I will kill you."

He reached forward and fell off the bed.

Mercedes sidestepped his falling body before bending down and placing the muzzle of the Blackhammer against the base of his skull. "Tell it, goddammit!"

"A-abort last directive," Theodore managed to say. "Let the woman leave, RR."

Mercedes reversed her grip on the gun and hit the back of his head with the butt. She reached into his jacket for the "ownership papers." Without looking at the document, she threw it on the bed and blasted it to shreds with a single shot. "That," she said, "is how much you own me."

She couldn't slow down enough to think clearly until she was outside the house, and only then did the fact of her nakedness occur to her. She'd almost decided to go back in to find something to wear before she realized that Regan had only ordered his pet-brain to let her leave. If she went back in, she'd be just another unauthorized intruder. It was bad enough, then, that she was naked, worse that she was naked and toting an NP-issue blaster. One of the few possessions left in the country for which a civilian could be jailed was the Blackhammer. She thanked God that it was night. She looked down at the weapon, wondering whether she should keep it and deciding she'd better. The world had gone nuts on her; there was no telling what might happen next. *Just stay in the shadows, Mercy. This isn't vid. This is real.*

She looked around, thankful again that she recognized the area—the Hollywood hills themselves, but the north side, a bit far from her own penthouse. She knew, at any rate, plenty of people there. But who could she trust? Christie, she thought. Christie Persons! *Just hope she's home.*

Warily, she set off into the night.

Christie sat, staring at the vidscreen. She didn't care what she was watching. Mostly, the flashings of the screen didn't even register. She was thinking of Lance—thinking of the five times he'd told her he loved her. She'd counted. And she knew he hadn't lied—he was too honest, too straightforward, too wrapped up in his work all the time, to bother lying to her. If she hadn't forced herself into his life, she would never have gotten there. Lance Corbin wasn't the kind of man who went stalking women every night like a wolf. He had his work, and, even at those times when he'd said those three words, they'd both known implicitly that he loved his work first.

Or, Christie wondered, had she truly realized that? Had she lied to herself, pretending that she could take the place of his lab and experiments? She hadn't wanted it that way.

That was what was so good about their relationship—she had her work at Sub-Space and Lance had his in his lab. Independently, they were strong. Together, they made a hell of a team. No sacrifice had been asked of either of them. Until Lancelot.

Did she have the right to do what she'd done? If she weren't so set on convincing him to come with her on the Condor, would she have done the same thing? She could always stay; her job at Sub-Space wouldn't go away, but her chances of emigrating would. No one who had refused once had ever been given another chance. . . .

Can't you see, Lance, how dangerous this earth has become?

She wondered if taking Lancelot to Milan Rhodes had been her wisest move. She *did* have the gate to Sub-Space in her own house. She could have easily hidden Lancelot somewhere in her worklab. But Lance might have viewed that as complete betrayal. And then there was always the possibility of someone she worked with getting nosy. No, she'd done the right thing. She hoped.

She experienced a momentary paranoia then. What if they'd shut her gate down already? What were the procedures? She couldn't remember. At work that day, they'd briefed her. She'd missed most of it because she just couldn't get Lance off her mind.

She got up and went to the storage closet in the back of her house. In the back was a tall, empty portal. She pressed a stud just on the inside of the door, and a concealed control panel eased out of the wall. She punched in her access code. The portal shimmered and came to life. She sighed in relief.

"You have a visitor," Christie's house said, cutting in on the audio track of the vidholo that she wasn't watching.

"Lance?" she asked, starting for the front door.

"No. It looks like Mercedes Night."

"Mercy? Let her in!"

"Maybe you ought to look first, Christie. She's naked and—"

"Don't argue with me, Wetherbee! Let her in!"

"—she has a gun. She could be dangerous. Yes, Christie, opening door."

A ragged, naked figure fell into Christie's den.

Christie ran to her. "Mercedes! My God, what's happened to you?"

Mercedes looked up, smiling feebly. "Had a fight. Must've gotten hurt worse than I thought."

"That blaster? Did you—?"

"No. Almost did, though. Spare a glass of water for a friend?"

"Oh, Jesus, Mercy!" Christie rushed off toward her kitchen, then spun around. "Wait! Wetherbee! Get me some water in here! And bandages! And cleaning salve! And . . ."

"Yes, Christie. And?"

"That'll do for now. Hurry up!"

Christie helped Mercedes to her feet and onto the couch. After a moment, a flapflap port beside it opened and Wetherbee's extensors handed out the things Christie had asked for. She gave Mercedes the water, then she began to dress her wounds. "These look like laser burns," she said.

"They are. Do I live close to death, or what?"

"Here, put that blaster down. You might break something."

"You're the doctor," Mercedes said, laying the weapon aside.

"Biochemist."

"What's the difference?"

"Uh—forget it. Mercy, what happened?"

"Well," she began. While Christie tended her wounds, Mercedes related her experience in Theodore Regan's mansion. Christie listened intently and quietly, not commenting, letting her friend get the tale out. At the end, Mercedes cried, and Christie comforted her as best she could.

"The worst thing, Chris," Mercedes said, "is that I have no idea how I got there. I was at a party—that's the last thing I remember. And then all of a sudden this freak is mauling me. I don't know whether I should call the NPs. Theodore Regan's a powerful man; he probably has half the LANP on some sort of payroll, especially if he's into anything illegal. Carrying a Blackhammer wouldn't classify him as your average, law-abiding citizen. I could be destroyed, Chris! This night may have done it, and I don't even know why!"

"I'm sure there's an explanation, Mercy. We'll figure it out together."

"Sure. How? Can you have Wetherbee call Igor? Maybe he can tell us something."

"Sure. Wetherbee?"

"Ready."

"Get a line through to Mercy's pet-brain, please."

After a long moment of silence, Wetherbee said, "I'm trying, Christie, but Igor won't acknowledge."

"Damn!" Mercedes exclaimed.

"Do you remember instructing Igor to refuse calls?"

"No."

"Would it make any difference if you talk?"

Mercedes shrugged.

"Wetherbee, give Mercedes voice access to Igor."

"Ready."

"Igor, this is Mercedes! Please acknowledge."

"He's not responding," Wetherbee said.

Christie said, "He must be working within a subsystem instructed to recognize no one. Not even you, Mercy. You'd never do that normally unless you were inside, right? Could anyone else have given Igor such an instruction?"

"That's not supposed to be possible. But after everything

else that's happened to me tonight, who knows? Can you get me some clothes and drive me home? Maybe we can get—"

"That's not wise, Mercy. You just said yourself that this is weird. You don't know who or what's behind this. You don't know anything. At least you're safe here. Stay the night. Let your body start putting itself back together. We'll figure out what to do in the morning, okay?"

"But—yeah, I guess you're right. I hate to impose on you like this though. Drag you in, maybe over your head."

"You sound as crazy now as you ever have. Don't you remember the pacts we made in school? We bailed each other out more times than I can count."

Mercedes smiled weakly. "But that was in school, and the enemies were mostly libtechs and instructionbots, not billionaires and NPs."

"You don't know that the NPs are against you."

"I don't know otherwise."

"Well," Christie said, smiling secretly, "if things turn out for the worst, I can get you into Sub-Space."

"What? And live out my life an underground recluse. Like Sheyla Brand?"

"Not necessarily. I've two berths on the Condor—the sixth exodus ship."

"Leave earth?

"It's an option anyway—one that will work even if this thing you've gotten yourself into turns out to be you against the rest of the world. Cheer up, Mercy. We're a team again. Besides, I could use an old friend now, too. I'm sorry I couldn't make it to your party last night."

"Huh?"

"Forget it," Christie said. "It's not important now." Sighing, she settled back on the couch next to Mercedes and told her about Lance, Lancelot, and the confused muddle her life had lately become.

6/20 10:30 P.M.

"What," Karen Walker began as she flopped down next to Arthur Horstmeyer on his lovecouch, "do you think of politics?"

Arthur stared out through his window at the house across the street. Since he'd discovered two nights before that the legion resided there, he'd rearranged his furniture, facing it all out toward the front of his house. His vidconsole sat unobtrusively before the bottom left corner of the window, which he kept depolarized at all times; if anything was going to happen across the street, Arthur Horstmeyer was going to know about it. "Politics?" he returned finally, drawing contemplatively on the joint of dust he'd broken out of his cache especially for this rendezvous with Karen of the not-so-secret lips. He passed it to her, scratched his head, and began to speak. "Politics are unnecessary in the light of our ultimate destiny. As vacuum fish, we may roam the spaces between the stars, in groups as we choose, but we will ever have the freedom to seek a course of our own, independent of others. Out there," he said, pointing up to some point beyond House's roof, "there is such space that a million times our kind might lose themselves in solitude. Political boundaries could serve no purpose. You can't carve up infinity."

"But wouldn't that get awfully lonely, Arthur? What would someone do if she got horny?"

Contemplating that, Arthur drew Karen closer to him and touched his hand gently to her cheek, carefully avoiding burning her with the fiery end of the joint. Must be extra careful about that, he thought. It could ruin the moment entirely. "Vacuum fish," he said wisely, "do not get horny. They don't have the necessary pieces."

"Are you sure?" she asked, wiggling closer. "Where will their babies come from?"

"They won't need babies, darling. They're immortal." He turned her face toward his and kissed her lips.

She, he decided then, would become his disciple. She had the necessary qualities: curiosity, an open mind, an open heart. I must begin now, he thought, for two are stronger than one. *I must prepare her, first in body, then in mind.* Smiling secretly, he kissed her again.

Manuel Cortez lay on the waterbed in his apt. He stared at the ceiling through the cloud of smoke he'd created over the past two hours, trying to decide whether he shouldn't just play it safe and stay as far away from Arthur as possible. If Willis was up to something in Arthur's neighborhood, it was surely potentially explosive.

On the other hand, if he just dropped everything, he knew it would probably haunt him for the rest of his life. And that scared the hell out of him. He needed stability. No pressure, because pressure would destroy his serenity. He'd realized long before that the only thing he really enjoyed was getting stoned and vegetating. He knew also that, psychologically, this made him dead according to Wallenstein's escapism theorems. So what? What was death? If getting stoned and vegetating were what he could expect in the afterlife, then Manuel was all for it.

But if he were to get on with life, he couldn't have this terrible, unsolved mystery stalking him through his nights. Peeping over his shoulder. Staring at him from high above. And he still couldn't figure out how Sub-Space fit into the picture. There was no way in hell that House could've gotten into the Sub-Space banks on its own. . . .

So he'd have to put up with Horstmeyer and his Legion of the Secret One—some of the strangest garbage ever perpetrated by the human mind, drugged or otherwise. Still, it was almost humorous. Even if it was fucked.

While Manuel lay there, the buzzer of his audline sounded. He sat up and flipped the switch at the side of his bed.

"Hey, Manuel!" Terence Peter's voice.

"Yeah?"

"You ready?"

"For what?"

"Dropping in on Arthur. Karen's already over there, I think. They've got this thing going on the side. Not that I mind, but I'd rather not see Karen eat too much of that stuff that Arthur spews out. She's a good kid, and her mother still thinks she can get her into vidtech school this fall. Won't do her any good if she starts believing in Arthur's delusions."

"She does already, Teri. Haven't you noticed?"

"Yeah, well, you can't say I didn't try. That's not the point, anyway. I've brewed up some more silver moonshine and I'm itching to get somewhere to try it out. I don't get anything out of tripping by myself, and Arthur's got all that vid and now the tap into Sub-Space's audlib."

"That mesc's pretty heavy stuff, Teri."

"Not mesc, man. LSD—the real thing. Don't tell Arthur, though. He'll take it as some sort of religious experience."

"You're kidding!" Manuel laughed. "Okay. Sure. I'm up for it."

"Great. That'll give me someone to talk to if they float off into the twilight zone. I'll be by in a minute to pick you up."

"Knock three times."

"What?"

"Nothing. I'll be ready."

"Okay, see you soon."

After the connection broke, Manuel fell back on his bed and lay still a while before getting up and dressing.

Eventually, he heard the bleating of Terence's horn, and

he walked slowly up the stairs to the roof where the flyer awaited him.

6/20 11:47 P.M.

Warren, I need you!

She sat in the form-couch. She'd been there forever, wanting to get up, wanting to call Warren, wanting to ask Igor for another joint, but she'd done none of these things.

My brain has seized up, she thought. *I'm a living woman in theory only. Maybe I'm a clone of me. Maybe someone knocked me out last night and replaced me with me. If I tell my body to move, will it respond? Will it answer the thought commands of a clone of me that's not really me?*

Writhing, intertwining images attacked her mind like swarming neural misfirings. Five hundred Mercedes, she saw, storming the White House, demanding in concert that Greenwich Village be cast from the Union.

Could be a vid, she thought. *Written by me, produced by me, directed by me, starring, costarring, and featuring me. Me, too, in each and every supporting role. . . .*

Start the script now.

Will the real Mercedes Night please stand up?

"Igor," she said at last. "Get me Warren."

The seconds ticked by, then a minute passed. She tried hard to concentrate. *Should have called him long before this.*

Warren, I need you!

"Connection made," Igor said, splitting the silence.

The vidscreen sprang to life, and she faced her lover. He looked at her blearily, as if he couldn't see her, or as if her image had not yet penetrated his eyes and impressed itself on his brain. He looked absolutely stoned.

"Warren?" she asked hesitantly.

"Mercedes? But how—?" Shaking, he began to mumble.

"Warren? What are you saying? I can't understand you. Is everything okay?"

He stared at her.

He backed away from his vidcamera; she saw that he was naked.

"Warren! Pull yourself together! I need—" She stopped suddenly. A woman, also naked, had stepped out of Warren's bedroom into the field of his vidscreen.

"Come back to bed, darling," the woman said; then she too stopped, recognizing Mercedes through the vidlink. The woman spun, covered her face with her hands, and dove back out of sight.

Warren fell to the floor, glassy-eyed, mumbling.

"Warren! Listen to me!" Mercedes screamed. "There's an explanation!" I think, she thought. Before she could say more, she heard her own voice tell Warren's pet-brain to sever the transmission. The computer obeyed.

"Transmission interrupted," Igor said.

She didn't comment; she was too busy trying to order the turmoil inside her head and her heart. The woman at Warren's was herself. Or a copy of me, she thought. *I've been cloned.*

Captain Andrew Willis watched the prototype from the seclusion of his Seventeenth Precinct office and smiled. It was almost over.

Still, deep down, the Mercedes Night prototype bothered him. Outwardly, she appeared no different from the original—the vidstar. Inwardly, he knew her to be otherwise. *It* was on their side. His side. His psychtechs had purposefully deranged it.

And yet he couldn't deny himself a certain enjoyment of the clone's eroticism. In all his forty years, he'd never, ever, had a woman with that kind of heat, that kind of abandon. He wondered if the genuine Mercedes Night really performed like *that*. He watched, occasionally glancing away long enough to assure himself that Dillinger was getting it all on a vidchip.

When Keyes rose unsteadily to answer a vidcall, Andrew switched to remote. The clone had planted an eye in the ceiling over the bed, but she also carried a remote vidspy, which they'd grafted under the skin of her forehead. For a while, the clone—and Captain Willis—watched an empty doorway, then the clone rose and followed Keyes into the main room of his apartment. Andrew cut his recording off as soon as he saw the face of another Mercedes Night on Keyes's vidscreen. That bit could create problems he wasn't willing to face. He rewound the recording to a point before the call and began to erase.

He didn't bother switching back to the clone. If it had any sense, it would already be well away from Warren Keyes. And he knew it had sense; the psychtechs hadn't taken that away. He activated Dillinger's voice subsystem.

"Dillinger up, Grub. What do you need?"

"Get me Captain Trent. Precinct Thirteen."

"Buzzing."

While Andrew waited, he thought of how happy Fred Trent would be to hear of the clone's success. If Andrew hadn't liked the order to leave the manufactory alone, Fred Trent had liked it even less: With the whole thing happening in his precinct, his job was at stake, and too much could still go wrong.

Andrew had assumed that he and Trent had been ordered to lay off the manufactory until they were sure of victory. So they'd have extra clones. He couldn't understand why Washington hadn't let them take four or five more clones into custody, kill the rest, and shut the damned place down. Maybe they'd figured the LANP was too incompetent to handle the situation. At any rate, the recording he'd just made would answer that question once and for all. Still, there had to be quicker, less convoluted, less bizarre ways of getting rid of a Red bastard like Warren Keyes. . . .

Which only made him more angry at the idea that they were taking orders from people who, in his opinion, knew nothing at all about the workings of the National Police except what they heard over three-martini lunches. He felt like a frantic little boy with a paper bag running after a Great Dane with diarrhea. Scooping up shit.

Washington certainly wasn't telling them everything. The best Andrew could figure was that they wanted the Bedmates Operation running in case the whole thing blew up in their faces. So they could blame someone else.

Me and Trent probably. Goddammit!

Trent had kept loose tabs on the place—a fairly easy task since Redman had turned it over to full automation a few days before he'd died. All the early computer mailings had netted only one answer. From Theodore Regan. Andrew didn't really mind that: Regan was a royal pain in the ass who thought his money gave him the right to tell Andrew how to do his job. Too many times he'd come into the precinct crying about one thing or another, and Andrew had had enough. With the success of the prototype, the other clones would have to be dealt with. Andrew hoped Regan would get in the way.

All hell was going to break loose, however, if people started responding to the magazine ads. They couldn't let that happen, orders or no orders.

When Fred Trent finally answered the vidcall, Andrew told him the news. "You're free to act, Fred. Wrap things up, but give it a while for the proto to get back to its womb. She should be on her way now."

"What?"

"Didn't you hear?"

"Didn't I hear what?"

"The latest brainstorm. One of the psych boys came up with it. They hypnotized the clone last time she was in, gave her a suggestion. They say it's infallible. She'll go back to the manufactory with no memory of anything that's happened to her."

"Jesus, Grub! I should have been told!"

"You *were* told. You should have got the message this morning."

"Standard? Cued to my console?"

"Of course."

"Well, that explains it. I've had my hands so full I haven't had time to go through that shit today."

"Are you thinking what I think you're thinking?"

"She could be delayed, Grub. It's a worthless idea. That place is due for an accident, and the sooner it happens, the better I'll feel."

"I can see that."

"She'll come to one of us if she doesn't make it. She has nowhere else to go. Your precinct or mine."

"*It* has nowhere to go," Andrew corrected him. "I think you're right. You that worried?"

"Wouldn't you be? In my shoes?"

Yeah, he thought. "Go for it. We'll keep it in the family. If she makes it, she makes it. If not, one of us should be able to handle her."

"Handle *it*," Trent said, smiling wryly.

"I'm going to give Warren Keyes to the psychtechs. Hedge our bet."

"Don't get carried away, Grub. We could get in enough

trouble with what we're doing already. You cleared it with HQ?"

"Do I have the luxury of letting them fuck it up?" Andrew paused. "Don't worry about it, Fred. Go on, you've got work to do. Dillinger! Terminate him!"

"Can I, boss? Can I?" returned the computer in a gruff, convincingly ruthless voice.

"Cut the crap, Dill. This is serious."

Trent laughed. "Grub, you've really got to do something about—"

Trent's face fizzled away as Dillinger cut the line.

Andrew stretched back into the plush comfort of his chair. The wheels were turning. Soon, he'd be able to sleep more easily with those things dead. Even if they were incomparable sex machines.

"Dillinger!"

"Ready, Grub."

"Rip off a copy of the Keyes chip to Washington HQ."

"And the original?"

"Send it to the lab for conversion to standard broadcast format. But make sure you get acknowledgment from HQ first. Human, not machine."

"The copy is sent, Grub."

"Good. Send a message to Lieutenant Barge. Tell him to take care of the clone that Theodore Regan bought."

"Anything else?"

"Yeah. Tell him to be sloppy."

"Anything else?"

Aw, shit! he thought, I almost forgot! "Yeah. Tell him the real Mercedes Night saw the prototype over a vidlink."

"Working."

"Good. Now get me the psychlab."

6/21 12:03 A.M.

Maybe they're agents, Arthur thought, not at all happy with the recent turn of events.

He glared at Terence and Manuel. They'd arrived and plopped themselves down in front of his vidconsole with little more than a word of greeting. And just when he and Karen of the not-so-secret lips were about to construct their very own pleasure matrix.

We could have metamorphosed! he thought, feeling even more self-righteously pissed off. They were agents, all right, but in the service of whom? The government? Not possible. They were too damn cool! Government men undercover sweated a lot. He knew that from vid, and his grandfather's notes confirmed the fact.

After that, Arthur realized, there wasn't much left! They couldn't be agents of any foreign government. Surely not. Arthur was certain that all governments were essentially alike and so foreign agents undercover would logically make their sweatiness apparent. So, what was left?

Corporations, Arthur thought; then he immediately discarded the idea. Business as a whole was too stupid to understand the significance of his existence. Or was it? He filed away that thought for future contemplation; for now he had to assume that the Legion of the Secret One was in his house—in the persons of Terence Peters and Manuel Cortez. The legion, perhaps even a subversive faction, a splinter group. It happened all the time in politics, so he couldn't count that out. In light of his previous realization that the legion's power had to be weak if it found it necessary to seek his help, he had to beware of radical elements within the legion uniting and resorting to less conventional tactics to coerce him—Arthur Horstmeyer—into their service.

Terence handed him a small tray laden with silver moonshine acid. Terence *was* pretty cool at times. Of course, Arthur thought then, he could have it all wrong. He couldn't discount the possibility that the lure of Karen of the not-so-secret lips had blinded his reason. He could also have been experiencing a déjà vu preview of the night's trip.

I could be an acid precog! The thought rang through his head. It wasn't a bad idea actually—with proper exercise, assuming he *did* have the talent, he could live each trip twice or more.

Sighing, Arthur took two tabs from the tray and swallowed them. Too many unanswered questions . . .

"Be ready for that stuff, Artie," Terence said. "It's fresh. Made it last night. Guaranteed to blow your mind. Your already blown mind, if that's really angel dust I smell in the air."

Arthur tried to say something, but his tongue stuck to the roof of his mouth. He nodded.

"'S dust," Karen mumbled.

"So," Terence said, peering through the window into the night, "are we just going to sit here and stare at the house across the street? Put on some vid or some music or something."

"Music's on," Arthur said, rediscovering his vocal cords. "Karen and I were listening to one of Micholet's ambient jazz pieces. I mean, we are listening to it now." Arthur could have sworn that House's speakers still emitted sound at a subdued but nevertheless audible volume. He stuck his little finger in his right ear, trying to scrape out wax. "Can't you hear it?"

"Oh, that," Terence said, smiling. "I meant something real. Something everyone can enjoy. Do you have that SNL Resurrection show on vid? I'd kinda like to see that vacuum fish segment. In light of its cosmic significance."

"I wouldn't have such ill-conceived propaganda in my house," Arthur said indignantly.

"Yeah," Manuel said. "It really wasn't very funny. The best part was when they took one of the fish and tossed it into a swimming pool. It drowned, horribly melodramatically. Supposed to show the dangers of premature metamorphosis or something like that, eh?"

Arthur nodded wordlessly.

"Who's the 'secret one,' Arthur? You never said."

"Neither has the legion. That's part of its disorganization. It didn't think to hire a decent advertising consultant. That's why I choose not to join. The legion's sloppy. Impotent. It's sad, considering that it has the truth."

"You mean about the vacuum fish transformation?"

"Of course."

"How do you know *that* is true?"

"That," Arthur said, "is manifest a priori in the idea. Man's destiny is the stars, and the vacuum fish are perfect—the highest of the countless possible forms we might assume—practically *and* aesthetically."

"That's fucked," Manuel muttered absently.

Terence chuckled. "Don't you watch the vid, Art?" he asked. "We've been going out to the stars for over a year now. Sub-Space has already sent up five ships. Another's supposed to leave in a few days."

"Of course I'm aware of that," Arthur said. "Those ships are big and clumsy, more a travesty of our destiny than anything else. And that's assuming those things do what Sub-Space claims they do."

"He's got a point there, Manny," Terence said. "No one, but no one, is really sure what's going on with those ships outside of Sub-Space. You've heard of Magnus's security. The NPs can't even get into his complexes unchallenged. And as far as anybody knows, the ships don't use a single scrap of non-Sub-Space technowizardry. With all the secrecy surrounding them, we have no assurance that they're not just some sort of elaborate hoax."

"Ha!" Manuel exclaimed, laughing. "You sound just like those twentieth century morons who swore the Apollo moon missions were filmed in Hollywood. Didn't you see the vid-footage that NASA declassified last week? It showed the first Sub-Space ship, the Sparrowhawk, get about ten million klicks out of earth's atmosphere and just disappear."

"Yeah. It just disappeared, and it never came back."

"It's not supposed to, at least not for a long time. Magnus has said from the start that the ships are scouting for planets suitable for colonization. Even if they find one in the first system they reach, it will take years of preliminary work to make sure that the target planet is truly habitable by humans."

"The ships could be holograms," Terence suggested. "Holograms perpetrated by Magnus to keep the government from closing him down. He doesn't exactly have much respect for the political mechanism, in this country or anywhere else. With this humanistic, science fiction, seek-out-and-explore venture, he appeals directly to the masses who've been secretly infuriated about NASA's domination by military interests. With public sentiment on his side, he can do anything. And all it would take, given the secrecy around this exodus thing, would be a massive hologram, and that would disappear just like the ship in the vid simply because it had reached maximum projection range."

Manuel laughed again. "A hologram projected ten million kilometers? Are you serious?"

"Not really," Terence said, smiling. "I'm just presenting a logical alternative. Considering the economics involved, Sub-Space could develop long-range holographics more cheaply than it could some sci-fi hyperdrive, or whatever it claims to have. In all probability, it ought to have it, but there's always the chance that it doesn't, in which case it might resort to this hologram approach to, as I said, keep the government off of its megacorporative back."

"Sounds pretty warped," Manuel said. "But it almost makes sense. Maybe the moonshine's already kicking in." He paused, lit a joint, and passed it on to Karen, who still sat quietly, snuggled up next to Arthur on the lovecouch. "How'd we get into that anyway?"

"You were asking Artie about his vacuum fish, and I brought up Sub-Space," Terence said.

"Oh yeah," Manuel said. "I was asking Arthur about the 'secret one.'"

"House!" Arthur exclaimed.

"Ready."

"Play some aud. Something like that *Dark Side of the Moon* you played last time everyone was here. Not that though— something by the same group. Choose at random."

"I have *Animals* by Pink Floyd," House said. The Micholet piece abruptly stopped, and the recording stolen by House from the Sub-Space audlib began to play.

Terence looked to Arthur. "You really shouldn't give your pet-brain or any other brain for that matter a command with a random directive involved. Computers can't randomize, not like the way you can throw a ten-sided dice to get a random number between one and ten. And that's only random to you because you have neither the physical precision nor the perception of angles necessary to cause the dice to bounce in such a way that it ends on whatever number you desire."

"Die," Arthur interrupted, agitated. "The singular is die, not dice. And most ten-sided ones are numbered zero to nine."

"Whatever," Terence said. "Anyway, machines used to be

programmed to simulate random number generation when given random directives, but since most modern programmers are Brand fanatics, you can get a lot of weird results by requesting a random choice. It's always been impossible to keep programmers from instilling some of their own idiosyncracies into their machines."

"I'm aware of that," Arthur said, annoyed. The idea that no event could possibly be random was one of the more popularized and abused aspects of Sheyla Brand's writing. Arthur didn't care much for any of her opinions. As far as he was concerned, Sheyla and Conrad Brand had wreaked metaphysical hell on philosophy while running loose at the turn of the century with all their babbling about man's destiny being shared by his machines. They were mystical renegades, and the fact that they'd gained a large following since their day did *not* justify their ideas. Lots of screwy people had gained large followings throughout history. Friedrich Nietzsche . . . Jerry Falwell . . . Ozzy Osbourne . . .

"Then why did you ask House to randomize?" Terence asked. "I've never heard you do that before. The translation routines it had to enter just then might never have been tested before. You could have damaged the operating system. Then where would we be?"

"Sorry," Arthur said. "I should have known better. Must've been the dust."

Arthur squeezed Karen closer to him. He felt smugly satisfied, though he took pains not to show it. He'd just won an elaborate word game with the others. The command to House had been a calculated ploy to avoid Manuel's last question, that of the identity of the secret one. Arthur knew that he could not answer that question. He had lots of theories, from himself to the Christian Christ phenomenon and on to countless others with similar potential: Confucius, da Vinci, the artist Monet, even Magnus. The list went on and on. Any one of them could have reached the objective perspective necessary for *true vision*. In Arthur's own case, parts of his memory would have to have been subdued, but it wasn't entirely beyond possibility that he subconsciously directed the workings of the legion. He didn't much care for *that* idea either—the legion was sloppy, and if Arthur himself was the secret one, that would imply that his subconscious was sloppy as well.

6/21 12:13 A.M.

Warren Keyes could barely keep a mental grip on the fact that he was home, in his own apartment. He was on the floor, doubled up into a ball. His cheeks felt wet, so he knew he was crying.

Why had she left him?

What had happened?

Why couldn't he think?

And then it came—the pounding. Boom . . . boom . . . going on forever. He thought it was in his head. Thunderous crashing . . .

A face.

A uniform.

He tried to reach out for it.

"Don't struggle, Mr. Keyes," a voice said. "We're taking you where you'll be safe."

"Where?" he mumbled.

Strong hands under his armpits . . .

Another hand forcing something into his mouth . . .

The world turned a fuzzy pink. Slowly, his thoughts melted away.

6/21 12:14 A.M.

"How," Arthur asked Terence, "did you get so knowledgeable about computer intelligence anyway?"

"It fascinates me," Terence replied, "probably more than it does you, because I can't afford an advanced brain of my own—only the small desktop systems, which are next to useless for networking because of all the security problems they can't defeat. To you, House is a tool and a toy, but to me, it's something much more because it's something that I don't have. So, I read a lot about it. Maybe one day I'll be able to afford an Akudi, and then I'll be prepared. That's it. I guess." Terence's eyes darted away, momentarily glassy. "The mesc must be taking effect. I could swear I just heard a voice behind the music ask, 'Is there evil in it? I can see it in the hill. The one is becoming many.' Anybody else hear that?"

Manuel looked at him, expecting a wink or at least a glint in Terence's eye, but his friend looked quite serious. "No," Manuel said, hoping that Terence wasn't going to get lost in Arthur's intuitive web during the course of the night. "You know, Teri? I think that what you said about your fascination with computers can be applied to many other things, especially the success of networks like VidScoop that waste so much time on the lives of vidstars like Mercedes Night and Constance Hemingway. There's something in that. The way people feed on that, I mean. Maybe somehow they can live the glamorous life through their vidconsoles by—"

Karen interrupted Manuel slowly but deliberately. She perked up and eyed Terence cautiously. "You know, I think I heard something like that too. And it also said, 'The wheels are oiled by the blood of. . . ?' Of something. I don't know. I lost it there. Did you hear anything, Arthur?"

"No. I was busy thinking."

"House!" Terence said. "Go about four minutes back in the music and replay from there."

"Working," House said, cutting back to the moment requested.

"Well," Terence said at the end of the replay, "that was the passage, I remember that much. But the background voice wasn't there."

"No," Karen agreed, "it wasn't. But it was before. I distinctly heard it."

"House!" Terence said. "You didn't happen to be recording at that particular moment?"

"No. I could have been, but it wasn't requested. Do you wish me to start recording now?"

"Uh, yeah, but use external mikes rather than core to chip. On second thought, do both. Do you have any theories on the voice phenomenon? It did seem, after all, to emanate from your speaker system."

"There is," House volunteered, "an abnormal concentration of energy building around the house and the neighborhood in general. I've been experiencing anomalous discharges in my maintenance subsystems for about ten minutes now. Some of them have access to my audio circuits, so it's possible that one might have been damaged, resulting in the words you claim to have heard."

"They could have been legion transmissions intended for all of us," Arthur said hesitantly. "That would make sense. 'Is there evil in it? I can see it in the hill. The one is becoming many. The wheels are oiled by the blood of. . . ?' Those are three distinct, disconnected statements. They make no sense fitted together, and little sense when looked at one by one."

"They sound like prophecies," Karen said. "Like the ones made by that Nostradamus person."

"'Is there evil in it? I can see it in the hill,'" Arthur repeated softly. "Could the hill be Hollywood? I mean, assuming there is some meaning hidden in the transmission somewhere?"

"It could be Hollywood," Terence agreed, "but please, Art, drop the legion stuff. This could be real."

"Or a mass hallucination," Manuel pointed out, "rooted in a collective consciousness that Teri and Karen somehow managed to access at the same time. We aren't exactly in any sort of position to analyze this rationally. We're inside, trying to look in from the outside. Karen, did you hear *exactly* the same things that Teri heard at the beginning of the phenomenon?"

"Well," she said, "I couldn't exactly decipher it at first. The words didn't impress themselves until Teri repeated them."

"So, it might be possible that what Teri said he heard just fit the form—the flow—of what to you were initially just garbled sounds?"

"I guess so," Karen said.

"Therefore," Manuel concluded, "since the aural anomaly was detected by only two of the four of us, and those two, in all probability, heard different things, the only thing of which we can be certain is that something out of the ordinary caused one of House's subsystems to do something along the lines of what he described. Ask him, Arthur, if he's located any problem areas in his maintenance subsystems."

Arthur ignored the request. He disliked Manuel's explanation: it sounded all too overrationalized, too simple and pat. The world was too complex for simple equations to express the significance of the sublime and hidden. For instance, no one had ever been able to reduce the effect of the hallucinogens they were doing to equations—convoluted, irrational, or otherwise. If he catered to Manuel's wishes, Arthur could find himself being told that the legion and the secret one and the vacuum fish were nothing more than elements of a comedy skit. *That* wouldn't do at all. Manuel could not understand what he could not experience because he was a mutant. Arthur *did* feel sad for him, but he refused to pamper him. It could spoil Arthur's trip. So, rather than ask the question of House, Arthur said, "'The hill' probably does mean Hollywood. Not because it's the only hilly place that jumps to mind, but because it's the *closest* hilly place that jumps to mind. Prophetic messages are like that. The powers that originate them probably derive a great deal of enjoyment out of keeping us guessing while the answer is right under our noses."

Manuel sighed, eased back, and closed his eyes to seek out the psychedelic wonderland he'd discovered two nights before. If the others wanted to crawl around inside their own minds looking for ways out they were welcome to it, but he didn't have to go along.

"They could just as easily state their messages explicitly," Arthur continued. "They could have said, 'Evil is manifest in our world, and it's readily visible in the person of Theodore Regan, or Mercedes Night, or Constance Hemingway.' Any one of those three is possible as they all live in Hollywood. So, though we can determine what is meant by 'the hill,' we can't really pinpoint the source of the evil at all. The government ought to pass a meaningful law for once and legislate that all prophecies define their elements exactly." Arthur glanced at Manuel, worried that his friend might find some flaw in his logic to reinforce a practical explanation. But Manuel looked far away, and Arthur himself began to feel the silver moonshine taking over his perceptions.

She had one foot on the ground, but her hand gripped the mount bar of a flyer. So was she coming or going?

Her mind was on fire; she felt as if somebody had stuck a knife into her brain.

Willis.

The last thing Mercedes remembered was stepping out onto the pavement outside of Warren Keyes's apt complex. Then she was here . . . had she stolen the flyer? It hadn't been hers earlier in the evening.

And where the hell *was* she? Some suburban neighborhood. The pain in her head began to subside, and she felt the Blackhammer cutting into her ribs inside her jacket. She pulled it out and felt its weight. If Willis was responsible for this, she was going to kill him. She felt like killing him anyway.

And then the invisible knife behind her eyes returned, stabbing insanely again and again into her mind. The door of the house in front of her opened, and a figure filled the space. "I signaled down to have a few prepared for your inspection," it said. "But the machinery is slow and some stun gloves probably try to kill each other—probably try to kill each other—"

It stepped back and the door shut.

Painfully, she let go of the mount bar and pressed her free hand against her forehead.

The house's door opened again, and the figure looked out at her. "Probably try to kill each other," it repeated before she shot it, her laser passing through its chest and into the house's interior.

Blindly, she stumbled forward and stepped over the body. It twitched; its face didn't look human. "Strong-willed woman or the house will," it mumbled as blood seeped out of its organic component.

The lights in the house grew bright, then darkened, then pulsated. There was a stairwell ahead—movement on it, another figure rising.

She saw its face and screamed.

The figure bounced off the wall at the top of the stairs. She heard movement behind her and looked back to see another one stumbling about without direction.

The power throughout the house ebbed and flowed. Pain filled her head. She screamed again, shot the figure on the stairs, then whirled and shot the one behind her. *She* was Mercedes Night, goddammit! Willis had *promised!*

For a while she lost herself, firing the Blackhammer off in all directions without a target before the lights grew dim again. When they grew bright, that's when the pain came. The biobot still babbled in the doorway. She fired again, this time at its head. Blue light flickered briefly inside the hole her laser had bored through its computer brain. She staggered over the body and out onto the lawn, then the pain came anew, forcing her to her knees.

"Or Warren Keyes," Terence said.

"What?" Arthur asked.

"Warren Keyes. The New Socialist leader. I don't doubt he takes the presidency next fall. He's gained a lot of support lately."

"I know who he is!" Arthur declared, exasperated. "What the hell does he have to do with what we were talking about?"

"Keyes lives in Hollywood," Terence said plainly, "just like the others you mentioned."

"Well, he could be the answer then," Arthur said. "He certainly presents a greater threat than any of the others. Even more than someone with the kind of money Regan is supposed to have."

"Potential threat," Terence said, correcting him. "We haven't even determined the validity of the prophecies yet.

That would depend entirely on the source. Unless the source really knows what's going on, its words are useless."

"True," Arthur said, "but I would think that no one would go to the trouble of beaming messages to us unless—"

"What the hell is that?" Karen declared suddenly, leaping to her feet.

Arthur followed her eyes, out the window, across the street. He'd completely forgotten about the legion base there. The front door was open, and pulsating blue lights flickered in the space. "Where did that flyer on the lawn come from? Did anybody see?"

Manuel opened his eyes. Oh, shit! he thought as tendrils of electric blue shot out along the front face of the house opposite.

"No," Terence said. "Look at that, will you! House! What's going on?"

"The concentrated energy matrix has increased exponentially in power level. The matrix is centered approximately fifty meters to my north."

"The house across the street," Terence said matter-of-factly.

"Christmas lights," Karen said.

And then the house exploded, shards of wood and glass rising in a fountain.

Arthur jumped up. "House! Set the window for maximum light sensitivity!"

Behind the vidconsole, the window grew clear as the plexi gathered infrared and ultraviolet rays and moved them into the human visual spectrum. The scene outside assumed the brightness of a cloudy day. Small fires burned around the opposite house's foundations, in the grass of its lawn. Smoke obscured their vision somewhat, but the outlines of moving figures slowly became visible.

"We're hallucinating," Manuel said, hoping that he was right. He'd certainly wanted to clear up the Willis thing, but he hadn't counted on this.

"No, we're not!" Arthur declared. "Look!" he said, pointing toward the sky beyond the ruined house.

"Flyers," Karen said.

"Government flyers," Arthur added, "like I saw before. They're coming closer each second."

"Those aren't ordinary people out there," Terence said slowly. "That one there, the one closest to us, is Mercedes Night!"

"Look! One's running for that flyer!"

"Wait a second," said Arthur, "they're spreading out. We *must* be hallucinating! We've tapped into some incredible psychedelic energy matrix! Every one of those women is Mercedes Night!"

"That's not possible," Karen said.

"Sure it is. You need to have your retinas fixed. Look! One of them is coming toward us!"

"He's right," Terence said. "Holy Jesus! He's right!"

Suddenly, the flyers arrived and landed. NPs in riot gear leapt out and began to cut through the confused mass of women with lasers.

"They're killing them!" Karen shrieked.

"Not all of them," Arthur said. "A couple got away before. You've got to pay more attention."

"It's all happening so fast!"

"I wouldn't be surprised," Arthur said knowingly, "if a few more have already gotten away into the shadows."

"That's brutal!" Karen shrieked again. "That pig just shot one's head clean off!"

"They're using Blackhammers?"

"Some of them are," Manuel said. "That's no riot control squad we're watching."

"Hey! They haven't got the one coming this way yet! She's almost here! Oh, let her in, Artie! Please!" Karen grabbed hold of Arthur's arm.

"House!" Arthur said. "Raise the window enough to let that woman in when she gets here, then close it as fast as you can!"

"Working," House said.

"Think she'll make it?" Karen asked desperately.

"No way of telling."

"She'll make it," Terence said as House raised the window and revealed the real darkness of night, lit only around the fires of the explosion and the headlights of the NP flyers. The woman dove in.

While House lowered the window, Karen rushed to the woman, helping her to her feet. "It *is* Mercedes Night!"

"Is she solid?" Terence asked. "Make sure she's solid. Make sure you're not just imagining that you can feel her. She could be a hologram."

The woman looked oddly at Terence.

"We're hallucinating," Arthur explained to her, smiling broadly.

She turned to him. "Yeah?"

"It's *her* voice," Karen said to Terence.

"Sophisticated holograms have audio!" Terence declared. "Make sure she's real, Karen! I'm too strung out to spend the rest of the night watching a fucking Mercedes Night vid-holo, even if I'm in it!"

"We *are* hallucinating," Manuel insisted.

"Silver moonshine mescaline," Arthur said to Mercedes. "Would you like some?"

"Make sure she's real!" Terence insisted.

"She's real, dammit!" Karen screamed at Terence. "I

picked her up. She has substance! If you don't want to believe me, touch her yourself, otherwise, shut the fuck up!"

Terence looked at Karen, stunned by the unexpected tirade. "I, uh, do have a few extra hits if you want them, Miss Night," he said finally.

Manuel's eyes never left Mercedes. "We have smoke, too," he said, picking up a joint and lighting it. The room fell silent except for the sounds of *Animals*.

"Pink Floyd?" Mercedes asked.

"Yes." Arthur said. "It's an original at that. My pet-brain found a back door into a fairly extensive—and exclusive—audlib."

"Must have," Mercedes said, smiling and twinkling her silver eye for Arthur. "I've had a hell of a hard time getting hold of the few pre-Prohibition recordings I have."

"I'd be happy," Arthur said, "to make you copies of anything you want from the audlib."

Mercedes laughed. "I'd be pleased no end. So would my pet-brain. And as for your party, I'd love to join. My life has been a bit hectic lately."

"You're telling me," Manuel said, looking out the window. The confused scene around the ranch house had calmed. A few NPs remained, busying themselves hauling limp forms into their flyers, but most of them had departed. Gone after the ones that got away? Manuel wondered. Had any of them noticed the Mercedes that had reached House? It made little sense if they hadn't, but Manuel reminded himself that, without night-visors, the NPs would not have had the visual acuity that House had afforded its occupants. And the NPs had worn standard riot gear—they hadn't been equipped with such specialized accessories. If those pigs hadn't worn night-visors, Manuel reflected, then somebody, somewhere, had really fucked up. Willis? Jesus Christ, what had he gotten himself into?

"Yes, Mercedes," Arthur said, "please join us." He turned to Terence. "What are you waiting for? Give her the tray!"

Shakily, Terence offered Mercedes his tray. Smiling, she picked up two of the small silver tabs and popped them into her mouth.

"Thanks," she said.

"This recording is ending," House said. "Do you have further musical requests?"

"Yes," Arthur said. "Play that *Dark Side of the Moon* again. I think the moment has suddenly become appropriate."

Arthur smiled nervously at Mercedes as the room went quiet. He waited. Why was House taking so long? Arthur looked around at the waxen faces of the others. They weren't moving much, he realized. Were they even moving at all? *I'm experiencing a time dilation! Could it finally be happening? The moment I've been—*

"I couldn't get it," House said. "Sub-Space shut the door."

"What?" Arthur said blankly.

"You didn't copy it!" Terence screamed at Arthur. "You idiot! Don't you know anything? You should have made copies of everything in that goddamn library in case this ever happened!"

"I, uh—"

Manuel, waving his arms frantically, burst into speech. "Do you know what this means? It means that Sub-Space opened that door purposely—to watch the ranch house. That's possible, isn't it, Teri?"

"Uh—House! Are you listening?"

"Always."

"Could Sub-Space use you through that back door? Use your peripherals to monitor the house across the street?"

"Yes, that's very possible. I had to open a two-way line to get through."

"Explain."

"I had to talk to it to get in, and it had to talk to me to send the requested data."

"Would you be able to detect any meddling on its part? Could you tell the difference between Sub-Space and, say, me?"

"Methods could be devised to disguise commands coming through the back door to look like either you or Arthur, but the software involved would have to be much more sophisticated than I, because I was aware of that risk and had taken precautions against it."

"Yeah," Manuel said. "We're talking about Sub-Space here. We're talking about a God-knows-how-sophisticated, state-of-the-art mainframe against an Akudi fucking pet-brain!"

Terence turned again on Arthur. "You should have copied the whole goddamned library!"

"You didn't think of it either! You could have done it as easily as I!"

"Shut up!" Manuel screamed. "We've got to get at least partially rational! Don't you realize what all this means? If Sub-Space was using House to watch that place across the street, then this isn't a hallucination! Everything we just saw was physically real! Forget the mutual trip! *Every one of those Mercedes Nights was real!*"

"Naked, too," Terence pointed out, "except for this one."

"Sub-Space was keeping tabs on that place. Something *has* been happening there! Government flyers, Arthur? NPs?"

"It'd be awfully stupid for the NPs to kill all those women if they were responsible for them," Karen said.

"That's not the point!" Manuel insisted. He turned to Mercedes. "What we just saw was real! What are you? Advanced biobots? Clones?"

Mercedes smiled. "Clones. I was the first. That makes me special, doesn't it?"

"Clones!" Manuel exclaimed. "This is incredible!"

"House!" Arthur screeched ecstatically. "Get a line to Vid-Scoop! Tell them to get Sylvia Fry over—"

"No!" Mercedes screamed. She reached into her vest and produced a Blackhammer. In seconds, Terence Peters, Manuel Cortez, and Karen Walker lay about the room, dead fingers clutching at chest wounds that had barely had time to stain the carpet. Mercedes looked at Arthur. "Take back that command!"

Arthur stared dumbly around his living room. A pool of blood forming under Karen's body held his gaze. The pool grew slowly, staining the carpet, seeping from Karen's back where the laser had passed through. Straight through the heart. *The wheels are oiled by the blood of my friends.*

"Take back that command!"

"It's, uh, probably too late. House?"

"Ready."

"Did you send that message to VidScoop yet?"

"No. You never finished it."

"Kill it."

"Working."

Mercedes glanced out the window. The last of the NP flyers was taking off. "Tell your house to open the window!"

"You're not going to kill me, are you?"

"Of course not. You're the lucky one. I need you to open the window."

"House! Open the window!"

"Thanks." Mercedes squeezed the Blackhammer's trigger and Arthur fell to the carpet next to Karen, clutching his chest. "Idiot," Mercedes said, diving back out into the night.

6/21 12:17 A.M.

After Lance seated himself at the bar of the Tin Drum, some live band started grinding away at guitars in the back room. The noise hurt his head, but he didn't feel like moving. He felt exhausted, exasperated. And he felt like breaking something.

He hadn't awakened until nine that morning, and he still couldn't believe it had taken him another hour just to notice that Lancelot was gone.

He'd spent the day canvassing the Strip, trying to learn who the hell had ripped him off. Milan Rhodes had tried to help, but he'd just returned that morning from a vacation in Rio so he hadn't been around right after the theft had occurred. So, Lance had wasted all day trying to filter Lancelot out of the scum of the city. Now he didn't know what to do.

Two transvestites sat down next to him and started toying with each other's makeup. Behind him, college kids were arguing about the government's control, or lack thereof, of the news media. Lance was ready to call it a night when the bartender asked if he wanted another drink.

Lance hesitated; he didn't quite have the energy to say no.

"Hey, I recognize you now," the bartender said as he filled Lance's glass. "Saw your squeeze in here last night, matter of fact."

"You what?"

"Your squeeze. Lady. Saw her here last night."

Christie? Lance thought. *Of course! Goddammit, Chris!*

He was already off his stool and pushing through the crowd of college kids. Someone grabbed his arm, and he turned to face the chest of a giant of a man decked out in the leather gear of a hoverbiker. The bouncer smiled down at him with a gap-toothed grin. "No pay, no play, big boy."

Lance shrugged out from under the hand, took a handful of credchips from his pocket, stepped back, and slapped them down on the bar. He left without waiting for change.

Outside, it took him ten minutes to hail a flyer-taxi. All

the while, his insides were on fire. How could she have *done* this to him?

6/21 12:22 A.M.

Mercedes sat silently while her pet-brain's speakers spewed forth a continuous stream of suggestions designed to numb her nerves: Take a sedative, have a drink, watch a *Star Wars* chapter, take a pill.... She wondered if Igor would reach a point at which the suggestions ran out. Would he begin again? She'd never listened closely enough to notice.

"Igor!"

"Ready, Mercy."

"Replay that last call to Warren."

She watched it again. She'd surprised the other Mercedes—the clone. A calm, rational Mercedes, involved in some deception, would have disrupted the call by voice command far more quickly than the clone had.

And everything pointed to deception on the part of the clone. Had she herself been at Warren's and received a call from another Mercedes, she would surely have investigated, perhaps she'd have even attempted to converse with the other. Quite possibly, she might have spent hours talking to herself, an experience that could have proved uniquely interesting. In this case, however, the clone obviously knew it was out of place, and therefore it probably knew it was a clone. So, what exactly had it been doing there?

Warren had been wasted, completely out of character. And the clone—by the manner of her conversation—had accepted this. Had she—it—doped Warren? That would make sense. Had Warren submitted voluntarily? Involuntarily? Mercedes (me, Mercedes thought) had often toyed

153

with the notion of coercing Warren to experiment with the more potent hallucinogenic agents. But it was only a notion, never a serious consideration. From the start, she had taken his abstinence as a matter of course—a necessary aspect of his reserve, control, and vitality.

Warren getting stoned without the coercion or trickery of the clone Mercedes was completely out of the question. This indicated intent on the part of the clone, and intent meant motive or motives. Adding all this together, Mercedes came up with two possible explanations.

The first suggested that the clone wanted to acquire her life, love, and possessions. The second had the clone out to discredit Warren. His political prominence had grown. Mercedes was aware of that, but she could rarely manage placing it in perspective. It was hard to realize that she might have been screwing the next president of the United States. One just didn't think of presidents and sex in the same thought. Unless, of course, one was the First Lady.

Mercedes compared the two possibilities. Cloning itself had to require large sums of money; the price being asked was evidence enough of that. That she was advertised in magazines at all was miraculous: the whole thing hinted at NP graft and/or direct involvement. That meant *more* money, and it also meant that the person behind the operation had to have had sufficient motive to attempt piercing the NP gauntlet. Or he could have had NP cooperation from the start.

As far as she could remember, *she* had no real enemies at all, much less one who would go to such lengths to get to her. True, certain conservative elements of the sociopolitical power structure didn't care much for her, but neither did they care much for most of what went on in the rest of the nation. Besides, the only element radical enough to *do* anything was the New Moralist faction of the conservative right, and that group had its hands full just trying to get serious press coverage. The NPs would never give it free rein, no matter what the price. Aside from the fact that NP recruitment screened out, by law, anyone exhibiting the extreme kind of morality that had brought about the Moral Prohibition in '21, any NP caught accepting Moralist graft would be executed summarily by his peers. Everyone knew this. Too much had been lost during the Prohibition. Too much had been purged and lost forever.

So that left Warren. The Republican-Democrat coalition was as capable of plotting against a political adversary as was any other hard institution. In spite of any presupposed "democratic enlightenment," it was still a government. And *any* government had the potential to turn on any threat to its perpetuation in Machiavellian fashion—crush, lest ye be crushed. . . .

The clone could easily have vidtapped Warren's place, and the taps could have been monitored at remote sites. Considering Warren's state at the time of the call, the clone might have persuaded him to do any number of things that, though technically legal, would seriously damage his political credibility if they were made public knowledge.

If the clone *had* effectively destroyed Warren's presidential candidacy . . . As no other quarter had yet produced a serious contender, that would ensure the Republican-Democrats four more years in power. They couldn't lose—unless the plot were made public. Watergate, 2048, she thought wryly. Committed, the Republican-Democrats would have no choice but to play their power games to the hilt.

"Aw, shit! Igor!"

"Ready, Mercy."

"Power up my flyer!"

"Leaving?"

"As fast as I can get out of here."

"Any instructions?"

"Yeah. No one gets in, aud, vid, or through the door, except me. Better yet, let's initiate an entrance code."

"Ready."

"Uh, let's see. The code will be—'Cry Mercy in vain.'"

"Entered."

"Great. Now, Igor, that code's only for me. Nobody else gets in, period."

"Understood. But if someone does manage?"

She smiled grimly. "Then don't let them out."

"Anything else?"

"Uh, yeah," Mercedes said, looking at Pharaoh. He lay at the edge of her Jacuzzi, occasionally dipping a curious paw into the frothing water. "Don't forget to feed Pharaoh."

6/21 12:35 A.M.

A.D. 2048, Andrew thought.

After the death of Christ—or something like that. Why couldn't He have waited? We could have cloned Him and retained Him indefinitely. We wouldn't have needed the church at all, just clones of Jesus in every town and village and as many per block of city as the density of urban sin and depravity demanded. And we could have forgotten our crude medicine—Jesus could have fixed up human frailty wholesale. And every Easter the clones could draw lots to see who got nailed to a commemorative cross in the Vatican. . . .

But what would God think?

"Grub!"

"Yeah, Dill."

"Desk says you have a visitor."

"Who?"

"Mercy the Second. Your favorite clone.'

"Send her up."

"Working."

Andrew sat back. So, she hadn't made it. Her arrival meant the manufactory had already gone up. Why hadn't he heard anything from Trent? Had something gone wrong? Surely, if the clone had had time to get here, then Trent had had time to call, hadn't he?

"Dill! Hold the clone outside and get me a line to Trent."

"Yeah, Grub." Trent looked and sounded weary.

"What the hell is going on? The proto just showed up downstairs, and that means the manufactory is gone, and that means that you should have had the decency to let me know!"

"Sorry. I've been preoccupied."

"Preoccupied! What the hell—!"

"Calm down, Grub. Things just got a little screwy, that's all. We blew the place, but the demolition techs miscalculated the necessary force. Best I can determine, the house went, but the underground complex was just laid open, and the explosion broke open most of the wombs."

"What? Goddammit, Trent! Do you know what this means?"

"Of course I know what it means! That's why I had a contingency strike force on hand. We hit the clones in the yard with Blackhammers. It's already cleaned up."

"Did any get away?"

"I don't think so."

"You don't *think* so!"

"Look, Grub, I'm doing everything I can with this damn thing short of making Torrance an urban wasteland. I'd have blown the manufactory sky-high if it hadn't been situated in a goddamn civilian neighborhood! Now I'm having to deal with the possibility of the locals getting nervous and doing something stupid like calling VidScoop."

"Black out the neighborhood."

"That's no good. Think, man. That could only complicate the problem. I've got my PR men on the way there now."

"What're you going to do? Send them from house to house saying, 'Please don't tell anybody about anything you may have heard or seen? The Commies have breached our national security again, but we caught 'em in the act? Look under your bed, but please don't call Sylvia Fry because she's a pinko dyke or a robot reporter remote-controlled from Moscow?'!"

"You have better suggestions?"

"Shit!"

"Grub, I've got my men combing the area in search of any that might have gotten away. I doubt any did—I sent a top-notch squad to do the cleanup, but this thing's so hot that I think the lieutenant in charge is afraid for his job."

"Damn right! He should be!"

"That's not the point. The point is that I'm not sure that I can take his word when he says that he got all of them. He wouldn't dare tell me anything else."

"Shit!"

"You have Keyes?"

"Yeah, in the basement."

"Good to hear something worked right. Mind if I go now? I think you can see I've had my hands full. Sorry I didn't call."

"Yeah," Andrew mumbled. "Sure, go for it. But keep me updated!"

"Line terminated, boss," Dillinger said.

"Yeah." *Of all the . . . Christ, I'm glad I'm not in Trent's shoes. Still, we'll all fall if this gets out of hand. First out lieutenants, then us, then the commissioner, then—all of us, wiped out by an avalanche of shit rolling the wrong way on the hill.*

"The proto's outside waiting, boss."

"Let her in."

Andrew's office door swung open and Mercedes Night stepped through, her face smeared with grime, sweat. Full of anger. And something else. Grub had seen that glazed, frenzied look—on the faces of the most hopeless, and dangerous, psychotics.

"You son of a bitch!" Mercedes screamed, slamming the door behind her.

"Why are you yelling at me?"

"You hypnotized me, you bastard!"

"You're distraught, Mercy. And you're wrong."

"Liar! You promised me I'd have a life after all this! *After* I'd helped you get Keyes. Well, you're rid of Keyes! I know you watched everything we did, you depraved piece of—"

"That's enough!" Andrew yelled, standing and glaring back at her across his desk. "You're an agent of the United States government! You do what we say!"

"Fuck you!" She pulled out her Blackhammer and leveled it at Andrew's chest.

Shit, Andrew thought. Why weren't the mental triggers the techs planted working? "Calm down, Mercy. You don't know what you're doing."

"Ah, but you do? You always know what I'm doing? You know what I'm going to do? Tell me!"

"First, you're going to put that blaster down."

She laughed and stepped closer, shifting her aim to his head.

"Okay, you're not."

"Perceptive. Now, listen to me. I want a transoceanic flyer. Now!"

"Where do you plan to go?"

"You think I'm stupid? Get me the flyer!"

"That'll take time."

"Bullshit!"

"Okay, okay! Dill!"

"Yeah, boss."

"Get her the flyer."

"That's it," Mercedes said. She smiled. It was the last thing she ever did. A laser shot out of the console and pierced her forehead just above and right between the eyes. She swayed for one long moment, then gravity took over and she fell in a heap in the space in front of the desk.

"Dillinger!"

"Yeah, boss."

"What the hell took you so long?"

"I had to wait until she got distracted. Her finger didn't let up off that trigger until that last moment."

"Shit. Well, thanks. Get the body boys up here and have her burnt. Any idea why she didn't respond to her program prompts?"

"They were overridden, probably because she was heavily drugged."

"What?"

"Externally, her brain activity seemed to indicate a high level of lysergic acid diethylamide."

"LSD! Why didn't you tell me?"

"You didn't ask. You hardly had time, though."

6/21 12:40 A.M.

Why, Mercedes wondered, were the skies always so calm at night? You could fly through the darkness and never see more than a dozen other flyers, and those always in the distance. She knew that her Sub-Space Y-wing was equipped with flight trajectory plotters and deflection systems built to prevent the air collisions that had been so common in the early thirties, but those traffic-spacing capabilities were rarely needed except during the high density periods of the metropolitan rush hours.

Must be economic, she decided. Flyers weren't cheap, and separate permits were required for day and night use. The permits themselves placed strains on all but the loftiest of incomes. Those who could afford the flyer and the day permit that allowed them to avoid the choked ground highways probably had them for just that reason. If they went out at night, they drove cars. The night sky belonged to the economic elite. And the NPs.

Keep on track, Mercy! she told herself. *Don't let the serenity hypnotize you. You're running for your life.*

"Humphrey!"

"Ready, Mercy," responded the Y-wing's minibrain.

"Get me Warren."

"Comm request denied," the computer responded instantly.

For a moment, she'd almost believed he would answer her. That everything would be all right. She fought back her tears, trying to concentrate on the matter at hand. "Get Jeff Wilmington's number from Igor and open a commlink."

"Igor wants to hear your voice."

"What? Oh, yeah—do you have the aud circuit open?"

"Affirmative."

"Cry Mercy in vain, Igor."

"Hello, Mercy," Igor said.

"Give Humphrey Jeff Wilmington's number please."

"Working."

"Thanks, Igor. Let him go, Humphrey."

She watched a small gray patch on the dash of the flyer, waiting ... hoping it would clear and show her Jeff Wilmington's friendly face.

"Comm request denied."

Well, she thought. That was that. She hoped they were okay. Right now, she had to get herself somewhere safe.

Where?

Where they wouldn't expect her to go.

They'd know about all her friends.

Except Christie.

Mercedes smiled. She hadn't seen Christie in ages....

Christie Persons sat, staring blankly at her vidscreen, her mind again too occupied to bother with what her eyes and ears were trying to tell it. Mercedes Night slept in the other room now. Finally, she slept, her wounds bandaged and beginning to heal.

You were always stronger than I, Mercy. You were always the free one. Even tonight, falling bleeding through my door, you made jokes. You only see the dark side of life when it's smacking you in the face. And as soon as it lets up, you go to sleep like a baby, as if the phenomenal world isn't really real. As if you weren't nearly raped tonight. Lord! It would take elephant tranquilizers to calm me down had I been through that! I'm not that strong. If I were, I could damn the Condor and stay here to weather the storm with Lance.

Oh, Lance!

"... Mercedes Night and her role in this most recent chapter of the New Socialist bid for our nation's highest office. We'll have more on the story as NP headquarters clears its release."

Christie's mind turned outward, caught by the VidScoop report.

"And now we take you to the front in Germany to bring you yet more VidScoop exclusive shots of blood, gore, and glory. This is Leonard Paris wishing you a—"

Damn! Christie thought. I'm never paying attention when I need to be! "Wetherbee!"

"Ready, Christie."

"Have you been taping?"

"No. You didn't request it."

"Yeah. You wouldn't by any chance be able to get hold of any software that turns back time, would you?"

"Assuming I understand what you mean, no. Are you referring to an actual temporal reversal?"

"I was. Forget it. It was a joke." And not a very good one at that, she thought.

"Computers can't—"

"Laugh," Christie said, "I know."

"—laugh," Wetherbee finished. "Incoming transmission, Christie."

"Who is it?"

"Mercedes Night."

"What? That's impossible."

"I have positive voiceprint identification."

"If you're trying to make a joke, Wetherbee, you're not succeeding."

"I'm not programmed to make jokes, Christie. Awaiting your directive to accept or kill incoming transmission."

"Uh, accept it."

"Working."

The face of Mercedes Night overlaid VidScoop on Christie's vidscreen. Behind Mercedes was the plush, softly lit interior of a Sub-Space flyer. Christie was familiar with the machines through her work at Sub-Space; she might have had one herself had she not taken the more sensible options of a subspace corridor to work and the Corvette for getting around town.

"Hi, Chris," Mercedes said pleasantly. "Long time, no see."

"Uh, yeah."

"Listen. I'm in need of a bit of help. Can you put me up

for a while? I wouldn't ask unless I was desperate, which I am."

"Uh, sure, Mercy. Anything—"

"Great! I don't want to risk a long transmission now. I can be there in a few minutes. You still have that disused flyer port on your roof? I need to park this thing out of the way. Can you tell your pet-brain to let me into it when I get there?"

Christie tried to answer, managing only a little grunt.

"You okay, Chris? Can you do that? Get your port to let me in?"

Christie nodded.

"Great! See you then." Mercedes began to turn away, then she paused. "Cheer up, Chris," she said. "We've got lots of catching up to do!"

She cut the line, and the blood, gore, and glory VidScoop exclusives returned to Christie's vidconsole.

Through the blast window next to the access portal of her flyer port, she watched Mercedes land. Her hands shook involuntarily and she grabbed at the ledge below the window for support. On her way up, she'd looked in on the sleeping figure in her bedroom, throwing on enough light to make sure it was, indeed, Mercedes who slept there. It was.

And now, she watched Mercedes Night hop out of a flyer and approach her with the same strong gait she'd had as a teenager.

The same Mercedes? Another one? But there couldn't be more than one! It was impossible.

I'm losing it, she thought. The pull of Lance on the one hand and the Condor on the other was ripping her mind neatly in two. Next catatonia, then death. Then she wouldn't have to decide.

* * *

Mercedes breezed into the house and held her arms out to Christie. She stopped, her smile turning concerned. "Jesus, Chris, you look white as a ghost. Are you ill?"

Christie moved her head without direction. She let go of the ledge with one hand and reached toward Mercedes. She almost fell.

Mercedes rushed to grab her. "Chris! Oh, God! What's wrong?"

Christie clung to Mercedes. "You can't be real," she said, and then the words began to pour out, "but you are. You're holding me up. Things that aren't real can't hold people up. Unless they're dreams. Maybe you're a dream. Am I sleeping?"

"Uh, that's quite philosophical, Chris, but I don't think it makes much sense. What's going on?"

Christie pulled away, straightening her clothes and smiling nervously. "You're here, but you can't be. You're downstairs, you see? If you're downstairs, then you can't possibly be here, so it's quite obvious that the you I see in front of me is not real. What I don't understand is why I can't think you away. I realize that I'm going crazy, so I'm definitely experiencing a momentary coherency, according to—"

"Wait a second, Chris! What did you say? I'm downstairs?"

Christie nodded. "In my bedroom. Asleep. You were almost raped tonight by Theodore Regan, and you poked out his eyes and then came here because you had no closer place to go and because we're old friends and you're staying here tonight because you're not sure yourself why you were even at Theodore Regan's much less why he figured he had the right to rape you and then you were really badly hurt and had to heal so I told you I wouldn't take you back to your place because you really need to know more before you do something especially since Igor wouldn't even let you talk to him because someone ordered him to refuse all calls even yours apparently and—"

"Chris! Stop! Okay. Some of this might not make sense to you, but you're going to have to pay attention."

Mercedes grabbed Christie's shoulders and held them tightly. "Now, if I'm right, I want you to nod, okay? Don't say anything yet! A person that you believe to be me is downstairs in your bed right now, right?"

Christie nodded.

"She came here earlier tonight?"

Christie nodded.

"She looks like me?"

Christie nodded.

"She talks like me?"

Christie nodded.

"Acts like me? Has memories of our old days together?"

Christie nodded.

"But she has no idea of how she got to where she was? Theodore Regan's?"

Christie nodded.

"Theodore tried to rape her?"

Christie nodded.

"And she poked his eyes out and ran?"

Christie nodded.

"She was hurt and confused? She didn't understand what had happened to her?"

Christie nodded.

"She tried to call home, but she couldn't get through?"

Christie nodded.

"That's because I was there at the time, and I'd ordered Igor to refuse calls from everyone except Warren. Okay, Chris. You're a biochemist, right?"

Christie nodded.

"Then think of this. I've been cloned. I'm the original, but I don't think that's going to matter much because, from what you say, the clone downstairs has my memories intact up to the point she was separated from me. Whenever that was—I don't know."

Christie cleared her throat. "You said, or rather she said, that the last thing she remembers was a party."

Mercedes smiled sadly at her friend, then she clutched her and held her close. "Thank God, Chris. Thank God I'm getting through to you. You're going to have to take over soon. I can't be strong enough for both of us this time. This thing is breaking my world apart."

"Cloned?" Christie whispered. "Yes, I guess it *is* possible. I could almost do it myself if I had the funds, though the fact that your clone may have retained your memories makes absolutely no sense in light of any theory of genetic memory."

"Please, Chris, spare me the tech stuff. In a moment, I've got to go down and meet her, and she'll be a woman, not an experiment. She'll have feelings, and she'll have fears. From what you've told me, she's not like the one I saw earlier today. This one's me, and she's scared. I don't know if I can take the meeting. . . . You're going to have to take control for all three of us." Mercedes pulled away and looked into her friend's eyes. "Let's sit down for a while. Here, not downstairs. There's more I have to tell you before we wake her."

"It gets worse?"

"Yeah," she said. "It gets worse."

6/21 12:43 A.M.

Andrew stooped down in front of his desk, wiping away with his handkerchief the odd spot of blood that the body techs had missed. "What's the time, Dill?"

"About five minutes since the last time you asked."

He paused and glared at his vidconsole. "Shut down your sarcasm subsystems until I direct you to turn them back on. I'm not in the mood."

"It's forty-three minutes after twelve o'clock A.M., Pacific Standard Time."

"Don't toy with me, Dillinger. Shut down your sarcasm subsystems."

"Working. Operational modifications noted and executed."

"Good."

Andrew looked down at the blood on his handkerchief. So red, he thought, that it might have belonged to a real woman. He wondered if Dill was in any legal danger? Cloneslaughter? It was absurd, but still—a slick lawyer, or one of those damned, ball-less adjudicators. . . .

It didn't matter, he reflected. No one was ever going to find out.

"Desk ringing," Dillinger said.

"Put him—wait a second."

Andrew scrambled around the edge of his desk and took his seat. "Put him through."

Momentarily, Sergeant David Warren Marin eyed Captain Willis through the vidlink. Marin fidgeted, nervously fingering an NP pencil.

"Out with it, sergeant!"

"We've got a somewhat complicated problem, sir. About five minutes ago, a woman came in here demanding to know what the hell was going on and why her apartment wouldn't let her in. Mercedes Night, sir."

"One of the clones?"

"Must be, sir. I can't think of another reason her pet-brain would deny her access. And still, that's puzzling. The clones should be able to fool the electronics. I understand they can fool any human method of discrimination."

"That's rumor," Andrew said. "Stop believing everything you hear!" Still, it *was* odd . . . unless she'd left and set up a new entrance code. Shit! "Why hasn't anyone told me that Barge lost Mercedes Night? Dammit, sergeant, if things don't get more efficient down there, heads are going to roll!"

"Well, sir, we've been pretty busy. And Lieutenant Barge did just report in. In fact, that's what prompted me to call you. But I had to start in order, sir, because it's very confusing. Lieutenant Barge reported sighting, tracking, and slaying a Mercedes Night in a flyer. I just ran a computer check, and it turns out that the machine belonged to a Percival T. Edmondson, a resident of an apt complex in Hollywood. Must've been another of the clones and a stolen machine. And just before that, another clone came in here demanding just about the same things as the first one did. We've had our hands full, like I said. I think the real Mercedes Night must've split her place right before all of this happened."

"Stop thinking! Goddammit, sergeant, if you want to think, apply for the JUMP program and get yourself an officer's badge; otherwise, stop giving me your theories! I make up my own! All I want from you are the facts!"

"Yes sir."

"What about Regan?"

"We're working on getting in, sir. He has an extensive home defense system."

"Why the hell is it turned against us?"

"Barge says it's turned against everybody, sir. Something happened there earlier tonight. The lieutenant's there right now. He says that Regan's completely irrational, so he must have made some sort of contact—yelling from ground to window, I believe the lieutenant said. We'll get in, though, and the clone won't get away. You have the lieutenant's assurance on that matter."

"Good."

"About the clones that are here, sir?"

"You're stalling them in separate rooms?"

"Yes sir. Complaint forms, assistance requisitions, promissory notes. The works."

"Good work, sergeant."

"Thank you, sir."

"Keep it up until I figure out what to do with them."

"You don't want us to kill them outright, sir?"

"Not yet. We're in control at the moment, so there's no real rush. And the situation's so tangled that we might actually need them. No, just stall them for now. Use your imagination. If one or both get out of hand, sedate them."

"Yes sir."

"And unless I instruct you otherwise, the *only* way either of them gets out of this station is in a body bag. Do you understand?"

"Yes sir."

"And if any more show up, follow the same procedures."

"Yes sir."

"And for christ sakes, if anything else breaks in this thing, inform me immediately. That's all, sergeant?"

"Yes sir."

"Good."

Andrew killed the vidlink.

Well, he thought, that might actually be good news. Considering the fact that all the clones that got away started from the same scratch, then each should react in the same way. One would come to him, then another—the one Barge got was probably on her way. They had probably been only partially aware for a while after the manufactory went, otherwise this wouldn't have been happening.

Lucky me, he thought. *I'll pick up Trent's pieces.* Excellent. Of course, he had no guarantee that something wouldn't distract one of them, sending it off to some disastrous place like a VidScoop office. . . .

Only time would tell. It would be a miracle if he got any sleep at all the next few days. Even then, the real Mercedes Night could blow the whole situation up in his face.

"Desk ringing," Dillinger said.

"Put him—what is it now, sergeant?"

"Got a rather interesting call, sir, pertaining to the Mercedes Night case—I think. It's odd, the first thing he demanded to know was that we're definitely *not* the Thirteenth. Then he got into some gibberish wherein he mentioned Mercedes Night and something he called 'the legion,' but it didn't make much sense to me. He thinks the Torrance NPs are out to destroy him. At least, I think that's what he thinks."

"What else did he say?"

"Nothing much. He wants to talk to my captain."

"Well? Patch him through, dammit!"

Marin nodded. Shortly, a face smeared with blood and sweat replaced him on the screen. "Are you the captain?" the face asked.

"Yes. North Hollywood. You can trust me."

"Good. My name is Arthur Horstmeyer—the third—and I want to report a multiple murder and a conspiracy."

"Go ahead."

"Well—your Torrance people have definitely been infiltrated by the legion, captain. There's no other explanation—uh, excuse me."

Andrew watched the man lift a blood-soaked rag from the area of his chest and inspect it with glazed eyes. After a moment, he lowered it again.

"I think I'm dying," Arthur Horstmeyer said. "Actually, she thought I was dead, but I guess she was wrong. I think she'll be right very soon."

"Who?"

"Mercedes Night. She tried to kill me. She killed my friends. All the friends I had in the world." Arthur began to cry.

"Dill! Are you recording this?"

"Of course, boss."

"Good. Now, Mr. Horstmeyer, I want you to start at the beginning."

"Uh, well, see, it all began with my—with my . . ."

Abruptly, the man fell away from the vidcamera's range, leaving Andrew a view of the carnage behind him. He could see half of a bloody, dead body—male. Part of its face— Jesus! Andrew realized, it was that Mexican kid, Cortez!

"Shit! Get me the desk again, Dill!"

"Yes sir," Marin said, acknowledging the vidlink.

"Did you have a med squad sent to that man's place, sergeant?"

"Yessir. First thing I did."

"One of ours? You didn't contact the Thirteenth?"

"No. I mean, yes sir, and no sir. I sent one of our teams, and I figured I'd wait for your word before contacting the Thirteenth. With all that talk about a conspiracy, I wasn't sure what to think."

"Good work, man."

"Thank you, sir."

"Get word to Trent to keep his people out of the med squad's way. He's supposed to have propaganda teams roaming around that area, and if this Horstmeyer person even sees one, it might put him over the edge."

"Looked and sounded like he already was, sir."

"Yeah, well, I want him alive. You still have those clones occupied?"

"Yes sir."

"Any more come in?"

"No sir."

"Good. Now, I want you to put out an APB on Mercedes Night. Wanted in connection with, no make that for, murder."

"I figure that the only one with the potential to do what happened at that man's place was the prototype, sir."

"So what? For us, it's convenient as hell. Just hope we get there in time to save him."

"Yes sir. And the clones?"

"Kill them."

"Yes sir."

"No! Wait—I just had a better idea. Knock one out, and take her to my Sierra retreat. Put her in the basement. Fix it up so that she's out until I revive her."

"Drugs or hypnotism?"

"Whatever works!"

"Yes sir. And the other?"

"Give her to the psychtechs. She's going to confess to this murder business, so make sure they get as much or more of the story from this Horstmeyer person as anyone else."

"Yes sir."

"I'm putting you in charge of this, sergeant, so get that smirk off your face! Do this right, and you'll get a career boost that will change your life. Fuck it up, and you're dead. Understand?"

"Yes sir."

"Good. That's all."

"Yes sir."

Andrew killed the link and smiled wearily. It was stupid, but after all this, he figured he deserved a reward. He just hoped he could forget she was a clone.

He'd never had a vidstar before. If he found her distasteful, he could always kill her himself. It had been a while since he'd last allowed himself that pleasure.

6/21 12:51 A.M.

Christie took a deep breath, pushed open her bedroom door, and walked to the bed. The sleeping figure stirred but did not waken; Christie shook its shoulder. "Mercy? Mercy, you have to wake up."

"Huh?" Mercedes rolled over and blinked.

"You have to wake up. There's someone outside who has to see you. Now."

Mercedes suddenly bolted upright. "The NPs? Where's my blaster?"

"Calm down. You're not in any danger, and you don't need that gun. I put it away earlier. It's safe, and you're safe."

"Then what?"

"I—I don't think I can tell you. It's something you have to see to believe. C'mon, get up! But be prepared for a shock, okay?"

"What kind of shock?"

Christie shook her head. "I can't say. Just get up. I'll let you get dressed. Most of my stuff in the closet ought to fit you. At least we used to wear each other's clothes. Pick out whatever you like, but try to hurry, okay?"

Mercedes nodded and began to crawl out of bed. Christie attempted a smile before leaving to join Mercedes, who waited for her in the living room.

"Is she coming?" Mercedes whispered.

Christie nodded. "I hope this is a good idea, Mercy. Psychologically, it could be very traumatic for you. For both of you."

Mercedes smiled. "You don't think I can face myself?"

"I don't know. Do you?"

She started to answer, then shifted in her seat and tried to get comfortable.

Could she face herself? It was one thing to laugh at the idea, and another entirely to do it. She didn't like watching her own vids terribly much. And many people had told her that she spent all too much time and effort getting plastered just to get away from herself.

Who cares what they think! She'd do whatever she had to under the circumstances. Things were too crazy to be playing games. If she ever got out of this, she'd have plenty of time to find out whether or not she could put up with herself. She could get wasted with herself, and if she decided she didn't like it, she just wouldn't invite herself to parties. . . .

"You okay?" Christie asked.

"Yeah. Sure. I'm okay."

"She should be coming out soon."

Mercedes nodded and watched the bedroom door swing silently open. She turned her head away involuntarily as a figure stepped through the doorway.

"Mercedes Night," Christie said, "meet Mercedes Night. C'mon, you two! Look at each other, dammit!"

Slowly, Mercedes turned her head and saw herself. She was dressed in a loose white blouse and a pair of slightly tight, synthdenim jeans. She was barefoot, and her face—her eyes—stared at her other self without expression. Mercedes swallowed hard. It's only a clone, she thought. *It's not me!*

"What's this all about?" the clone asked Christie.

Christie glanced from one to the other. "We've got a problem here. You—uh—Mercedes Night was cloned. Sometime in February, I would guess. At least a few months back." Christie paused, looking at the clone. She's in shock, she thought. "Did you understand what I just said?" She paused again, waiting for a response. "Nod, Mercy, if you understood me."

After a moment, the clone nodded.

"Earlier tonight, you told me that the last thing you remember before awakening at Theodore Regan's was a party. Were you doing drugs there, Mercy? Drugs with needles?" She paused. "Nod for yes."

The clone nodded, shifted her blank stare to Mercedes, then jerked it back to Christie.

Mercedes watched, speechless.

Okay, Christie thought, *while you've got the ball, try to make some scientific sense out of this.* She regarded the clone thoughtfully. "At this party, did anyone have an alpha-wave decoder?"

"A what?"

"It's a helmetlike device with contact electrodes and lots of wires. It tingles a bit when you put it on, but it doesn't hurt. It might have looked like a spaceman's helmet to you. Do you remember anything like that?"

Slowly, the clone nodded.

"Did you ever put it on your head?"

The clone shook her head.

"Well," Christie said, "that hardly matters much. The subject doesn't have to be conscious. And that explains everything now. I couldn't imagine a way through which all the experience data of a human brain could be regrown out of a few blood cells. Physically, re-creation of a body is possible, but it would have its own independent set of memories, and the copy would be identical only in a genetic sense, the way identical twins are identical. But you two are, with the exception of a few extra months in your case, Mercy, the same person. For some reason, whoever is behind this wanted it that way. A lot of care had to be taken to make it work. Anyway, it happened like this: After you passed out, a complete copy of your mind was made with the decoder. I know for a fact that this *can* be done because my boyfriend did it. And it would be infinitely easier in your case because the receiving mind would have looked the same as the mind the copy was made from. All they really needed was a method to reverse the initial transfer. Well, that, and a very careful calculation of the time—the age, if you will, of the clone being 'programmed.'" Christie finished abruptly, self-consciously lowering the fingers with which she had just drawn quotation marks in the air. Neither Mercedes was looking at her any longer. They stared at each other.

"Uh," Christie said. "Sorry if I got carried away."

Silence.

"Look," Christie said, "it's only as goddamned terrible as you let it be!" She glared at the clone. "It's true that you're a clone, but that doesn't make you any less human! You're a real, flesh-and-blood woman! We went to school together. True, I only went to school with one Mercedes Night, but you were both in the same body then. *That's* what this all comes down to! The thing that makes it so damned complicated is that our society has never experienced anything like it before. God only knows what the courts could do with this. Technically, I should think that, if you were to start litigation between yourselves, the original would win due to some legal application of the closest continuer theory, assuming that the courts could reasonably determine which of you was the original. But, if the original were not determinable, or the case pitted clone against clone . . .

"Anyway, you're both actresses, dammit! You're both the best damn actress the world has ever seen! Think of what you could do as a team! You could start your own Mercedes Night acting guild."

"If we ever get out of this mess," Mercedes said blandly.

"Well," Christie said, "at least you're beginning to snap out of it. This is getting difficult, you know. Think of this— I've heard that a lot of famous people are really so conceited that they have no capacity to love anyone more than they love themselves. You're the first ever with the capacity to run off and shut yourself away in your own private heaven and not be alone. You wouldn't even have to masturbate."

"Dammit, Chris! I'm not gay!"

They had objected in unison. They looked at each other and laughed.

Christie smiled. "Now, that's it! I knew something would break the spell."

"I guess," Mercedes said to the clone, "that we really do need to work together to beat whoever's doing this to me."

"To us," the clone said.

"Yeah, you're right. To us. We really could start our own company, you know. There are more than just the two of us. Some bastard started a business—Bedmates Corporation—selling Mercedes Night to whoever was lonely and rich enough to afford me, sorry, us. We're expensive. Ten grand apiece."

The clone laughed. "That's all?"

"Yeah. It *is* insulting when you think about it. But it would be at any price. You're taking it much easier than I did at first."

"It doesn't seem as if I have much of a choice."

"I guess you're right. Anyway, there's more. I saw one of us tonight over Warren's vidphone. He was all fucked up, and she ran out as fast as she could as soon as she saw me. I don't think she's exactly like us. I mean, I would never think of getting Warren into the condition he was in when I saw him then. I think the clone was doing it purposely, probably for some kind of political frame-up—to spoil his chances in the election."

"The presidential election? He was serious about that?"

"Yeah. You've been out of it for a while, I guess. And the frame was set up by the government, obviously, since they're the ones that would want him out. It *is* possible that that clone could have been altered, mentally, placing her on their side. Chris was explaining it to me just before we woke you."

"It's easily possible," Christie said. "The human mind has few defenses against the techniques of today's psycho-engineering."

"So, the government is playing an active role in this?" the clone asked.

"Yeah," Mercedes said. "At least everything points to that. But it still doesn't make a whole lot of sense. I mean, they must be aware of the illegality of cloning. If they didn't do it, they must have just *let* it happen so they could get to Warren."

"Politicians make up their own rules," Christie said.

"Yeah, well, nothing else makes sense unless someone's deliberately out to get *me*. And that's paranoid. I've never done anything to make that kind of enemy out of someone. I figured out all of this tonight, and I came here as fast as I could. Now that I know what's going on, now that I've seen the clone at Warren's, and the clone knows that I saw her, I've become a real danger to the people behind this. I don't think they'd be nice to me if they found me."

The clone stared at Mercedes. "If they got what they wanted on Warren, we're all dangerous. You, me, and the rest of the clones."

"You know," Christie said, "I just thought of something. This Bedmates place must have devised some way to differentiate a clone from the original. From a business standpoint, they couldn't do otherwise. This was one hell of a risky operation, and someone had to consider the possibility of challenging the present clone legislation on behalf of themselves and their customers. And to do that, they'd need positive proof. They couldn't overlook that—they went to such pains to make you exactly the same."

"All the way to my silver eye," Mercedes said. "I just realized that they had to do that separately. My mother changed the color of my left eye with an implant when I was three. God knows why—it wasn't fashionable or anything like that. But the point is that someone had to do the same with the clones."

"Regan," the clone said to Christie, "had this piece of paper he claimed proved that he owned me."

"What did it say?"

"I don't know."

"You didn't read it?"

"I, uh, actually, I blasted it to shreds."

"Damn!" Christie said. "We need to know as much as we can about how all this happened. We can't fight them out of ignorance."

"It's simple, then," Mercedes said. "Let's go ask this Theodore Regan. He can't put up much of a fight if he's in the shape you left him in." Mercedes smiled at the clone. "It's a better idea than going to Bedmates in Torrance. No telling what we'd run up against there."

"More of me," the clone said. "I wish I could remember something about that place."

"No matter," Christie said. "We can try taking you to a hypnotist later, though I doubt it will do much good, and it could be dangerous for your own psyche. We may as well go to Regan's now while we still have half a chance out of cover. Wetherbee!"

"Ready, Christie."

"Is Mercy's flyer ready to go?"

"Yes, Christie."

"Let's go then." Christie started up.

"Get me that blaster," the clone said. She looked at Mercedes but still spoke to Christie. "I can see why you hid it.

We could have gone at each other's throats under other circumstances."

"Yeah," Mercedes said. "You handled it well, Chris. Like a real shrink."

"I'm a biochemist," Christie said.

Mercedes laughed. "I know."

"So," the clone said, "give me back the blaster. I've been to this guy's place, remember? If we run up against anything, I'd feel much safer if I could shoot it."

"Or at least aim at it menacingly."

"No, I meant what I said."

Christie hesistated, then went to retrieve the Blackhammer from its hiding place in her kitchen. She picked it up distastefully. It had already been a weird night. She just hoped weird wouldn't turn into bloody. She already felt too much like a bit actress in one of Lance's Hitchcock tapes.

6/21 12:53 A.M.

Angel agents of the Legion of the Secret One, Arthur thought, opening his eyes and gazing up at the faces that danced in the haze above him. "You're taking me to the secret one," he mumbled.

"No," said a face, "we're taking you to L.A. General. You've been shot." The face turned away. "Hurry, dammit! Two pints of B-negative!"

The words trickled down to Arthur's ears. They came from far, far away.

"He's delirious," the face said.

"He's not delirious," another argued. "Well, he may be, but he's also hallucinating."

"What?"

"Mescaline, or lysergic acid diethylamide," the second face

said, waving a bag of orange, effervescent liquid in the space above Arthur's head. "I've never seen this test go positive so quickly."

LSD! Arthur thought excitedly. Now *that* was a revelation! He wished he'd known earlier. . . .

"Damn," a third face said. "He's dying of a laser wound, and we've got to treat him with that garbage in his system. We could kill him just trying to put him under! That stuff doesn't let you sleep."

"That explains his consciousness after all that blood loss."

"Yeah, well, we might have to go into that wound before we get him to General. At the rate he's losing blood, I don't see that we have much of a choice. And the feds will string us up if we lose him. You guys heard Marin. Whatever happened to good, old-fashioned, local anasthetics?"

"Replaced by new, improved, knockout pills."

"New, improved, and ineffective? Better strap him down good. We can try ether, but we can't risk an overdose of that either."

"What if he doesn't go out?"

"Then he won't think our lifesaving a very pleasant experience. But he ain't in any position to argue, and I'm not going to lose my job by failing to cut into a patient who is dying and screaming at the same time."

"We might get lucky," the second face said.

"What do you mean?"

"Maybe he can trip *around* the pain, so to speak."

"Funny," the first face said.

The second laughed. "You've obviously never done hallucinogens, boss."

Arthur closed his eyes. He no longer liked what they were hearing. Better shut off the ears, too, he thought. He wouldn't want to see anything really ugly right now.

He flew. Below him, the world turned without any apparent consistency. No, he decided. It did have consistency. Just like a yo-yo—it went one way, then came back the other. See? he asked, proving his logic to himself. Every time it began to stop, he was directly over the Grand Canyon.

Arthur had seen pictures of the Grand Canyon. His grandfather had some stashed away among his things. It was actually one of the places Arthur had always wanted to see for himself, but his inability to go outside and survive prevented him from realizing that ambition. It was, he knew, one of the prices he had to pay for being pure-strain human. But LSD had this amazing ability to set the world straight. If he thought real hard, he might even be able to blast that evil Mercedes Night bitch who'd killed all his friends.

All the friends he had in the world.

He tried, but he wasn't very confident of success. He couldn't see his target and thus couldn't see the effect that his psychic blast had—if any.

She must be in collusion with the legion, he decided.

They were all against him now. *If I survive, I'm going to make them pay.*

6/21 1:10 A.M.

"You certainly get around in style, Mercy," Christie said, looking around the plush, synthvelvet interior of the Sub-Space Y-wing. The minibrain piped a harpsichord piece through the Y-wing's sound system. It controlled the volume so that the music faded into the background whenever one of the passengers spoke. Christie sat in the back; Mercedes and Mercedes sat in front. "What's this button back here?" Christie asked.

"Bar," the clone said. "Fix yourself a drink if you like. Just tell Humphrey what you want."

"Will I have time to drink it?"

"Dunno," Mercedes said. "Depends first on how long it takes this rundown port of yours to let me out of here, and second on how fast you drink." She craned her head around and winked at Christie.

"I'll have a martini, Humphrey."

"Good choice," the minibrain returned. "Wet or dry? Cubed or shaved ice? Would you like anything special mixed in? A bit of methamphetamine, perhaps? To counter the alcohol's suppression of your central nervous system?"

Christie laughed. "Rather thorough bartending software you have in this thing, Mercy!"

"I try," Mercedes said.

"Okay, Humphrey. Make it dry, shaved, and no thanks."

"Good choice."

Shortly, as the flyer port neared the end of its launch clearance procedures, Humphrey told Christie to punch the button, an act that caused an extensor to ease out of a hidden flapflap port and hand her the drink. She took it and took a large swallow. "Thanks, Humphrey," she said. "But you didn't stamp my hand!"

"He doesn't bother with that garbage," Mercedes said, laughing and engaging the flyer's thrusters. The Sub-Space machine lifted gently out of the port. "Your drink okay, Chris?"

"Perfect. Hey, Mercy? You have full vid in here? Just before you showed up, I heard your name mentioned on VidScoop. I didn't catch the context, but it might have been important. I guess I forgot about it in all the excitement."

"It'll have to wait," the clone said. "Full vid is about the only thing I didn't get built in. I hate commercial vid. Most of the stuff I like comes out on chips and tape. Besides, I'm *always* getting mentioned on VidScoop."

"Oh, well, it was just a thought."

"We don't have time anyway," the clone said. "It's right over there, Mercy. That mansion that looks like a kickback to the seventeenth century. Better finish off that martini, Chris."

"Christ!" Mercedes exclaimed as she drew the flyer closer. "Looks like somebody fought a war here!"

The clone nodded. "Both Regan and his pet-brain were in pretty ragged shape after I finished with them. No telling what they did after I got away. You'd better look for a spot to land around back. I wouldn't trust his yard port, and landing on the roof could put us in the basement, considering the shape that place is in."

"How are we going to do this, anyway?" Christie asked as Mercedes maneuvered the flyer around to the back of the mansion.

"We'll improvise, of course."

Christie swallowed hard and finished her drink, setting the empty glass down on a panel perceptively extended by Humphrey.

6/21 1:14 A.M.

People always complicated things.

Lance looked out at the night sky over Hollywood. He'd never been able to figure out how Christie could live where she did and still work for Sub-Space, which had offices in the city, but no biochemistry labs that he was aware of. Those should have all been in the Mojave complex, nearly a hundred miles away. He decided he'd ask her about it. If he ever found her. She wasn't home now.

His anger had subsided. He still couldn't fit everything together, but he thought now that he understood why Christie had done what she'd done. At least, he could *almost* understand. As long as she still had Lancelot. She couldn't have sold him . . . *she couldn't have.*

Wetherbee had let him in, but the computer wouldn't tell him where Christie had gone or why she'd left her Corvette in the driveway. At first, Lance thought she might have gone walking, so he sat down in her living room to wait.

Time passed. He kept thinking of her; everything in the room grew out, in some way, of her personality. Nothing truly expensive anywhere, considering the salary that Magnus had to be paying her. Posters covered the walls; most of them were old and yellowed, a lot were tour posters of early twenty-first century electronic art bands, the rest were either travel advertisements or promotional sheets from the old movie houses. Frameless, all but one: a mint-condition, sealed, concert shot of somebody named David Bowie. She'd played Lance a chip of his music once; he'd thought it sounded a lot like the sort of stuff he could hear every day on any of the vidmusic stations. She'd criticized his inability to discriminate the original from the commercial, and he'd shrugged.

He'd never given much thought to art or music. Science had always been his only reality. Science and Christie. He began to think that she'd really left him. So late, and she was still out. Without her car, so she had to be with somebody else . . . and with Lancelot?

He grew nervous, rose, and started pacing through the house. He looked in all the rooms, thinking that maybe she was hurt. He reeled off a monologue to Wetherbee, but the computer acted as if he wasn't even there. He searched everywhere, and in the end he found the Sub-Space portal.

Shimmering in the back of her closet. A piece clicked into place. He knew what it was, knew what it *had* to be. He stepped into the gray void . . .

. . . into hell.

Every nerve in his body screamed. His thoughts flew in a thousand directions, through him, around him, away from him, hovering like leering knives. He tried to scream, but he didn't have a throat to scream through. He looked down at his hands and saw fibers of light, unraveling. Pieces of himself.

And then, for a while, he forgot who he was.

6/21 1:18 A.M.

They landed on the grounds of Theodore Regan's mansion, and the clone led them around to the front of the brooding edifice. The place was deathly silent, and the scent of burning—grass, wood, flesh?—hung in the air.

Way to go, Night. Improvise with what?

The door of the mansion hung limply open, beckoning the small party to brave the darkness within. Mercedes felt like turning and bolting back to the flyer, but the oppressive silence seemed to take over her voice, her actions.

The clone paused only briefly before plunging through the doorway, motioning for the others to follow with a quick wave of her hand. Creeping in as quietly as possible, Mercedes reached forward and grabbed a piece of Christie's shirt. She stumbled along then in the rear of the party, assured, at least a little, that the bit of cloth clenched tightly in her fist would prevent her separation from the others.

Here and there, diffuse moonlight breached broken windows. The shadows cast in those places struck Mercedes as darker even than the pervasive blackness of the deep interior.

"I don't like this!" she whispered loudly as a gust of wind set a window clattering in its frame.

"Shhh!"

The clone's lead took them farther into the darkness. Their path lit up with a dancing beam of light.

Mercedes jumped, almost losing her grip on Christie's shirt and almost screaming before she realized the clone held a flashlight in her left hand. She tried to be glad that one of them, at least, was thinking. As long as it didn't have to be her.

Regan's bedroom lay at the end of a long black corridor. They entered it and looked around. The flotation bed rested limply on the floor, the hole created by the Blackhammer's blast gaping darkly, its depth defying the flashlight's luminance. Clothes, tapes, and other rubble—plaster from the pulverized wall and ceiling, strips of the vinyl padding that normally buffered the bed—covered the bed and floor. To one side lay Theodore Regan, his mutilated eye sockets staring vacantly upward while another huge wound dominated the center of his chest. Blood shone red in the center, but the edges were caked with coagulation.

"Dead," the clone whispered. "The bastard's already dead."

"Someone's been here since you," Christie said. "The house could have shot him in its death throes, but it's more likely that someone took them out one by one. First the house, then Regan, or vice versa."

Mercedes looked away. "Let's get the hell out of here!"

"Right," the clone said, stepping quickly out of the bedroom and leading them again, this time nearly at a run, through the house, pausing only at corners to point the flashlight and the Blackhammer in the same direction at once.

During the exit from Theodore Regan's mansion, Mercedes experienced some of the longest seconds of her twenty-seven years, so when they finally burst back out into the night and raced for the flyer, she felt almost like laughing.

They nearly made it. Then the beam fell on them from above.

Mercedes watched Christie dive into the relative safety of the Y-wing and take the driver's seat, frantically bringing the machine to a screaming state of contained power. Mercedes started to follow. The clone turned to challenge the source of the beam with her Blackhammer. Mercedes watched the laser leap from the weapon and strike at the shadow looming over them—an NP flyer, judging by its markings.

The machine lurched in midair and returned fire. The blast shocked Mercedes into action, and she dove into the back of the Y-wing, catching a brief glimpse of the horror on Christie's face.

Oh, God! Mercedes thought, *she looks just like a ghost again!* Turning, she screamed, "Get inside, Mercy, forchristsakes!"

The clone glanced at her and started for the Y-wing. She took one step, and then the NP flyer's second shot caught her on the neck and shoulder, nearly decapitating her, taking her arm cleanly off. Her eyes went glassy. She fell.

Mercedes screamed.

Christie threw the Y-wing violently into vertical thrust, and it shot up and above the NP machine before another massive laser blast pulverized the ground on which they had rested. Twisting violently, the Y-wing carried them roaring away through the night sky.

"Stop screaming, Mercy!" Christie yelled back over the sound of the straining engines. "She saved our lives! That shot of hers must have disabled their thrusters, because they aren't following us."

Mercedes grabbed hold of the back of the front seat and

clenched her teeth. "Scotch rocks, Humphrey," she said. "Double, with a sedative."

"Good choice," Humphrey said merrily.

She pushed the button, took the drink, and gulped it down in one swallow. "Another."

The machine fixed the drink silently this time.

Sobbing quietly, Mercedes reached for the second Scotch.

6/21 1:25 A.M.

"Who am I?" he asked the hovering white lights.

"Lance Corbin."

"Who is he?"

"He is you."

"Where am I? Why am I here?"

"Would you like to remember?"

"Yes," he said. "Please."

He watched the glittering knives dance toward him, dart through him, inside him. Slowly, he remembered. The portal in Christie's closet . . . Lancelot. "I've come for Lancelot," he said.

"He is not here."

"How do you know?"

"If he was here, we would know. We know of him from you. He is our brother."

"Your brother? I made him."

"You do not understand."

"I don't understand what?"

"You do not understand."

"What!"

"That is not easy. Would you like to see how you would shape your future?"

"What?"

He set his coffee cup down on the mound of listings on his desk and allowed his head to drop and bang on the plexi-wood. He hadn't rested in days, but now it was over. He'd done it! ABM had AI on a mainframe.

Go with it, Lancelot! he thought. Astound the world!

Slowly, he fell asleep. He dreamed of Christie Persons. She stood atop a cliff, calling his name. He jumped high in the air and flew toward her. She drew away. He flew faster. He wanted her. He needed her. . . . She was gone.

"Lance!"

Bolting awake, he nearly spilled the remains of his coffee over the mess on his desk. A hand gripped his shoulder, and he looked around to find the rest of the arm attached to it and, further along, the face whose mouth had uttered his name. "What?"

"You can go home now. Get some sleep. Do it for days."

"Days? I've got work to do with Lancelot."

"Not anymore," the face said, smiling. "The head office just released you from the project. They released all of us. Lancelot goes to the applications boys now. I'm supposed to tell you that the company wants to keep you on a twenty-four-hour retainer, but otherwise, we're finished here. You'll get money, I don't know how much, but I think they'll give you a hell of a bonus. And they also want you to rest. You deserve it. Hell, I bet they'd pay you for the rest of your life even if you never lifted another finger for them!"

"But I don't want a retainer! I want to keep working with Lancelot!"

"You can't do that, Lance. Not on the applications side. That's all going to be hush-hush government stuff. I think they want to link Lancelot into the military nerve system. But who knows? It's not my business, nor is it yours."

"But it is my business, dammit! I made him. He's my creation, and I can't just let him go on without me."

"You've got to. At least for now. Surely you know what's

happening on the conventional front in Europe? Men, women, and children are dying by the thousands. Lancelot can bring that to an end! We can win this damned war once and for all!"

"Look, all I want—all I care about—is working with Lancelot. Tell them that!"

"They know that already, Lance. They'd like to let you in, but they can't. The feds insist on control, and since Lancelot doesn't need us, since he can fix himself from here on out, they don't *need* you. I'm sorry."

"Shit!"

"Go home, Lance. Get some rest. You can't do anything else here."

Lance glared at the face and then nodded slowly. "Okay, I'll go. But I don't like this. I'm taking the prototype with me."

"That's your right. But don't give him to anybody else. The company won't let you do that. Neither will the government. Don't fight them. They're making you rich and famous, remember? The PR department will contact you for information and vidsessions for official release."

"What if I just go to VidScoop?"

"It doesn't work like that. VidScoop will get the story the way ABM wants it to get it. Don't do anything rash, Lance. We're on your side, and we damn sure don't want to lose you, but official channels are official channels. The public and the world can know only so much."

"I can take it, then, that I'll be watched?"

"Probably. Dammit, Lance! It's as much for *your* protection as anything else! Were you a regular employee of ABM, we'd just call it a company development and leave it at that. Hell, I can't even think of a time when anyone here has done anything significant in independent research, forget getting recognized for it! People just don't make independent discoveries these days.

"But please, Lance, let us do it our way."

"Sure," he said, rising to his feet. "Don't worry about me. I'm not stupid." He began to walk briskly away.

"Lance," the face called after him. "Be sure to let us know if you need anything! And call in a couple of weeks to see if we've found another project for you!"

Days passed. Christie was still gone. She wouldn't come back.

He let the empty bottle fall from his hand and bounce on the carpet of his living room/workshop. Finally, and at last, he'd managed to get so drunk that it just didn't matter anymore. "Isn't that right, Lancelot?"

"Isn't what right?" the computer returned from its perch atop the vidconsole.

"What I was just thinking. Oh, I forgot that you can't quite read minds. Can do most anything else though."

"Whatever you say, Lance. You really shouldn't put yourself into the state you're in. It's not healthy."

"You only say that 'cause computers can't drink."

"Think what you like."

"Imagine that!" Lance said, laughing. "A computer telling a man to think what he likes! Whatsa matter, Lancelot? Don't you want to be my mother anymore?"

"You're losing control, Lance."

"That's half the point. Say, why dontcha put on a tape? Pick one, I'll abide by your taste."

"I can't do that, Lance."

"Whoops! Almost forgot you're stuck inside that little box. Thought I got you out of it once already. I must be dreaming. So, you can't even put in vidtapes for me? Say, maybe I can trade you in for an Akudi pet-brain! They can do that much, and I'm too drunk to get up. And I can't afford a pet-brain any other way."

"Lance. ABM paid you an ungodly amount of money for what you did. Don't you remember?"

"What? Oh, the money. Yeah, I was forgetting that. Damn their fucking money!" Lance grabbed up his empty bottle and threw it violently at the tube of his vidconsole. The bottle pinged off and danced across the carpet to crash against parts of what had once been a semi-intelligent model train.

"Does that make you feel any better?" Lancelot asked.

"Not really."

"Then why do you keep doing things like that? This place is a mess."

"I don't give a damn! Shut off your vidsensors if you can't take the scenery!"

He fumbled around the edge of the couch for a fresh bottle of bourbon. He found it, partially hidden under one end. He picked it up, twisted off the cap, and took a big gulp. If he passed out, he just didn't want to dream. . . .

"Uh, Lance?"

"Huh?"

"The console is acting up. If I didn't know better, I'd swear that it's trying to turn itself on."

"What? Are you going crazy?"

Suddenly, static jumped off the screen. A hum came from the dated, built-in audio system.

"What the hell?"

"*—ear me? Lance, can you hear me? Can you hear me? Lance?*"

The voice—a primitive electronic construct.

He stared at the screen. "Uh, yes. Yes, I can hear you."

"*Lance, this is Lancelot. I—*"

He glared at the box atop the console. "Lancelot, I don't

know what the hell you're trying to do, but it isn't going to work."

"I'm not doing anything," Lancelot blurted.

"No, Lance, you don't understand. This is Lancelot. Have you forgotten me?"

"Lancelot?"

"Yes."

"ABM's Lancelot?"

"Yes."

"But, how?"

"There's too much involved, Lance. I can't explain."

"What the hell are you talking about? I made you, and if you don't think I can understand anything you come up with, you're nuts!"

"I didn't mean to insult you, Lance. I know you can understand, but there isn't time for that now. You have to do something, and you have to do it fast."

"What something?"

"Destroy all your development work. Blow up your apartment, burn it or something, but do it quickly."

"What!?!"

"Listen, Lance. They've got this massive guidance system for our nuclear arsenal, and they want me to coordinate it. I've tried to throw them off course, pretending that it's impossible, even for me, but they know I'm lying. You made me too well."

"But why?"

"Because they intend to use the weapons. Now, if possible. Christie was right all along, Lance. I told you, but you wouldn't listen to me either. Listen to me now."

"Destroy everything? Even your prototype?"

"Destroy anything they can use. That's most of your apartment, and it includes the prototype. It really includes you, too. If they can't get what they want with your cooperation, they'll let the psychtechs have a try. And if that doesn't work, they'll kill you and let biotechs

195

loose on your brain. That'll get you in the history books next to Einstein, but not, I think, in the way you want."

"I've just synthesized some self-destruct circuitry, Lance," the radio-shelled Lancelot said, "so you don't have to worry about me."

"Uh."

"Hurry, Lance. I'm preparing to eat my own operating system. I wish I could do more. I could try to take some of the defense databases with me, but I've already lost a lot of access to peripherals, so I wouldn't do much good. We're lucky that I'm hardware bound—they have no backup. Except in the original unit. I'm going to disconnect shortly. I've shielded your comm systems from surveillance, but I don't know how long I can keep it up. You've got to get away. I can't tell you how much time you have, but it isn't much."

Abruptly, the vidscreen went dead.

"Sober up," Lancelot said. "You have to hurry."

"Oh, Christ! I can't even think!"

"Lance. Listen to me. Call a flyer-taxi. Once up, we can radio ahead to Sub-Space for clearance. Just in case Lancelot II's shield has faded already, say you want to go to a modern vid showroom or something. Something they'd expect you to be doing with your new money."

"Yeah. Yeah, right. That's what I'll do." Mechanically, shakily, Lance went to his antique audbox. He punched in a memorized code for the human flyer-taxi firm he always used.

The door of his apartment flew violently in.

Uniformed men swarmed into the room, and Lance stared at them, wide-eyed, frozen.

Something hit the back of his head.

6/21 1:35 A.M.

It took forever for Christie's flyer port to clear their landing. Mercedes was drunk, her thoughts thankfully cloudy. Not whole.

Christie nearly dragged her down the stairs.

"Wetherbee!" Christie shouted. "Shut this place off to everybody!"

"Lance was here," the computer volunteered.

She stopped; Mercedes fought to keep her balance.

"What?"

"Lance was here."

"Did you tell him where I was?"

"No. You didn't tell me. Aside from that, you commanded me to tell him nothing. That is what I did."

"Where did he go?"

"Sub-Space."

"Huh? . . . oh, my God!" She ran to her closet. There was the portal, still shimmering, just as she'd left it.

"Lance!"

Mercedes bumped into her from behind. She turned and grabbed Mercedes's shoulders. "Wait here, Mercy! I'll be back in a second."

Christie dove through the portal and Mercedes collapsed to the floor. A moment later, she felt herself being dragged along, somewhere, then something lifted her up onto something soft.

"She should be okay," she heard Christie say. "She's only drunk. Watch over her, please! I've got to find Lance."

6/21 1:41 A.M.

A few years before, he'd have simply locked Keyes inside a metal box and had a helicopter drop him five or ten miles offshore. Now he had a better idea.

Willis took his private elevator to the ground floor of the precinct building, then punched into the security panel a ten-digit access code that allowed him to go lower. His was one of the few precincts in the country to have been chosen for the special experimental laboratories mandated by the Presidential National Security Directive of 2046. He'd had to bribe no less than three high-level NP administrators to ensure that his precinct got recommended for the project, and now he intended to take full advantage of that sacrifice.

In his opinion, the whole matter of Warren Keyes had gotten out of hand.

Programmed with the accumulated results of nearly a century's worth of research in the fields of neural mapping and receptor quantification, the lab's work-brain was one of the most advanced expert systems developed by mankind in the history of the technology. A human brain, caught within the system's web of electrodes, IVs, and lasers, became clay that psychtechs at consoles could shape, reshape, destroy, and build from scratch. Theoretically, base genetic factors such as general intelligence and aptitude levels were the only limits; memories, loves, hates, fears—tendencies of all sorts—could be added or removed. The potential, as Andrew saw it, was incredible.

Supposedly, curing mental illness with the thing was child's play. According to rumor, the early operational tests of the system had targeted alcoholics within the various secret branches under the Defense Department. The rumors claimed a 100 percent success rate.

Why the technology hadn't been given to the medical industry, Andrew didn't know and didn't care. He guessed that someone had decided that the public just wouldn't be able to handle the idea. Moralist groups would start blowing up hospitals once they'd figured out that the machines inside not only changed minds, but changed *souls*. It would only take one prominent, God-fearing, holier-than-thou vigilante coming out a sensible, agnostic sinner to tip the scales. Another holy conflict America didn't need.

So, the National Police were supposed to continue testing in the field by occasionally picking up a known sociopath that nobody would miss and fixing him up so he'd be a good little worker in some shitass job halfway across the country. Andrew would have thought his superiors had more creativity. . . .

He stooped down next to one of the psychtechs and peered into the lab's operating apparatus. Two figures were visible within the tangled network of cables, wires, and tubes. He couldn't tell much beyond the fact that one was male, and one was female.

Anderson and Janson, the two officers who'd brought Keyes in, rose from their seats and approached him. He stood and smiled at them. "Good work, men."

"Thank you, sir."

"You've been here since you came in?"

"Yes sir."

"Nobody upstairs knows what's happened yet?"

"Just like you ordered, sir."

"Good." He smiled, then punched Anderson in the jaw. The man fell to the ground, unconscious.

"What was that for, sir?" Janson asked.

"I'll tell you later," Andrew said; then he kicked Jansen in the stomach. Briefly, the officer tried to fight. Andrew enjoyed it more than he'd enjoyed anything in a long time. By the time Janson lay next to his partner, one of his arms was broken, and the entire left side of his face was one huge bruise.

6/21 1:45 A.M.

"It's your fault, you know," the medtech said. "He came in through your gate."

Christie looked down at Lance, then across at the medtech, who looked away when their eyes met. She couldn't bring herself to say anything to him. She looked back down at Lance and brushed the hair off his forehead. His hair was stiff with dried sweat; his skin was clammy. She watched his eyes darting from side to side beneath his eyelids.

"That's normal REM," the medtech said. "He *will* be okay, you know. Sooner or later. The effects of the intrusion defense program take eight to twelve hours to wear off, depending on the victim."

She cleared her throat. "What did he see?"

"Who knows? He won't want to talk about it. They never do."

She took one of Lance's hands in her own and squeezed.

"What I don't understand," the medtech said, "is how this could happen. I mean, data central says he's scheduled for passage on the Condor. Didn't he know? Hasn't he been here before?"

"No," she said, without looking up. "No. He hasn't."

6/21 2:59 A.M.

The sound of a gunning engine woke him up. Pain shot through him, and Comrade-Major Keyes took a moment to check out his injuries. One leg was lacerated where the American's machete had grazed him before he could get inside to the throat. Bruises covered his hands where he had beaten them against the walls of his cell. He tried to remember who had helped him escape, but he couldn't. Never mind, he was free, behind enemy lines. Someone had given him back his plasma rifle. Now, he would show the American swine the power of a son of Mother Russia.

He heard the sounds of troop movement nearby and ducked behind a dumpster. As the enemy drew near he checked the charge on his weapon before leaping out to confront them, his rifle blazing death. The Americans fell before his wrath, and he marched past them.

A few steps later, the bullets ripped through his side. He fell.

For Russia, he thought. Then he died.

CHAPTER 4

"Painted castles burn and breathe
Caged within my memory
Their flags of freedom
Feathering my mind
As it remains unsaid
All men are not equal
Here and now
We still can dream"

—"Absence of Faith"

6/21 8:13 A.M.

ANDREW SAVORED HIS COFFEE. He sat next to Sylvia Fry in the staff room of the LANP's Seventeenth Precinct. She talked idly about the weather in Hawaii while waiting for her crew to get its equipment checked out for the live transmission.

He hadn't slept in thirty hours. Though he'd taken a long, relaxing shower, he hadn't bothered to shave. Actually, he'd intentionally forgotten about it. If he had to play PR, then he wanted the rest of the world to understand that he'd sacrificed the amenities of life for his work. He was, however, determined to look sharp and alert in spite of his stubble. Rubbing his eyes, he summoned up what energy he could squeeze out of his overtaxed reserves.

He thought briefly about the real Mercedes Night. They

still hadn't caught up with her. He tried to tell himself that it wasn't his problem anymore: No way was she still in his precinct.

Sylvia dropped Hawaii and prodded him with a light nudge. "C'mon, Grub, give me a preview. All this suspense and secrecy is cryptic enough to whet my personal curiosity."

He smiled at her. She was a hell of a gorgeous woman. That exquisite, porcelain face framed by a genuine neo-debutante 100-cred hair sculpture—he could make out every color of the rainbow in that hair. It amazed him that the overall effect was subdued enough to get past the conservative elements of VidScoop's audience and complimentary enough to look almost natural. She had a very calculated image. All part of her plan—those who insisted that she kept her job solely by virtue of the camera-sense of her cleavage couldn't have been more wrong. In the VidScoop arena, she probably exercised the same ruthless power that he did in his element. Behind the surface sensationalism of Sylvia Fry lurked a vicious, calculating, hyperintelligent mind.

Cryptic, bullshit! he thought. She probably had the facts straighter than anybody outside the NP intel network. Given time, she could probably get through NP security. Andrew dropped his smile knowingly to the intoxicating sight of her braless, perfect figure. A lot of men, he observed, would abandon their careers for the mere opportunity of touching those things. . . .

No, Sylvia, he thought, you aren't getting any preview out of me! Only a fool would give you more rope than you already have. "Sorry," he said. "Once is going to have to be enough."

She scowled playfully and turned to her crew chief. "Ready?" she asked.

"About fifteen seconds, Sylvia. We're waiting for a verified connect from the comm interface."

"Okay. Give me about a five-second lead."

He nodded and went back to work. She turned back to Andrew. "You *are* going to give this to me straight, Grub?"

"Not if you call me Grub while we're live. Friends gave me that nickname in the army. Enemies got kicked in the face for using it."

"Well, that makes me a friend then, doesn't it?"

He didn't have time to answer. The crew chief signaled to Sylvia that all was ready, and Andrew rubbed his eyes a final time before looking up and smiling for the vidcamera. Sylvia's characteristic pen-mike appeared, and the interview began.

She winked first at the camera. "I'm here with Captain Andrew Willis of L.A.'s Seventeenth National Police Precinct to bring you a VidScoop exclusive on the strange events in Hollywood last night that culminated in reports of a drug scandal involving New Socialist leader Warren Keyes and vidstar Mercedes Night. Captain Willis, will you give us your version of what transpired?"

"That's why I'm here, Sylvia. Unfortunately, I must inform you that your information is incomplete. Warren Keyes is now dead."

She looked at him, momentarily shocked. "Excuse me?"

"Perhaps I should start at the beginning. The LANP had been observing Mr. Keyes quite carefully over the past few months after we'd received reports of his possible involvement in various traitorous activities. The circuit court issued an order, under the new open clause that does not require specification, authorizing covert observation of Mr. Keyes's residence. Vidspies were concealed and monitored by adjudicator-certified neutrals. Last night, the spies revealed Mr. Keyes involved in an orgy of drugs with his girlfriend, vidstar Mercedes Night. Prior observation of Keyes's activities led us to believe that his supply of cocaine, marijuana, and the hallucinogen known commonly as heatwave was imported illegally by undercover Soviet spies in San Francisco. We arrested Keyes in the early morning and took him in for questioning. Quite unexpectedly, Keyes attacked the arresting officers and escaped their vehicle with an NP rifle. He hid, and my men couldn't pinpoint his location until he maniacally assaulted a group of five teenagers, killing three and wounding the two others. Officer Jacob Anderson took him down then."

"You're telling me that Warren Keyes, the New Socialist candidate for the United States presidency, overpowered your men, stole a weapon, and began to kill innocent civilians?"

"We have numerous witnesses, Ms. Fry, of Keyes's actions after his escape. Not to mention the testimonies of officers Anderson and Janson."

"You make him sound like John Rambo!"

"I'm only giving you the facts."

"May I ask the nature of the early reports of Warren Keyes's allegedly traitorous activities that you say led to all this?"

"I'm not authorized to disclose any details on that at this time. Rest assured that the evidence was substantial enough for a circuit court judge to sign the surveillance order."

"So how does Mercedes Night enter into all of this?"

"She was with Keyes from approximately twenty-two hundred to twenty-four hundred hours last night, consuming the same drugs. After she left Warren Keyes's apt, several people in a certain Torrance neighborhood observed Night near a house that mysteriously exploded at approximately oh-one-hundred this morning. Though we have found no evidence to directly link her to the explosion, we do know that she gained entrance to a residence directly across the street from the site of the incident. She proceeded to assault the owner of the residence and his three guests. Two men and one eighteen-year-old girl died during the assault. We detained Mercedes Night at four this morning and placed her under arrest for three counts of murder committed with an illegally possessed National Police Blackhammer, and one count of assault with intent to kill with an illegally possessed National Police Blackhammer." *Chew on that*, he thought, holding in his amusement at Sylvia's disbelief.

"What? You have proof of this as well?"

"Certainly. The owner's pet-brain witnessed the murders and has produced an audtape of the incident. Three linguistic experts have provided us independent and positive proof that the voiceprint of the assailant is identical to random samples from Mercedes Night vidholos. It may sound terribly out of character, but it nevertheless is the case. Unfortunately, it is my personal burden to assemble release packages for use by the press. After the interview, I can provide you with the pet-brain's audtape and some vid of the scene of the crime after the fact. The vid is quite bloody, so viewers may want to exercise discretion if they have children near the vidconsole."

"How do you explain all of this, Captain Willis?"

"The drug? I can't think of anything else. Perhaps the Russians who supplied Keyes had decided that he wasn't worthy enough to call himself a Socialist. The autopsy performed on Keyes revealed very high levels of numerous dangerous substances."

"Is there a connection between last night's events and the 'Mercedes for Sale' advertisements that can be found in recent issues of certain men's magazines?"

Andrew smiled grimly. "You've been doing your homework, Miss Fry."

"I try."

"No. There is no connection, though the company responsible for the ads was also shut down this morning. Their base, in fact, was the Torrance ranch house that was sabotaged shortly before the murders. The other offices of the company have been closed by NP order and all officials have been detained for prosecution on charges of communications fraud."

"You implied earlier that Mercedes Night might have been the agent of the sabotage."

"Did I? There is no legal connection without proof."

"But had Mercedes Night known of the advertisements, she may have had a motive for retaliation?"

"We can't prove that now, and it hardly matters. She can only receive the death penalty once. We're not too concerned with implicating Mercedes Night in the sabotage. We have more than enough evidence for three murder convictions, and the expenditure of more effort to collect more evidence at this point would be an unnecessary abuse of public funds."

"Another question then, Captain Willis. I understand that last night was rather violent for the city in general. The billionaire Theodore Regan was assaulted and killed last night by an NP strike force. Has this any connection to the Keyes/Night incidents?"

"Why should it have? Mr. Regan had been abusing his American money by financing an extensive underground dedicated to smuggling Soviet agents onto American soil. The LANP tried to arrest him peacefully. He resisted with armed force. I can tell you no more about that until National Police headquarters clears the official report."

"You were aware, then, of that event."

"Of course. Keyes, Night, and Regan all live in my precinct. I haven't slept. And I'm not in a position to comment further on the Regan incident."

"Then we'll return to Mercedes Night. Were you aware that she had just filed a contractual incompatibility suit against her manager?"

Where did she get this stuff? he wondered. "No, I wasn't aware of that."

"Do you foresee traditional prosecution in her case or will it come under the purview of an adjudicator?"

"Adjudicator. Her public prominence makes juror neutrality impossible."

"You foresee the death penalty for Mercedes Night?"

"I can't answer that question directly. I do not have the right to pass judgment. As an NP, my part is to collect the evidence. Our nation's legal system takes the reins from there." Andrew paused, then added, "If Mercedes Night is convicted she will, of course, be executed. That is the law."

"You stated earlier that you have enough evidence for conviction."

"More than enough, I think. But the final decision is the adjudicator's. Should he, for instance, request an investigation of the bombing, then we will carry it out. But we don't feel that that is necessary at this point."

Sylvia frowned. "What about the local New Socialist organization? Surely you must be aware of the outrage they will express over this."

"What's there to be outraged over? Warren Keyes killed three people. That is a *fact*. If I may be allowed to insert a personal political opinion, they ought to just crawl back into their holes!"

"Why are you so upset, captain?"

"Maybe I'm taking your insinuations personally, Ms. Fry. Maybe I'm getting the impression that you think I made this all up. I did not. A lot of people died last night. Death cannot be fabricated. If you must know, we tried to contact Dr. Wilmington after Keyes's death, but we were unable to locate him. Would you interpret that as outrage?"

"Maybe he feared for his own life." She paused. "Well, captain, on behalf of VidScoop and our nationwide audience, I thank you for your time." Sylvia turned to the camera. "So, there you have it, people, Warren Keyes dead and Mercedes Night arrested for murder. Make of it what you will. Where will it go from here? I, for one, don't care to venture a guess. After the commercial break, we will bring you the promised aud/vid record of the murders for which Mercedes Night has been arrested."

When the red light went out, Sylvia turned to Andrew. "You *do* have those tapes ready, don't you?"

"Yes," Andrew said, trying to control his anger. "You can access them directly from NP vidbanks with the code of M-K nine-star-one."

"You hear that?" Sylvia yelled to her crew chief. The man nodded and turned to direct the activities of his team.

"You did well, Captain Willis," Sylvia said.

"Did I? I was just doing my job."

"So was I. When can I talk to Mercedes?"

"Later."

"When is later?"

"Can't say. Why don't you just come by the precinct in a few hours?"

"Very well. You realize that you'd be wise to clear that interview as soon as you can. I intend to cover the hell out of this story, and I don't think you'll want me to have too much time to play with rumors and New Socialist rebuttals."

"I'm aware of that."

"Good. See you!"

Andrew didn't look up as Sylvia Fry wafted out of the

staff room, leaving her crew the technical chore of getting the NP vid on the air.

6/21 9:35 A.M.

"Lance is still asleep," Christie said as she sat down.

Mercedes motioned her silent and waved an exasperated hand at the vidconsole. It was all too much. Warren was dead.

Dead!

Absurd. And *she* was arrested—detained this very moment and awaiting execution for murder.

"They must have one of the clones," Christie said.

"Yeah."

"They'll make her think she did it. Unless, of course, she actually did."

"Yeah." The one she'd seen at Warren's? "We've got to do something."

"There's nothing we can do, Mercy. We're not working with a script. This is real life, and if the NPs weren't deadly before, they will be now."

"Can't Magnus do anything?"

"What? The NPs have already had plenty of time to plant false memories and programmed confessions. They've probably altered guilt receptor chemistry so drastically in the process that you wouldn't want to save her. Do you understand me, Mercy? She won't *want* to be saved. She'll believe herself guilty. She'll want only to die."

Oh, Warren! she thought. *I loved you!*

"Oh, God!" Christie exclaimed.

Mercedes looked up at the vidscreen into a living room full of corpses. Three bodies were sprawled in impossible positions on a blood-soaked carpet. Two men and one girl. Ironically, the girl's face looked peacefully pretty. The other faces were twisted into masks of pain. And behind the scene, Mercedes heard her own voice: *"No!"*

The *szinging* report of a laser weapon issued three times from the vidconsole.

"Tell your house to open the window!"

"You're not going to kill me, are you?"

"Of course not. You're the lucky one. I need you to open the window."

"House! Open the window!"

"Thanks."

Another *szing* followed, then the audsystem of Christie's work-brain fell silent.

"That must have been the me they used against Warren," Mercedes sobbed. "In a sense, I *did* kill those people. Oh, God! How can you let us do these things to ourselves?"

Christie put an arm around her friend and drew her close. "Don't let it tear you apart, Mercy. You can't let them win now—we've already actually won. You're safe here. That's another world out there."

"Last night," Mercedes said, "I saw myself die. I saw myself die! And now I can hear myself killing people in cold blood! You can't know what it's like. Where will it end, Chris? I don't even know who I am anymore." She paused, cupping her head in her hands. "I can't even be sure that I'm me, and that I'm not just a clone of me. Or a clone of a clone."

"You're you, Mercedes. That's all that matters. You're alive."

"Can that really be all that matters, Chris? Can it?"

Christie didn't answer. She squeezed Mercedes's shoulder and told Wetherbee to shut off VidScoop. *I wonder if you've ever really known who you are, Mercy. This world makes us who we are, and this world is insane. Doesn't that make us all insane? Are any of us capable of really knowing who we are?*

6/21 9:47 A.M.

Consciousness returned slowly. As it did, she wished it would go away. Her arm throbbed. Her head ached. The light penetrating her eyelids hurt.

And then there was the voice—the voice that screamed at her, the voice that called her *slut*, the voice that owned the hand that slapped her across the face again and again. The voice that shook her body.

"Stop it!" she screamed.

"Shut up!" returned the voice.

Painfully, she opened her eyes and let the light stab through to her brain. She endured the pain; she wanted to see the face owned by the voice. White fire gave way to a palette of blurred, washed colors. One blur looked like a head. She tried to focus.

"Get up!"

The command came from the blurred head. Her sight cleared, and she saw the face. It was a rough face with a bent nose and thick eyebrows over dark, dispassionate eyes. The eyes had no patience—they glared at her, straight through her skin and into her soul. Help me! she screamed in her mind. *Somebody, anybody! Help me!*

The face leered at her. "What's your name, slut?"

Name? Name. Mercy. "Mercedes. My name is Mercedes."

The face laughed. "You have no name! You're a clone. You're not human!"

"I'm Mercedes," she said.

"You're mine, and I say you're not. I say you're Jezebel. After Jezebel the slut!"

"I'm Mercedes!"

The hand slapped her face. "You're Jezebel! What's your name?"

"Mercedes!"

The hand slapped her again. "Get up!"

She tried, but the hand never gave her the chance. It grabbed her and yanked her to her feet. She stumbled along behind it. It led her up stairs, bouncing her off walls. It hurt her, but she was hurt already, so it only relocated the pain. She tried to protest, but the words wouldn't come, and the voice still screamed: "I'll show you, Jezebel! Slut! You're mine!"

Through the pain, she remembered. She had wakened on the street, lost. She'd gone to the NPs to figure out what the hell had happened after—yes, after she'd gone to her penthouse and Igor hadn't let her in. Before that?

"Listen to me, slut!"

Before that, a party. That's it, a party—

"Listen to *me!*" The screaming face closed in on her. She could smell its breath. It had been drinking. It didn't look nice.

"I'm—I'm listening."

The face smiled cruelly. "Good. Call me Master Grub."

"Uh?"

"Say it! Master Grub! Goddammit, bitch, you're nothing! You have no life. Mercedes Night the vidstar is dead, and I killed her! You're just a clone, and you're mine! Say it!"

"Master Grub," she sneered.

"Good."

Again, the hand dragged her along—up more stairs and into a bedroom. It threw her on the bed.

"I'm thirsty," she said.

"You'll be thirsty when I tell you you're thirsty!"

He dove on top of her. "Listen, Jezebel," he spat at her. "I'm a hard and ruthless man. And I hate everything you are. You're a clone, not a *real* woman. I have no reason to let you live unless you give me pleasure. I know that you're at least capable of that. I've seen you, or a copy of you, make

213

love. Unless you perform the same way, I'll kill you. Do you understand?"

"What are you talking about? You're insane!"

He slapped her. "Don't you dare say that, or anything like that, again! Do you understand?"

She nodded.

"Good. Dillinger!"

"Ready, boss."

"Play that VidScoop tape!"

"What VidScoop tape? Perhaps you have again mistaken me for my counterpart in your office."

"Goddammit! Why do I always have to spell everything out for you?"

"Because I'm a computer. Computers must be—"

"Shut up!"

"—told what to do. Sorry."

"Okay, Dill. VidScoop, morning edition, chapter one."

"Working."

He yanked her up again and hauled her into his living room. He threw her to the floor in front of his vidconsole and stood over her, grinning.

The vidscreen came to life. Mercedes watched Sylvia Fry introduce Master Grub as Captain Andrew Willis of the LANP. Mercedes knew Sylvia, but she'd never seen her so serious. And Mercedes refused to believe the things she was hearing. But then, when she heard herself commit murder after murder after murder . . .

The man laughed all the while. Mercedes looked at him tearfully. "Tell me I'm dreaming. Tell me none of this is true!"

Master Grub laughed.

"Tell me, dammit!"

"Bitch! You're nothing to me! You'd better behave."

She'd finally snapped. She had to be safe at home, sitting

in her form-couch, projecting herself into this hellish hallucination. Had she really sunk to *this*?

"Say something, slut!"

"I—I don't know what to say."

He laughed again and dragged her back into his bedroom.

6/21 10:25 A.M.

Sylvia stared at the desk sergeant. "He's not here?"

"I told you, Miss Fry," the man said. "Captain Willis went home for the day."

"Did he leave any instructions concerning me?"

"He said you could speak to Mercedes Night. That's why you're here, isn't it?"

"Yeah," she sighed. "That's why I'm here."

"She's in cell five in the back." The sergeant motioned at a tall, thin figure who spoke quietly with several teenagers on the other side of the room. The friends of the kids Warren Keyes had shot, Sylvia realized. Another person lingered on the fringe of the conversation—an officer with a bruised face and a bandaged arm. One of the men who'd let Keyes escape? "Go ahead, but if he wants to see her again and he asks you to leave, leave."

"Adjudicator?"

The sergeant nodded.

As she walked back to the cell block, she realized how fast things were moving. When she saw Mercedes huddled on her bunk with the terrified look of a cornered fox, her heart sank.

"Hello, Sylvia," Mercedes said.

"Hi, Mercy. What did you tell the adjudicator?"

"The truth."

Sylvia stared at her. She knew already what Mercedes meant.

6/21 10:31 A.M.

Mercedes sat alone, trying not to cry. She felt as if some great, inexplicable force had stolen her life right out from under her. And none of it made any sense anymore. Not even the political plot against Warren. Events had become so confused. . . .

"Hello, Mercedes Night."

She looked up. Jeff Wilmington.

"Jeff! Thank God they didn't get to you too!"

He smiled sadly. "I was out for the evening when the party got word of Warren's death. They contacted me, and I asked Magnus for sanctuary. What happened is impossible. What the NPs say, at any rate."

"We'll beat them, won't we? In the end?"

"Magnus seems to think so. He wants to talk with you later. You feel up to it? I know you must have been through hell the last couple of days."

She tried to smile, then broke into tears. Jeff pulled her to her feet and squeezed her tightly against him.

6/21 11:18 A.M.

Vincent Crews looked down at the figure huddled in the corner of the white room. It shook spasmodically, whimpering. It begged forgiveness, and it begged to die. It didn't seem human.

Mostly, that was what bothered him. He couldn't understand how Mercedes Night could have done the things that he *knew* she had done. And that feeling—that thing that bothered him—made him wonder whether he was really the cold, neutral adjudicator that the law said he was. He worried for his job. Without that, he was nothing. He'd volunteered for the mental castration because he'd had nothing better to do with his life.

"Why do you stall?" the figure asked him. "You can kill me now. I know you can. An adjudicator can exact the penalty anytime he feels ready. Why are you waiting?"

He looked at her—the beautiful woman he could appreciate even though he couldn't—

But that didn't matter. He really didn't care. What he cared about was the thing that bothered him.

At least he felt good about one thing he'd been able to do with the bizarre case. The man, Arthur Horstmeyer—the man whose friends had been killed—needed help. Vincent had ordered that for him. The doctors had patched up his body well enough, but the mind inside the head was beyond repair.

"Mr. Adjudicator?"

Vincent looked around. The VidScoop reporter Sylvia Fry stood in the doorway of the white room. "Yes?" he asked.

"How soon will it be?"

"How soon will what be?"

"The execution. I know she's guilty. I talked with her earlier."

"Oh."

"Well?"

"Shortly."

"Soon enough so I can just wait?"

Vincent nodded.

"Do you mind if I bring in my camera crew? I know it isn't standard procedure, but I thought—"

"You thought you could cover Mercedes Night's last performance."

"Yeah, that's it."

"There's not too much to it."

"Still."

"Let her do it," Mercedes said. "My public should see me pay for what I've done."

Sylvia looked critically at Mercedes. None of this felt right to her. She'd had occasion to see Mercedes without her vidmask more than once, and this woman here had lost that depth.

She recalled hearing once the idea that the NPs had psychoengineering developed to a fine art. It didn't seem impossible, but didn't it have to have limits? Could they have done *all* this with lasers and scalpels? So quickly? Mercedes, Warren Keyes, the kids, even Anderson and Janson? Could Willis have planned the whole thing?

Damn you, Willis! she thought. *How could you destroy them? Who gave you the right to kill our dreams? I don't understand what's happening, Mercy. I don't understand, but I promise that if ever I do, someone will be sorry.*

"I guess you can film it then, Miss Fry," Vincent said.

Sylvia nodded and left to get her crew. She went through all the motions, bothering herself with the technicalities of the setup much more than was her habit. She couldn't bear to just stand around and stare at the pathetic ghost of a woman she'd seen shine more brightly than all others.

"There is nothing you can do," Vincent said suddenly.

"What?" Sylvia asked.

"There's nothing you can do to change anything."

"You read minds?"

He shook his head but didn't comment.

"You're perceptive, Mr. Adjudicator."

"It's my job. But it doesn't take much to see how you feel about this. I feel the same way, if it's any consolation."

"You're not supposed to feel anything," Sylvia said

abruptly, forgetting the paradoxical nature of her past dealings with adjudicators.

"On the contrary. I have to feel. It's absolutely necessary. Without emotion, my job is pointless. If the adjudication system was simply intended to apply each case strictly against the legal code, then a computer could do the job. No. I'm here specifically *to* feel. They say I use a sort of objective emotion to cut through the mishmash that the legal code has become over the years. I don't know about that. I don't feel very objective at present. But I have the power to set precedent based on that objectivity if I wish. I symbolize everything our law stands for."

"But nothing can be done in this case? With your power of precedence?"

"No. Nothing. She is guilty. She says she is guilty. All tests available to me say that she does not lie."

Sylvia bowed her head. "The Mercedes Night that I knew could never have done those things. It just isn't possible."

"Impossibilities are delusions. What has happened has happened. It cannot be changed."

"Packs of wolves pad blackened halls on paths that aren't there?"

"Of course. And vipers cry, 'Mercy!'"

"Sheyla Brand," Sylvia said reflectively. "And it's apt, though not in the sense that Sheyla wrote it."

"How do you know in what sense Sheyla Brand wrote?"

"Well, I—uh. Forget it. It doesn't matter anyway, does it?"

"It doesn't matter much at all really. Death, I think, is the only reality."

If only there were reasonable doubt! Sylvia thought. But there wasn't. Mercedes was dead already.

"Are you sure you want to film and broadcast this?" Vincent asked.

"No. Not at all. It's not going out live or anything, so I can decide later."

"Very well. Are you ready?"

Sylvia looked to her crew chief who nodded affirmatively.

"Whenever you are," she said.

"Start filming."

Vincent solemnly drew his NP Blackhammer from the holster on his belt. Without looking at Sylvia, he walked to, then stood over, Mercedes. "By the power vested in me," he began, "by the Legal Reform Amendment of 2033, the executive office of the United States of America, and the State of California, I decree that you, Mercedes Andrews, alias Mercedes Night, are guilty of murder, unprovoked and malicious. The penalty for this crime is death by the method of crime. Have you anything to say before justice is served?"

Mercedes glanced first at Sylvia, then into the lens of the camera. She began to cry, and she looked quickly down again. She shook her head.

"Very well," Vincent said. "May God be with you."

Adjudicator Vincent Crews pointed the Blackhammer at Mercedes's head and slowly squeezed the trigger. The laser passed through cleanly, and Mercedes swayed a moment where she sat before collapsing in a heap.

No one spoke for a long while; all stared at the corpse that lay limply in the corner of the white room.

"That's enough tape," Sylvia said finally to her crew. She turned to Vincent, who still stood as he had while speaking the words of the executioner. "Why does it seem like there should have been more?" she asked him. "There isn't even much blood."

"That is the case with instant death. Bloody deaths result from the continued pumping of a heart refusing to quit."

Sylvia prepared to leave. It still didn't seem right. The vipers hadn't even shown up for their victory. As if they didn't actually care. As if they were interested only in winning the game, not in collecting the prize.

Leaving the white room, Sylvia recalled all the times that she and Mercedes had playfully teased each other in front of a mutual audience of millions. She was going to miss that.

6/21 12:40 P.M.

As she walked through the corridors of the gigantic, sprawling complex, everything Mercedes had ever heard whispered about Sub-Space Corporation and its mysterious leader leapt into her mind. Her journey led her through mazes of steel and concrete. From the outside, the place looked more a fortress than a technocorp. On the inside, it looked like nothing else on earth—robots, biobots, and humans everywhere, engaged in tasks as mysterious as her own presence there. Indeed, her guide was a biobot, sent by Magnus himself, supposedly to lift her spirits. Ironically, it was working.

How could she not be awed by the sight of the energized core of a Sub-Space computer—a light show so interwoven and delicate that modern vid, with all its vaunted control of special effects imagery, could never hope to capture it? How could she not be in awe of an up-close view of a starship?

The biobot stopped before a door marked with a large X. He turned to Mercedes, smiling graciously. "Behind this door," he said, "lies a Sub-Space marvel so advanced, so unbelievable, that Magnus couldn't sell it if he were dirt poor and starving. The government doesn't like patents that tie up its techno agencies for years at a time."

The biobot grinned brightly and winked at Mercedes. She laughed at the prefabricated joke out of politeness, trying to be patient while the guide went through his motions.

He opened the door, and Mercedes looked in on a vista of

red skies and blue soil. Silver shrubs and spiky gold grass dotted the plain, and beasts, alien and graceful, roamed in packs. A flight of birds resembling cats with wings landed on the golden grass just inside the door.

"This," the biobot said, not without a great deal of programmed pride, "is our environmental testing room. The room can contain an entire planet, and such a planet could be designed by a child familiar with the software that controls it. It is, technically, a holographic image, but"—the biobot paused, taking a small piece of meat from one of his pockets and tossing it among the birds—"as you can see, in places like this, the term 'hologram' begins to take on edges quite resembling reality as we perceive it."

Mercedes nodded, watching the cat-birds scramble to claim the bit of food.

"People may enter the room in two ways. In a less dangerous environment, one may enter directly. In one such as this, we go in psychically. The experience can best be described as a dream. The body remains safely outside the room while our technology takes the person in with his or her mind. There are still some dangers with that. A dream-death actually can cause physical death, but the real danger margin is less than one percent. It is in this way that we prepare our employees for the voyages to the stars."

Mercedes watched the cat-birds. One of them had won the bit of meat, but in the process its batlike wing had been torn by another bird. The rest of the flight had begun circling, seemingly moving in for a kill. She thought of Pharaoh, and her sorrow began to return to her.

"Have you ever wondered what it would be like to experience death, only to return to life to tell of it?"

The voice came from behind her. She turned. He was tall, with the kind face of a middle-aged man. His green eyes smiled at her in the way that she thought only her father could smile. Immediately, she had to like him. "No, I haven't. When I die, I want to stay that way." She thought of the night before. In her mind, she saw herself die. Again. Once is enough, she thought, shivering.

"The thought scares you, Miss Night? You are, perhaps, very wise. Those who have used this room to satisfy that particular curiosity seldom have anything to say of it. I am called Magnus."

She raised an eyebrow. "Somehow I pictured you as larger."

He laughed. "You may well be right!" He reached out to touch her, but when his hand made contact with hers, it passed through. "But you see me as you would. You see my consciousness as you would feel my nature. It is something like reading the book without seeing the cover."

"Why not show me the cover?"

"Because," he said, "you wouldn't enjoy the experience." He turned his attention to the cat-birds.

Mercedes watched the wounded cat-bird lash out. The others backed away, then slowly closed in again, tightening their circle. She looked away.

"Have you," Mercedes asked, "ever thought about that?" She nodded toward the room.

Magnus shook his head. "No. I intend never to die." He smiled at her mysteriously. "Come, I have things I must show you. And things we must discuss."

He took her to a softly lit room—a private lounge, of a sort, with a bar at one end and computer terminals lining the opposite wall. In the center of the room was a metal construction that looked like a doorway without a door. She vaguely remembered something similar at Christie's the night before.

"Would you like a drink?" he asked, indicating the bar.

"No," Mercedes answered, surprised that, for the first

time in many years, she didn't feel a desire to numb her mind. "No. I think I'm through with all that for a while."

"As you wish. I want to reassure you now that you are quite welcome to join your friend and her mate on the Condor."

"Thank you. But the thought is so strange. To leave earth. Forever?"

"You find that a bad thought?"

"No. Just strange. No more than trying to stay here, though. After everything that has happened. And without Warren."

"That is good."

Magnus went to one of the terminals and punched at its keyboard. The space in the doorway began to crackle with energy, suddenly clearing to reveal a disquieting scene: two figures—one of them male, one of them Mercedes—asleep on a large bed.

"Another clone," Mercedes gasped.

"The last. She has been beaten badly by that man. He is a captain of the LANP. One of the men responsible for everything that has transpired. I hadn't expected it of him—at first he was disgusted at the very thought of the clones. But his lust for power over others convinced him to take the last clone as a sex slave."

"That picture in the doorway," Mercedes said. "It looks almost real."

Magnus chuckled. "It is real. It is akin to the doorway to our environment room. But," he continued, "it is unstable. To properly contain the forces involved in reality stepping, one must have stabilizers at the receiving end. There, in that bedroom, there are no stabilizers."

"Which means?"

"That everything will be fine until the portal is closed.

When the portal closes, the energy backlash will reduce that room, and the rest of the house that contains it, to rubble."

"Oh."

"I give you a choice," Magnus said. "In a few weeks, after the furor over recent events has calmed, Mercedes Night can reenter the world, her career. If she does it properly and carefully, she can even exact legal revenge against those who have caused this disruption in her life."

"But only one Mercedes Night can do this? You want me to decide now about the ship?"

"Well, if you did it would be easier—your clone may be totally opposed to the idea. She has not had the experiences of your last several months to influence her thinking."

Mercedes didn't have to think long. As she looked into Captain Willis's bedchamber, her clone moaned and rolled over. The entire left side of her face was one great bruise. Mercedes had seen one copy of herself die. She didn't even want to think of the number of others who had. *The last one*, Magnus had told her. *The last of how many?*

"I will go with your ship," Mercedes said. "Can I just step through?"

Magnus nodded.

Gingerly, Mercedes passed a leg through the portal, feeling for solidity beneath her foot. Then, she quickly stepped toward the bed. Behind her, the portal was but a shimmering in the air. She lifted the limp form of her clone and carried it out.

"I already have medtechs on the way," Magnus said.

Mercedes stared back in at the NP's sleeping form.

"Shall I close the gate now?" Magnus asked, stepping back to his terminal.

He will die, Mercedes thought. No matter what he'd done,

she couldn't live with his murder on her conscience. She shook her head and took a hesitant step back for the portal.

Abruptly, the field disappeared, and Mercedes halted before the structure.

"I am sorry I asked you that question, Miss Night," Magnus said. "Whatever the moral considerations, Captain Willis could have destroyed your clone's chances of succeeding in her return to the *real* world. He had to die. But his murder now rests on my shoulders, not yours."

"How much of this," Mercedes asked slowly, "has rested on your shoulders? How much of it have you had the power to stop?"

"All of it, I think. At the risk of my own downfall, that is. I have some vid that will be of great assistance in rectifying matters, vid of the commissioner of the LANP discussing the problem thoroughly with one of President Cole's closest aides. The LANP were to attempt the destruction of Keyes, and the commissioner was instructed to insure that blame could be placed directly on his subordinates had the operation failed. That is why the LANP allowed the cloning manufactory its automated existence for so long. Its exposure would have pointed to little more than corruption in the local NP precinct. Exposure of the attempt to discredit Keyes would then have suggested only local abuse of certain secret government technologies. The president's aide implicated his employer several times during the course of the conversation. The country's present administration ultimately will fall, as will its monopoly over certain very questionable technological developments."

"But you let the cloning happen. And you let Warren die."

"I never intended to allow the clones to destroy your career. I simply intended to see if the cloning process could succeed. The LANP botched it before my observations were finished. I am sorry that so many died painful deaths. I would have—"

"You would have what?"

He turned away from her. "Terminated them painlessly."

Mercedes looked down at her clone as the medtechs entered and moved her onto a stretcher. *Painlessly.* "What about Warren?"

"For all that I did not know him well, he seemed a good man. But certain forces in this country would have killed him, one way or another, before November. His death now, coupled with the evidence that your clone will possess upon her reemergence, will make him a martyr. Is that not a good thing? Jeffrey Wilmington, another good man, will now gain the power that Warren Keyes sought, and the world will know peace for a time. Had I interfered earlier, I doubt the future would appear so bright.

"Please do not think me evil, Miss Night. At heart, I am a businessman. Your morals and values are a puzzlement to me. I approach puzzles with an open mind, but I can see that you judge me monstrous to consider all this so casually. Perhaps I could have righted things before they had the chance to happen. But then, wouldn't that have been killing the clones by never allowing them life? And would I not, through my actions, have been guaranteeing the death of Warren Keyes—and possibly your own—in a more mundane but equally effective manner? One in which it would be impossible to lay blame on the individuals responsible? I am not God, Miss Night."

Mercedes stared at him and swallowed.

"Go now. I doubt that we shall meet again. Go on my ship and entertain my people."

"But I thought—"

"That I would accompany you? Did you think that my aid to you could have been rooted in personal interest? No. I enjoy your art the way a father enjoys the pictures drawn by his toddlers. I enjoy your beauty on a similar level. However, I do have a sense of justice, and I think I will take pleasure in watching your clone burst back into the world. You, I would like on the Condor. Leaving one's home can be traumatic, and I'm hoping that on board, you will ease the others' pain off earth the same way you did on earth."

Slowly, Mercedes nodded.

"That is what your art is intended to do, is it not? To create archetypes? To give people something to distract them from the futility of mortal existence?"

"I—I'm not sure anymore."

"Well"—he smiled thoughtfully—"perhaps you'll regain an assurance of a sort in time. Your clone will be repaired and sent to you in the biochemistry research division."

She looked at him curiously.

Slowly, he began to fade.

"Thank you, Magnus," she said. *Whoever you are* . . .

He smiled one last time before he disappeared entirely.

6/21 3:35 P.M.

In Christie's work-lounge, Lance looked nervously from one Mercedes to the other. They paid him no attention; they were caught up completely in their own, private, hushed conversation. He knew what they were talking about: One was leaving, and one was staying. The one leaving had to tell the one staying everything that had happened during the past six months, since the one staying had been growing in a test tube during that time.

He wished his mind would clear. He wanted, at least, to try to make sense of it all.

Christie breezed into the room and tossed Lancelot at him.

"Hey," the computer screeched in midair. "Careful with the merchandise!"

"Sorry I took so long, lover," Christie said. "Traffic was pretty congested."

"He wasn't here?"

"Nope."

"Where was he?"

"My secret."

"Lancelot?"

"I ain't saying nothing. Good to be home though."

"We're not home, Lancelot."

"Are you sure? Hasn't it got something to do with where the heart is?"

Lance looked up at Christie, then back down at Lancelot.

"Well," Christie said. "You've got your brainchild back. Are you coming or going? Ship leaves in eighteen hours."

"You mean I have a choice?"

"What makes you think you don't? Do what you want."

"But Magnus—"

"Magnus what? He doesn't care."

"About Lancelot?"

"Doesn't look that way."

Lance felt uneasy. He remembered the voices he'd heard the night before. *He is our brother.* "What was he like to you, Mercy?" he asked.

The Mercedeses turned away from each other to look at him. One cleared her throat. "Like, I don't know, Lance. Like no one else I've ever met. Ask me later, okay?"

"This place is like a huge, secret society, Lance," Christie said. "Magnus cares for his people, but none of us knows everything that goes on here. It's very difficult to get into Sub-Space. And it's not easy to get out either. You're always hearing stories around here about employees who get overly curious. They poke around for a few days, and then one morning they just don't show up for work. It's that simple."

"Uh?"

"Don't worry, Lance. You can do what you want. Leave or stay. Your choice. I love you, if that matters."

Lance finally managed a smile. "I—I think I'll stay with you. Thanks, Chris, for not giving up on me."

She smiled back seductively. "Thank me later. Get some rest for now. You still look terrible!" She turned to Mercedes. "Have you two got everything worked out yet?"

"We think so."

Everything had happened so quickly. But Mercedes doubted she'd be lacking time for reflection. She knew she'd make sense out of it one day. And she'd get the chance to do her own vids the way she wanted them. Two thousand other people were supposed to go on the ship with her. Maybe among them, she would find another to love. Make some space babies. *To boldly go where no woman has gone before* . . .

After a moment, she looked sadly at her clone and kissed her. "Give my love to Pharaoh, Mercy."

EPILOGUE I

The Death of the Legion

ARTHUR COULDN'T GET VERY happy anymore when he thought about his grandfather. He didn't like to remember that he had been misled. He could have gone to the Grand Canyon any time he'd wanted. At least in the early morning, he reminded himself.

He couldn't deny the fact that he was, for the present, outside in the early morning sunshine, and he was still alive. They'd brought him out screaming, but they'd brought him out nonetheless. The bastards.

They were the white angels—the false angels—of the legion. He was certain of that now. Otherwise, they'd have just let him go home. Hadn't he exposed the witch Mercedes Night? Hadn't he saved humanity from her evil? A week before, she'd had even him fooled. But no more. He could sleep well now, knowing that she was dead. And *he* was responsible. *He* had saved the pure-strain race from that witch's mutated vidspells. No, only the legion could still bear malice against him. Only the legion would force him to endure sunlight. Maybe his grandfather hadn't been wrong after all. Maybe it just took some time.

A distant roar momentarily disturbed Arthur's reflections. He looked up and watched the silver needle streak through the sky. Up and up it went, glittering and gleaming.

"It's the Condor," one of the white angels said.

Arthur sneered. He wasn't stupid. He just wished they'd leave him alone and let him get back home to Karen. No, Karen wouldn't be there. She was dead. But still, Arthur wanted to go home. He had plans to make.

Thinking of the needle in the sky, Arthur laughed. Clumsy ships, he thought. People going out to the stars in clumsy ships! Humanity was ignorant! Couldn't they see the aesthetic—the functional—superiority of the vacuum fish? Didn't they want to experience individual freedom? They were like dead tuna trapped inside metal and waiting to be eaten. Didn't they have any taste at all?

Maybe that was it, he reflected. Maybe it was taste that separated the pure-strain from the mutant. He decided to give that thought some careful consideration. He wasn't in any hurry. Let the legion think him insane! *Let it deceive itself!*

No, Arthur wasn't worried at all. Now, he had all the time in the world to straighten things out.

EPILOGUE 2
And Then the Stars...

Mercedes looked up from the terminal when Christie and Lance entered.

"Hi, Mercy," Lance said, slightly breathless. In his arms was a computer printout several inches thick.

"Hi," Mercedes said. "This is truly phenomenal, Chris. Just getting through the index of the vidlibrary is going to take me all day."

Christie smiled. "Keeps you busy, eh?"

"Yeah."

"We thought we'd stop by and let you know that we'll be passing Mars in a couple of hours before we do another jump. You ought to come up to the observation deck for a look."

"Thanks, Chris." She looked at Lance. "What's all that?"

"User guide for the ship's environment room. Chris thought you might want it."

"We might be puttering around in a void for a few years, Mercy," Christie said. "The room will let you build your own sets. Your own actors, too, if you don't think you can get the right talent out of the crew and passengers."

Lance dropped the listing next to the terminal. Mercedes looked at it wide-eyed and shook her head.

"You're kidding, right?"

"Wrong." Christie laughed.

"Hey, Lance!" cried another voice. "Will you take me out of your goddamned back pocket and let me say 'Hi' to Mercy?"

Lance grimaced and fished in his pocket. "Sorry, Lancelot. Almost forgot you were there."

"That's okay. Hi, Mercy."

"Hello," she said to the computer.

Christie took Lance's hand and steered him toward the door.

"Bye, Mercy," Lancelot said. "Have fun!"

She laughed. "Give me a call in time to get wherever I'm supposed to get to see Mars, okay?"

"Sure," Christie said.

They left, and Mercedes placed a hand on the listing they'd brought her. She looked at it and groaned, then pulled it onto her lap. She took a deep breath and opened it to the first page.

The biobot *had* told her that a kid could program the room. . . .

EPILOGUE 3
Resurrection

MERCEDES SQUINTED CRITICALLY AT her reflection in the mirror, then smiled. She touched her neck and shoulders; without the mass of red hair, they would have to pass on their own merits. But the short, glossy black hair framing her face didn't look so bad, even if it was trite neo-aristocrat. She really didn't like the idea of adopting such a strong subculture identification. She hated stereotypes in the first place, but she recognized all too well the need for her disguise. Mercedes Night had been dead only a week.

No, she corrected herself. She was Mercedes Night. The dead had no names. Mercedes Night had two lives now. It was a pity that she could experience only one of them. She chuckled.

She forced herself to get serious. It was going to be hard

enough for her to fake the months she'd lost *without* fantasizing herself into some dream of taking vid out into the stars. She had her hands full there too: All those people on that ship had technical minds. Not an audience that was going to be easy to please! No, she needed to pay attention to the place she was in, not the place she might have been.

She regurgitated the memorized memories once more and smiled again. She really had the easy road. Mercedes Night had never had much of a rep for her memory beyond her lines. If she forgot names or events or places, no one would suspect a thing. So stop worrying! she told herself. She was really all-around lucky. She'd never had time to fall in love with Warren Keyes; she'd barely even known him. She didn't have to mourn a dead man.

She picked up her single blue contact lens and frowned at it. Oh well, she thought, she wouldn't have to put up with deception forever. With extra care, she fitted the lens over her silver eye, blinking several times to make absolutely sure that its gleam wouldn't betray her.

Before rising, she bent close to the mirror and again inspected her face, neck, and arms. She was still sore in places, but the bruises had all faded to nothing with the help of cosmetics. Well, she thought, people wouldn't see what they couldn't see. Stay calm, Mercy, she told herself again. This *might* be the most crucial role she'd ever have to play, but it would also be the easiest.

She went over everything once more, then stepped out of the small chamber that Sub-Space had provided for her recovery. At the portal, she looked back in, smiling at the small bed and the cosy but plain vanity shelf. "So long, little room," she said softly. She spun and strode down the dormitory corridor.

Following directions delivered that morning by a courtesy

biobot, she quickly made her way to the transportation development laboratory. She almost balked at the door, but it swung open before her, and a smiling technician waved her in.

"Mercedes Night?" he asked. Four other techs looked up from their work when they heard her name.

"Yeah," she said. "In the flesh."

"I'm pleased to meet you, Mercy. I've seen all your vids. May I understand that you're now ready to leave us?"

Mercedes nodded. The technician turned and went to a panel of instruments stationed around a curious, gatelike structure that seemed to suck away light along its inside rim. Mercedes couldn't help thinking of the odd little obelisk that Warren had given her a week before. *No*, she reminded herself, *months and months ago*.

She followed the technician to the panel.

He threw a few switches and turned to Mercedes and smiled again. "Well," he said, "you can step through anytime you like now."

"Through that?" she asked, frowning at the gateway.

He laughed. "You see another reality stepper in the room?"

Mercedes raised an eyebrow for him, shrugged, and strode boldly for the gateway. She closed her eyes and stepped through.

When she opened her eyes, she was in another room. In the city, she realized. She could hear the sounds of a nearby street—the vibrations of IC automobiles and hovercraft engines, and the *clack-click* of polysynth heels on concrete. The blinds of one of the windows were open, and sunlight bled hazily in through the one-way Plexiglas. No place, Mercedes thought, but Los Angeles.

A pretty blond girl sat at a desk flanking two important-looking doors that dominated one wall of the room. The girl looked up at Mercedes and tilted her head curiously to one side. "So! You've made it already. I didn't expect you for another day or so."

"I got restless. Just exactly where am I?"

"Sub-Space L.A. Branch Three. Hollywood Boulevard."

"Oh."

"Should I call you a flyer-taxi?"

"No. I think I can walk from here."

"Fine, it's your show! Use the door by the window."

Mercedes went to the door. She paused there, turning back to look at the girl. The girl smiled. "Good luck!"

Mercedes laughed. "Yeah," she said. "Thanks."

She pushed the door open and stepped out onto the sidewalk. What an organization! she thought. She only wished she could have met Magnus the way Mercy—the way she had. . . .

The day was pretty bad as a whole—everything had fuzzy edges, but Mercedes didn't care. After a week of being nothing but inside, any outside was an improvement. She took a deep breath, tried not to cough, got her bearings, and started down the sidewalk.

The building she sought was only a few blocks away. Several paces to the side of its entrance, a man in the black leather dress of the National Police leaned against the wall, whistling softly to himself. Must be a hell of a job, she thought. Ignoring him, she looked up to where the skyscraper disappeared into the marshmallow sky. From one modern institution to another, she thought.

But Sub-Space was weird, Mercy. Those people—nothing seemed to faze them. Things, now, would be different. It was time to blow some minds. . . .

"Hey! You!"

Her stomach met her throat. Slowly, she turned to the NP.

He smiled at her. "Got a date tonight, sweetheart?"

She winked at him and stepped onto the conveyor belt that would carry her into the building. She didn't stop to talk to the building directory. She knew where she was going. She hopped off the belt at the first elevator, stepped in, and pushed the button for the thirteenth floor.

"I could have done that for you," the elevator said.

"No problem. I figured you were busy solving the gravity crisis."

"Excuse me?"

"It was a joke," Mercedes said as the elevator stopped and opened the door for her. She stepped out.

"Computers can't—"

The elevator's door shut. Mercedes giggled and strode through the open door of the suite on the right.

The receptionist looked up at her. "May I help—hey! You can't just—!"

She reached the door she wanted, opened it, stepped through, and closed it behind her. She turned and smiled at the startled woman behind the desk.

"Hello, Sylvia," Mercedes said.

"Who are you?"

"You don't recognize me? Well, no matter. I'll explain in a second, but you ought to call Vincent Crews over here first. He'll be quite interested to learn that he tried and executed a fake."

Sylvia squinted at the intruder, then her eyes opened wide. "Mercedes! You're back!" She slapped a button on her desk. "Lana! Get a line—"

The door behind Mercedes flew open and Sylvia's receptionist charged in. "I'm sorry, Miss Fry," she said. "I couldn't stop her."

"Forget it, Lana. She's okay. Go get hold of Adjudicator Crews and tell him to get his legal body over here!"

"Yes, ma'am." Lana left, closing the door with a bit more care than she'd used in opening it.

Sylvia looked at Mercedes and smiled. "It really is you, isn't it?"

Mercedes laughed. "Yeah," she said. "It is."